Center Point
Large Print

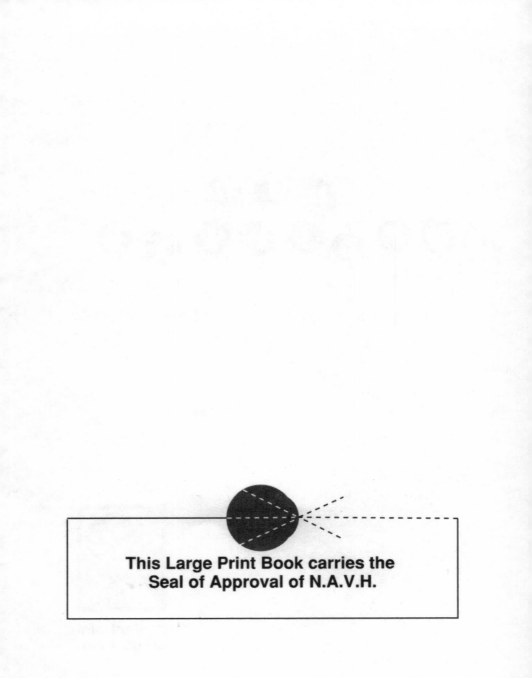

**This Large Print Book carries the
Seal of Approval of N.A.V.H.**

A Western Quartet

Louis L'Amour
edited by Jon Tuska

A Circle Ⓥ Western

CENTER POINT PUBLISHING
THORNDIKE, MAINE

This Circle V Western is published by Center Point Large Print in 2008 in cooperation with Golden West Literary Agency.

The text of this Large Print edition is unabridged. In other aspects, this book may vary from the original edition. Printed in the United States of America. Set in 16-point Times New Roman type.

ISBN: 978-1-60285-184-9

Library of Congress Cataloging-in-Publication Data

L'Amour, Louis, 1908-1988.
    Big medicine : a western quartet / Louis L'Amour ; edited by Jon Tuska. -- 1st ed.--Center Point large print ed.
        p. cm. -- (A Circle V western)
    ISBN 978-1-60285-184-9 (lib. bdg. : alk. paper)
      1. Large type books. I. Tuska, Jon. II. Title. III. Series.

  PS3523.A446B54 2008
  813'.52--dc22

2008009492

Acknowledgments

"Big Medicine" under the byline Jim Mayo first appeared in *Thrilling Western* (1/48). Copyright © 1948 by Standard Magazines, Inc. Copyright not renewed.

"Trail to Pie Town" under the byline Jim Mayo first appeared in *West* (2/48). Copyright © 1948 by Better Publications, Inc. Copyright not renewed.

"McQueen of the Tumbling K" under the byline Jim Mayo first appeared in *Thrilling Western* (12/47). Copyright © 1947 by Standard Magazines, Inc. Copyright not renewed.

"A Man Called Trent" under the byline Jim Mayo first appeared in *West* (12/47). Copyright © 1947 by Better Publications, Inc. Copyright not renewed.

TABLE OF CONTENTS

Introduction
by Jon Tuska

Louis Dearborn LaMoore (1908-1988) was born in Jamestown, North Dakota. He left home at fifteen and subsequently held a wide variety of jobs although he worked mostly as a merchant seaman. From his earliest youth, L'Amour had a love of verse. His first published work was a poem, "The Chap Worth While", appearing when he was eighteen years old in his former hometown's newspaper, the *Jamestown Sun*. It is the only poem from his early years that he left out of SMOKE FROM THIS ALTAR, which appeared in 1939 from Lusk Publishers in Oklahoma City, a book which L'Amour published himself; however, this poem is reproduced in THE LOUIS L'AMOUR COMPANION (Andrews and McMeel, 1992) edited by Robert Weinberg. L'Amour wrote poems and articles for a number of small circulation arts magazines all through the early 1930s and, after hundreds of rejection slips, finally had his first story accepted, "Anything for a Pal" in *True Gang Life* (10/35). He returned in 1938 to live with his family where they had settled in Choctaw, Oklahoma, determined to make writing his career. He wrote a fight story bought by Standard Magazines that year and became acquainted with editor Leo Margulies who was to play an important rôle later in L'Amour's life. "The Town No Guns Could

Tame" in *New Western* (3/40) was his first published Western story.

During the Second World War L'Amour was drafted and ultimately served with the U.S. Army Transportation Corps in Europe. However, in the two years before he was shipped out, he managed to write a great many adventure stories for Standard Magazines. The first story he published in 1946, the year of his discharge, was a Western, "Law of the Desert Born" in *Dime Western* (4/46). A call to Leo Margulies resulted in L'Amour's agreeing to write Western stories for the various Western pulp magazines published by Standard Magazines, a third of which appeared under the byline Jim Mayo, the name of a character in L'Amour's earlier adventure fiction. The proposal for L'Amour to write new Hopalong Cassidy novels came from Margulies who wanted to launch *Hopalong Cassidy's Western Magazine* to take advantage of the popularity William Boyd's old films and new television series were enjoying with a new generation. Doubleday & Company agreed to publish the pulp novelettes in hard cover books. L'Amour was paid $500 a story, no royalties, and he was assigned the house name Tex Burns. L'Amour read Clarence E. Mulford's books about the Bar-20 and based his Hopalong Cassidy on Mulford's original creation. Only two issues of the magazine appeared before it ceased publication. Doubleday felt that the Hopalong character had to appear exactly as William Boyd did in the films and on television and thus even the first two novels had to be revamped to meet with this requirement prior to publication in book form.

L'Amour's first Western novel under his own byline was WESTWARD THE TIDE (World's Work, 1950). It was rejected by every American publisher to which it was submitted. World's Work paid a flat £75 without royalties for British Empire rights in perpetuity. L'Amour sold his first Western short story to a slick magazine a year later, "The Gift of Cochise" in *Collier's* (7/5/52). Robert Fellows and John Wayne purchased screen rights to this story from L'Amour for $4,000 and James Edward Grant, one of Wayne's favorite screenwriters, developed a script from it, changing L'Amour's Ches Lane to Hondo Lane. L'Amour retained the right to novelize Grant's screenplay, which differs substantially from his short story, and he was able to get an endorsement from Wayne to be used as a blurb, stating that HONDO was the finest Western Wayne had ever read. HONDO (Fawcett Gold Medal, 1953) by Louis L'Amour was released on the same day as the film, HONDO (Warner, 1953), with a first printing of 320,000 copies.

With SHOWDOWN AT YELLOW BUTTE (Ace, 1953) by Jim Mayo, L'Amour began a series of short Western novels for Don Wollheim that could be doubled with other short novels by other authors in Ace Publishing's paperback two-fers. Advances on these were $800 and usually the author never earned any royalties. HELLER WITH A GUN (Fawcett Gold Medal, 1955) was the first of a series of original Westerns

L'Amour had agreed to write under his own name following the success for Fawcett of HONDO. L'Amour wanted even this early to have his Western novels published in hard cover editions. He expanded "Guns of the Timberland" by Jim Mayo in *West* (9/50) for GUNS OF THE TIMBERLANDS (Jason Press, 1955), a hard cover Western for which he was paid an advance of $250. Another novel for Jason Press followed and then SILVER CAÑON (Avalon Books, 1956) for Thomas Bouregy & Company. These were basically lending library publishers and the books seldom earned much money above the small advances paid.

The great turn in L'Amour's fortunes came about because of problems Saul David was having with his original paperback Westerns program at Bantam Books. Fred Glidden had been signed to a contract to produce two original paperback Luke Short Western novels a year for an advance of $15,000 each. It was a long-term contract but, in the first ten years of it, Fred only wrote six novels. Literary agent Marguerite Harper then persuaded Bantam that Fred's brother, Jon, could help fulfill the contract and Jon was signed for eight Peter Dawson Western novels. When Jon died suddenly before completing even one book for Bantam, Harper managed to engage a ghost writer at the Disney studios to write these eight "Peter Dawson" novels, beginning with THE SAVAGES (Bantam, 1959). They proved inferior to anything Jon had ever written and what sales they had seemed to be due only to the Peter Dawson name.

Saul David wanted to know from L'Amour if *he* could deliver two Western novels a year. L'Amour said he could, and he did. In fact, by 1962 this number was increased to three original paperback novels a year. The first L'Amour novel to appear under the Bantam contract was RADIGAN (Bantam, 1958). It seemed to me after I read all of the Western stories L'Amour ever wrote in preparation for my essay, "Louis L'Amour's Western Fiction" in A VARIABLE HARVEST (McFarland, 1990), that by the time L'Amour wrote "Riders of the Dawn" in *Giant Western* (6/51), the short novel he later expanded to form SILVER CAÑON, that he had almost burned out on the Western story, and this was years before his fame, wealth, and tremendous sales figures. He had developed seven basic plot situations in his pulp Western stories and he used them over and over again in writing his original paperback Westerns. FLINT (Bantam, 1960), considered by many to be one of L'Amour's better efforts, is basically a reprise of the range war plot which, of the seven, is the one L'Amour used most often. L'Amour's hero, Flint, knows about a hide-out in the badlands (where, depending on the story, something is hidden: cattle, horses, outlaws, etc.). Even certain episodes within his basic plots are repeated again and again. Flint scales a sharp V in a cañon wall to escape a tight spot as Jim Gatlin had before him in L'Amour's "The Black Rock Coffin Makers" in *.44 Western* (2/50) and many a L'Amour hero would again.

Basic to this range war plot is the villain's means for crowding out the other ranchers in a district. He brings in a giant herd that requires all the available grass and forces all the smaller ranchers out of business. It was this same strategy Bantam used in marketing L'Amour. *All* of his Western titles were continuously kept in print. Independent distributors were required to buy titles in lots of 10,000 copies if they wanted access to other Bantam titles at significantly discounted prices. In time L'Amour's paperbacks forced almost every one else off the racks in the Western sections. L'Amour himself comprised the other half of this successful strategy. He dressed up in cowboy outfits, traveled about the country in a motor home visiting with independent distributors, taking them to dinner and charming them, making them personal friends. He promoted himself at every available opportunity. L'Amour insisted that he was telling the stories of the people who had made America a great nation and he appealed to patriotism as much as to commercialism in his rhetoric.

His fiction suffered, of course, stories written hurriedly and submitted in their first draft and published as he wrote them. A character would have a rifle in his hand, a model not yet invented in the period in which the story was set, and when he crossed a street the rifle would vanish without explanation. A scene would begin in a saloon and suddenly the setting would be a hotel dining room. Characters would die once and, a few pages later, die again. An old man for most of a story would turn out to be in his twenties.

Once when we were talking and Louis had showed me his topographical maps and his library of thousands of volumes which he claimed he used for research, he asserted that, if he claimed there was a rock in a road at a certain point in a story, his readers knew that if they went to that spot they would find the rock just as he described it. I told him that might be so but I personally was troubled by the many inconsistencies in his stories. Take LAST STAND AT PAPAGO WELLS (Fawcett Gold Medal, 1957). Five characters are killed during an Indian raid. One of the surviving characters emerges from seclusion after the attack and counts *six* corpses.

"I'll have to go back and count them again," L'Amour said, and smiled. "But, you know, I don't think the people who read my books would really care."

All of this notwithstanding, there are many fine, and some spectacular, moments in Louis L'Amour's Western fiction. I think he was at his best in the shorter forms, especially his magazine stories, and the two best stories he ever wrote appeared in the 1950s, "The Gift of Cochise" early in the decade and "War Party" in *The Saturday Evening Post* (6/59). The latter was later expanded by L'Amour to serve as the opening chapters for BENDIGO SHAFTER (Dutton, 1979). That book is so poorly structured that Harold Kuebler, senior editor at Doubleday & Company to whom it was first offered, said he would not publish it unless L'Amour undertook extensive revisions. This L'Amour refused to do and, eventually, Bantam started a hard cover publishing program to accommodate him when no other hard cover publisher proved willing to accept his books as he wrote them. Yet "War Party" possesses several of the characteristics in purest form which I suspect, no matter how diluted they ultimately would become, account in largest measure for the loyal following Louis L'Amour won from his readers: the young male narrator who is in the process of growing into manhood and who is evaluating other human beings and his own experiences; a resourceful frontier woman who has beauty as well as fortitude; a strong male character who is single and hence marriageable; and the powerful, romantic, strangely compelling vision of the American West which invests L'Amour's Western fiction and makes it such a delightful escape from the cares of a later time—in this author's words from this story, that "big country needing big men and women to live in it" and where there was no place for "the frightened or the mean."

A Western Quartet

Big Medicine

Old Billy Dunbar was down flat on his face in a dry wash swearing into his beard. The best gold-bearing gravel he had found in a year, and then the Apaches would have to show up!

It was like them, the mean, ornery critters. He hugged the ground for dear life and hoped they would not see him, tucked away as he was between some stones where an eddy of the water that once ran through the wash had dug a trench between the stones.

There were nine of them. Not many, but enough to take his scalp if they found him, and it would be just as bad if they saw his burros or any of the prospect holes he had been sinking.

He was sweating like a stuck hog bleeds, lying there with his beard in the sand and the old Sharps .50 ready beside him. He wouldn't have much a chance if they found him, slithery fighters like they were, but if that old Sharps threw down on them, he'd take at least one along to the happy hunting ground with him.

He could hear them now, moving along the desert above the wash. Where in tarnation were they going? He wouldn't be safe as long as they were in the country, and this was country where not many white men came. Those few who did come were just as miserable to run into as the Apaches.

The Apache leader was a lean-muscled man with a hawk nose. All of them slim and brown without much meat on them, the way Apaches were, and wearing nothing but breechclouts and headbands.

He lay perfectly still. Old Billy was too knowing in Indian ways to start moving until he was sure they were gone. He lay right there for almost a half hour after he had last heard them, and then he came out of it, cautious as a bear reaching for a honey tree.

When he got on his feet, he hightailed it for the edge of the wash and took a look. The Apaches had vanished. He turned and went down the wash, taking his time and keeping the old Sharps handy. It was a mile to his burros and to the place where his prospect holes were. Luckily he had them back in a draw where there wasn't much chance of their being found.

Billy Dunbar pulled his old gray felt hat down a little tighter and hurried on. Jennie and Julie were waiting for him, standing head to tail so they could brush flies off each other's noses.

When he got to them, he gathered up his tools and took them back up the draw to the rocks at the end. His canteens were full, and he had plenty of grub and ammunition. He was lucky that he hadn't shot that rabbit when he saw it. The Apaches would have heard the bellow of the old Sharps and come for him, sure. He was going to have to be careful.

If they would just kill a man, it wouldn't be so bad, but these Apaches liked to stake a man out on an anthill and let the hot sun and ants do for him, or maybe the buzzards—if they got there soon enough.

This wash looked good, too. Not only because water

had run there, but because it was actually cutting into the edge of an old riverbed. If he could sink a couple of holes down to bedrock, he'd bet there'd be gold and gold aplenty.

When he awakened in the morning, he took a careful look around his hiding place. One thing, the way he was located, if they caught him in camp, they couldn't get at him to do much. The hollow was perhaps sixty feet across, but over half of it was covered by shelving rock from above; the cliff ran straight up from there for an easy fifty feet. There was water in a spring and enough grass to last the burros for quite some time.

After a careful scouting around, he made a fire of dead mesquite, which made almost no smoke, and fixed some coffee. When he had eaten, Dunbar gathered up his pan, pick, shovel, and rifle, and moved out. He was loaded more than he liked, but it couldn't be helped.

The place he had selected to work was the inside of the little desert stream. The stream took a bend and left a gravel bank on the inside of the elbow. That gravel looked good. Putting his Sharps down within easy reach, Old Billy got busy.

Before sundown he had moved a lot of dirt and tried several pans, loading them up and going over to the stream. Holding the pan under the water, he began to stir the gravel, breaking up the lumps of clay and stirring until every piece was wet. Then he picked out the larger stones and pebbles and threw them to one side.

He put his hands on opposite sides of the pan and began to oscillate it vigorously under water, moving it in a circular motion so the contents were shaken from side to side.

With a quick glance to make sure there were no Apaches in sight, he tipped the pan slightly, to an angle of about thirty degrees so the lighter sands, already buoyed up by the water, could slip out over the side.

He struck the pan several good blows to help settle the gold, if any, and then dipped for more water and continued the process. He worked steadily at the pan, with occasional glances around until all the refuse had washed over the side but the heavier particles. Then, with a little clean water, he washed the black sand and gold into another pan, which he took from the brush where it had been concealed the day before.

For some time he worked steadily. Then, as the light was getting bad, he gathered up his tools and, concealing the empty pan, carried the other with him back up the wash to his hide-out.

He took his Sharps and crept out of the hide-out and up the wall of the cañon. The desert was still and empty on every side.

"Too empty, durn it!" he grumbled. "Them Injuns'll be back. You can't fool an Apache."

Rolling out of his blankets at sunup, he prepared a quick breakfast, and then went over his takings of the day with a magnet. This black sand was mostly particles of magnetite, ilmenite, and black magnetic iron oxide. What he couldn't draw off, he next eliminated by using a blow box.

"Too slow, with them Apaches around," he grumbled. "A man workin' down there could mebbe do sixty, seventy pans a day in that sort of gravel, but watchin' for Injuns ain't goin' t'help much."

Yet he worked steadily, and by nightfall, despite interruptions, he had handled more than fifty pans. When the second day was over, he grinned at the gold he had. It was sufficient color to show he was on the right track. Right here, by using a rocker, he could have made it pay, but he wasn't looking for peanuts.

He had cached his tools along with the empty pan in the brush at the edge of the wash. When morning came, he rolled out and was just coming out of the hide-out when he saw the Apache. He was squatted in the sand, staring at something, and, despite his efforts to keep his trail covered, Dunbar had a good idea what that something would be. He drew back into the hide-out.

Lying on his middle, he watched the Indian get to his feet and start working downstream. When he got down there a little farther, he was going to see those prospect holes. There would be nothing Dunbar could do then. Nor was there anything he could do now. So far as he could see, only one Apache had found him. If he fired to kill the Indian, the others would be aware of the situation and come running.

Old Billy squinted his eyes and pondered the question. He had a hunch that Indian wasn't going to go for help. He was going to try to get Dunbar by himself, so he could take his weapons and whatever else he had of value.

The Indian went downstream farther and slipped out of sight. Billy instantly ducked out into the open and scooted down the cañon into the mesquite. He dropped flat there, and inched along in the direction the Indian had gone.

He was creeping along, getting nearer and nearer to his prospect holes, when suddenly instinct or the subconscious hearing of a sound warned him. Like a flash, he rolled over, just in time to see the Indian leap at him, knife in hand!

Billy Dunbar was no longer a youngster, but he had lived a life in the desert, and he was as hard and tough as whalebone. As the Apache leaped, he caught the knife wrist in his left hand, and stabbed at the Indian's ribs with his own knife. The Apache twisted away, and Billy gave a heave. The Indian lost balance. They rolled over, and then fell over the eight-foot bank into the wash.

Luck was with Billy. The Indian hit first, and Billy's knife arm was around him, with the point gouging at the Indian's back. When they landed, the knife went in to the hilt.

Billy rolled off, gasping for breath. Hurriedly he glanced around. There was no one in sight. Swiftly he clawed at the bank, causing the loosened gravel to cave down, and in a few minutes of hot, sweating work the Indian was buried.

Turning, Billy lit out for his hideaway, and, when he made it, he lay there, gasping for breath, his Sharps ready. There would be no work this day. He was going to lie low and watch. The other Indians would come looking, he knew.

After dark, he slipped out and covered the Indian better, and then he used a mesquite bush to wipe out as well as possible the signs of their fighting. Then he cat-footed it back to the hollow and tied a rawhide string across the entrance with a can of loose pebbles at the end to warn him if Indians found him. Then he went to sleep.

At dawn he was up. He checked the Sharps, and then cleaned his .44 again. He loaded his pockets with cartridges, just in case and settled down for a day of it.

Luckily he had shade. It was hot out there, plenty hot. You could fry an egg on those rocks by 10:00 in the morning—not that he had any eggs. He hadn't even seen an egg since the last time he was in Fremont, and that had been four months ago.

He bit off a chew of tobacco and rolled it in his jaws. Then he studied the banks of the draw. An Apache could move like a ghost and look like part of the landscape. He had known them to come within fifteen feet of a man in grassy country without being seen, and not tall grass at that.

It wouldn't be so bad if his time hadn't been so

short. When he had left Fremont, Sally had six months to go to pay off the loan on her ranch, or out she would go. Sally's husband had been killed by a bronco down on the Sandy. She was alone with the kids, and that loan was about to take their home away.

When the situation became serious, Old Billy thought of this wash. Once, several years before, he had washed out some color here, and it looked rich. He had left the country about two jumps ahead of the Apaches and swore he'd never come back. Nobody else was coming out of here with gold, either, so he knew it was still like he remembered. Several optimistic prospectors had tried it and were never heard of again. However, Old Billy had decided to take a chance. After all, Sally was all he had, and those two grandchildren of his deserved a better chance than they'd get if she lost the place.

The day moved along, a story told by the shadows on the sides of the wash. You could almost tell the time by those shadows. It wasn't long before Dunbar knew every bush, every clump of greasewood and mesquite along its length, and every rock.

He wiped the sweat from his brow and waited. Sally was a good girl. Pretty, too, too pretty to be a widow at twenty-two. It was almost mid-afternoon when his questing eye halted suddenly on the bank of the wash. He lay perfectly still, eyes studying the bank intently. Yet his eyes had moved past the spot before they detected something amiss. He scowled, trying to remember. Then it came to him.

There had been a torn place there, as though some-body had started to pull up a clump of greasewood and then abandoned it. The earth had been exposed and a handful of roots. Now it was blotted out. Straining his eyes, he could see nothing, distinguish no contours that seemed human, only that the spot was no longer visible. The spot was mottled by shadows and sunlight through the leaves of the bush.

Then there was a movement, so slight that his eye scarcely detected it, and suddenly the earth and torn roots were visible again. They had come back. Their stealth told him they knew he was somewhere nearby, and the logical place for him would be right where he was.

Now he was in for it. Luckily he had food, water, and ammunition. There should be just eight of them unless more had come. Probably they had found his prospect holes and trailed him back this way.

There was no way they could see into his hollow, no way they could shoot into it except through the narrow entrance, which was rock and brush. There was no concealed approach to it. He dug into the bank a little to get more earth in front of himself.

No one needed to warn him of the gravity of the sit-uation. It was 150 miles to Fremont and sixty miles to the nearest white young man, Sid Barton, a cowhand turned rancher who had started running some cattle on the edge of the Apache country.

Nor could he expect help. Nobody ever came into this country, and nobody knew where he was but

Sally, and she only knew in a general way. Prospectors did not reveal locations where they had found color.

Well, he wasn't one of these restless young coots who'd have to be out there tangling with the Apaches. He could wait. And he would wait in the shade while they were in the sun. Night didn't worry him much. Apaches had never cared much for night fighting, and he wouldn't have much trouble with them.

One of them showed himself suddenly—only one arm and a rifle. But he fired, the bullet striking the rock overhead. Old Billy chuckled. *Tryin' t'draw fire*, he thought, *get me located*.

Billy Dunbar waited, grinning through his beard. There was another shot, and then more stillness. He lay absolutely motionless. A hand showed, and then a foot. He rolled his quid in his jaws and spat. An Indian suddenly showed himself, and then vanished as though he had never been there. Old Billy watched the banks cynically. An Indian showed again and hesitated briefly this time, but Dunbar waited.

Suddenly, within twenty feet of the spot where Dunbar lay, an Indian slid down the bank and, with a shrill whoop, darted for the entrance to the hideaway. It was pointblank, even though a moving target. Billy let him have it.

The old Sharps bellowed like a stricken bull and leaped in his hands. The Apache screamed wildly and toppled over backward, carried off his feet by the sheer force of the heavy-caliber bullet. Yells of rage greeted the shot.

Dunbar could see the Indian's body sprawled under the sun. He picked up an edged pieced of white stone and made a straight mark on the rack wall beside him, then seven more. He drew a diagonal line through the first one. *Seven t' go*, he mused.

A hail of bullets began kicking sand and dirt up around the opening. One shot hit overhead and showered dirt down almost in his face. "Durn you," he mumbled. He took his hat off and laid it beside him, his six-shooter atop of it, ready to hand.

No more Indians showed themselves, and the day drew on. It was hot out there. In the vast brassy vault of the sky a lone buzzard wheeled.

He tried no more shots, just waiting. They were trying to tire him out. Dog-gone it. In this place he could outwait all the Apaches in the Southwest—not that he wanted to!

Keeping well below the bank, he got hold of a stone about the size of his head and rolled it into the entrance. Instantly a shot smacked the dirt below it and kicked dirt into his eyes. He wiped them and swore viciously. Then he got another stone and rolled that in place, pushing dirt up behind them. He scooped his hollow deeper and peered thoughtfully at the banks of the draw.

Jennie and Julie were eating grass, undisturbed and unworried. They had been with Old Billy too long to be disturbed by these—to them meaningless—fusses and fights. The shadow from the west bank reached farther toward the east, and Old Billy waited, watching.

He detected an almost indiscernible movement atop the bank in the same spot where he had first seen an Indian. Taking careful aim, he drew a bead on the exposed roots and waited.

He saw no movement, nothing, yet suddenly he focused his eyes more sharply and saw the roots were no longer exposed. Nestling the stock against his shoulder, his finger eased back on the trigger. The old Sharps wavered, and he waited. The rifle steadied, and he squeezed the trigger.

The gun jumped suddenly and there was a shrill yell from the Apache, who lunged to full height and rose on his tiptoes, both hands clasping his chest. The stricken Indian then plunged face forward down the bank in a shower of gravel. Billy reloaded and waited. The Apache lay still, lying in the shadow below the bank. After watching him for a few minutes, alternating between the still form and the banks of the draw, Dunbar picked up his white stone and marked another diagonal white mark, across the second straight line.

He stared at the figures with satisfaction. "Six left," he said. He was growing hungry. Jennie and Julie had both decided to lie down and call it a day.

As luck would have it, his shovel and pick were concealed in the brush at the point where the draw opened into the wider wash. He scanned the banks suddenly, and then drew back. Grasping a bush, he pulled it from the earth under the huge rocks. He then took the brush and some stones and added to his parapet. With some lumps of earth and rock he gradually built it stronger.

Always he returned to the parapet, but the Apaches were cautious and he saw nothing of them. Yet his instinct told him they were there, somewhere. And that, he knew, was the trouble. It was the fact he had been avoiding ever since he had holed up for the fight. They would always be around somewhere now. Three of their braves were missing—dead. They would never let him leave the country alive.

If he had patience, so had they, and they could afford to wait. He could not. It was not merely a matter of getting home before the six-month period was up—and less than two months remained of that—it was a matter of getting home with enough money to pay off the loan. And with the best of luck it would require weeks upon weeks of hard, uninterrupted work.

And then he saw the wolf.

It was no more than a glimpse, and a fleeting glimpse. Billy Dunbar saw the sharply pointed nose and bright eyes and then the swish of a tail. The wolf vanished somewhere at the base of the shelf of rock that shaded the pocket. It vanished in proximity to the spring.

Old Billy frowned and studied the spot. He wasn't the only one holed up here! The wolf evidently had a hole somewhere in the back of the pocket, and perhaps some young, as the time of year was right. His stillness after he had finished work on the entrance had evidently fooled the wolf into believing the white man was gone.

Obviously the wolf had been lying there, waiting for him to leave so it could come out and hunt. The cubs would be getting hungry. If there were cubs.

The idea came to him then. An idea utterly fantastic, yet one that suddenly made him chuckle. It might work! It could work! At least, it was a chance, and somehow, some way, he had to be rid of those Apaches.

He knew something of their superstitions and beliefs. It was a gamble, but as suddenly as he conceived the idea, he knew it was a chance he was going to take.

Digging his change of clothes out of the saddlebags, he got into them. Then he took his own clothing and laid it out on the ground in plain sight—the pants, then the coat, the boots, and, nearby, the hat.

Taking some sticks, he went to the entrance of the wolf den and built a small fire close by. Then he hastily went back and took a quick look around. The draw was empty, but he knew the place was watched. He went back and got out of line of the wolf den, and waited.

The smoke was slight, but it was going into the den. It wouldn't take long. The wolf came out with a rush, ran to the middle of the pocket, took a quick, snarling look around, and then went over the parapet and down the draw.

Working swiftly, he moved the fire and scattered the

few sticks and coals in his other fireplace. Then he brushed the ground with a branch. It would be a few minutes before they moved, and perhaps longer.

Crawling into the wolf den, he next got some wolf hair, which he took back to his clothing. He put some of the hair in his shirt and some near his pants. A quick look down the draw showed no sign of an Indian, but that they had seen the wolf, he knew, and he could picture their surprise and puzzlement.

Hurrying to the spring, he dug from the bank near the water a large quantity of mud. This was an added touch, but one that might help. From the mud, he formed two roughly human figures. About the head of each he tied a blade of grass.

Hurrying to the parapet for a stolen look down the draw, he worked until six such figures were made. Then, using thorns and some old porcupine quills he found near a rock, he thrust one or more through each of the mud figures.

They stood in a neat row, facing the parapet. Quickly he hurried for one last look into the draw. An Indian had emerged. He stood there in plain sight, staring toward the place.

They would be cautious, Billy knew, and he chuckled to himself as he thought of what was to follow. Gathering up his rifle, the ammunition, a canteen, and a little food, he hurried to the wolf den and crawled back inside.

On his first trip he had ascertained that there were no cubs. At the end of the den there was room to sit up, topped by the stone of the shelving rock itself. To his right, a lighted match told him there was a smaller hole of some sort.

Cautiously Billy crawled back to the entrance, and, careful to avoid the wolf tracks in the dust outside, he brushed out his own tracks, and then retreated into the depths of the cave. From where he lay he could see the parapet.

Almost a half hour passed before the first head lifted above the poorly made wall. Black straight hair, a red headband, and the sharp, hard features of their leader.

Then other heads lifted beside him, and one by one the six Apaches stepped over the wall and into the pocket. They did not rush, but looked cautiously about, and their eyes were large, frightened. They looked all around, then at the clothing, and then at the images. One of the Indians grunted and pointed.

They drew closer, and then stopped in an awed line, staring at the mud figures. They knew too well what they meant. Those figures meant a witch doctor had put a death spell on each one of them.

One of the Indians drew back and looked at the clothing. Suddenly he gave a startled cry and pointed—at the wolf hair!

They gathered around, talking excitedly, and then glancing over their shoulders fearfully.

They had trapped what they believed to be a white man, and, knowing Apaches, Old Billy would have guessed they knew his height, weight, and approximate age. Those things they could tell from the length of his stride, the way he worked, the pressure of a footprint in softer ground.

They had trapped a white man, and a wolf had escaped! Now they found his clothing lying here, and on the clothing the hair of a wolf!

All Indians knew of wolf-men, those weird creatures who changed at will from wolf to man and back again, creatures that could tear the throat from a man while he slept and could mark his children with the wolf blood.

The day had waned, and, as he lay there, Old Billy Dunbar could see that while he had worked the sun had neared the horizon. The Indians looked around uneasily. This was the den of a wolf-man, a powerful spirit who had put the death spell on each of them, who came as a man and went as a wolf.

Suddenly, out on the desert, a wolf howled!

The Apaches started as if struck, and then as a man they began to draw back. By the time they reached the parapet, they were hurrying.

Old Billy stayed the night in the wolf hole, lying at its mouth, waiting for dawn. He saw the wolf come back, stare about uneasily, and then go away. When light came, he crawled from the hole.

The burros were cropping grass and they looked at him. He started to pick up a pack saddle, and then dropped it. "I'll be durned if I will!" he said.

Taking the old Sharps and the extra pan, he walked down to the wash and went to work. He kept a careful eye out, but saw no Apaches. The gold was panning out even better than he had dreamed would be possible. A few more days—suddenly he looked up.

Two Indians stood in plain sight, facing him. The nearest one walked forward and placed something on a rock, and then drew away. Crouched, waiting, Old Billy watched them go. Then he went to the rock. Wrapped in a piece of tanned buckskin was a haunch of venison!

He chuckled suddenly. He was big medicine now. He was a wolf-man. The venison was a peace offering, and he would take it. He knew now he could come and pan as much gold as he liked in Apache country.

A few days later he killed a wolf, skinned it, and then buried the carcass, but from the head he made a cap to fit over the crown of his old felt hat, and, wherever he went, he wore it.

A month later, walking into Fremont behind the switching tails of Jennie and Julie, he met Sally at the gate. She was talking with young Sid Barton.

"Hi," Sid said, grinning at him. Then he looked quizzically at the wolf-skin cap. "Better not wear that around here! Somebody might take you for a wolf!"

Old Billy chuckled. "I am," he said. "You're durned right, I am. Ask them Apaches."

Trail To Pie Town

Dusty Barron turned the steel-dust stallion down the slope toward the wash. He was going to have to find water soon or the horse and he would be done for. If Emmett Fisk and Gus Mattis had shown up in the street at any other time, it would have been all right. As it was, they had appeared just as he was making a break from the saloon, and they had blocked the road to the hill country and safety. Both men had reached for their guns when they saw him, and he had wheeled his horse and hit the desert road at a dead run. With Dan Hickman dead in the saloon it was no time to argue or engage in gun pleasantries while the clan gathered.

It had been a good idea to ride to Jarilla and make peace talk, only the idea hadn't worked. Dan Hickman had called him yellow, and then gone for a gun. Dan was a mite slow, a fact that had left him dead on the saloon floor. There were nine Hickmans in Jarilla, and there were Mattis and three Fisk boys. Dusty's own tall brothers were back in the hills southwest of Jarilla, but with his road blocked he had headed the steel-dust down the trail into the basin.

The stallion had saved his bacon. No doubt about that. It was only the speed of the big desert-bred horse and its endurance that had got him away from town before the Hickmans could catch him. The big horse had given him lead enough until night had closed in, and after that it was easier.

Dusty had turned at right angles from his original route. They would never expect that, for the turn took him down the long slope into the vast, empty expanse of the alkali basin where no man of good sense would consider going.

For him it was the only route. At Jarilla they would be watching for him, expecting him to circle back to the hill country and his own people. He should have listened to Allie when she had told him it was useless to try to settle the old blood feud.

He had been riding now, with only a few breaks, for hours. Several times he had stopped to rest the stallion, wanting to conserve its splendid strength against what must lie ahead. And occasionally he had dismounted and walked ahead of the big horse.

Dusty Barron had only the vaguest idea of what he was heading into. It was thirty-eight miles across the basin, and he was heading down the basin. According to popular rumor, there was no water for over eighty miles in that direction. And he had started with his canteen only half full.

For the first hour he had taken his course from a star. Then he had sighted a peak ahead and to his left and used that for a marker. Gradually he had worked his way toward the western side of the basin.

Somewhere over the western side was Gallo Gap, a green meadow high in the peaks off a rocky and rarely used pass. There would be water there if he could make it, yet he knew of the gap only from a story told him by a prospector he had met one day in the hills near his home.

Daybreak found him a solitary black speck in a vast wilderness of white. The sun stabbed at him with lances of fire and then, rising higher, bathed the great alkali basin in white radiance and blasting furnace heat. Dusty narrowed his eyes against the glare. It was at least twelve miles to the mountains.

He still had four miles to go through the puffing alkali dust when he saw the tracks. At first he couldn't believe the evidence of his eyes. A wagon—here!

While he allowed the steel-dust to take a blow, he dismounted and examined the tracks. It had been a heavy wagon pulled by four mules or horses. In the fine dust he could not find an outlined track to tell one from the other.

The tracks had come out of the white distance to the east and had turned north exactly on the route he was following. Gallo Gap, from the prospector's story, lay considerably north of him and a bit to the west.

Had the driver of the wagon known of the gap? Or had he merely turned on impulse to seek a route through the mountains. Glancing in first one, and then the other direction, Dusty could see no reason why the driver should have chosen either direction. Jarilla lay southwest, but from here there was no indication of it and no trail.

Mounting again, he rode on, and, when he came to the edge of the low hills fronting the mountains, he detected the wagon trail running along through the scattered rocks, parched bunch grass, and grease-wood. It was still heading north. Yet when he studied the terrain before him, he could see nothing but dancing heat waves and an occasional dust devil.

The problem of the wagon occupied his mind to for-getfulness of his own troubles. It had come across the alkali basin from the east. That argued it must have come from the direction of Manzano unless the wagon had turned into the trail somewhere farther north on the road to Conejos.

Nothing about it made sense. This was Apache country and no place for wagon travel. A man on a fast horse, yes, but even then it was foolhardy to travel alone. Yet the driver of the wagon had the courage of recklessness to come across the dead white expanse of the basin, a trip that to say the least was miserable.

Darkness was coming again, but he rode on. The wagon interested him, and with no other goal in mind now that he had escaped the Hickmans, he was curious to see who the driver was and to learn what he had in mind. Obviously the man was a stranger to this country.

It was then, in the fading light, that he saw the mule. The steel-dust snorted and shied sharply, but Dusty kneed it closer for a better look. It had been a big mule and a fine animal, but it was dead now. It bore evi-dence of that brutal crossing of the basin, and here, on the far side, the animal had finally dropped dead of heat and exhaustion.

Only then did he see the trunk. It was sitting between two rocks, partly concealed. He walked to it and looked it over. Cumbersome and heavy, it had evidently been dumped from the wagon to lighten the load.

He tried to open it, but could not. It was locked tight. Beside it were a couple of chairs and a bed.

"Sheddin' his load," Dusty muttered thoughtfully. "He'd better find some water for those other mules, or they'll die, too."

Then he noticed the name on the trunk: D.C. LOWE, ST. LOUIS, MO.

"You're a long way from home," Dusty remarked. He swung a leg over the saddle and rode on. He had gone almost five miles before he saw the fire.

At first, it might have been a star, but as he drew nearer, he could see it was too low down, although higher than he was. The trail had been turning gradually deeper into the hills and had begun to climb a little. He rode on, using the light for a beacon.

When he was still some distance off, he dismounted and tied the stallion to a clump of greasewood and walked forward on foot.

The three mules were hitched to the back of the wagon, all tied loosely and lying down. A girl was bending over a fire, and a small boy, probably no more than nine years old, was gathering sticks of dried mesquite for fuel. There was no one else in sight.

Marveling, he returned to his horse and started back. When he was still a little distance away, he began to sing. His throat was dry and it was a poor job, but he didn't want to frighten them. When he walked his horse into the firelight, the boy was staring up at him, wide-eyed, and the girl had an old Frontier Model Colt.

"It's all right, ma'am," he said, swinging down, "I'm just a passin' stranger an' don't mean any harm."

"Who are you?" she demanded.

"Name of Dusty Barron, ma'am. I've been followin' your trail."

"Why?" Her voice was sharp and a little frightened. She could have been no more than seventeen or eighteen.

"Mostly because I was headed thisaway an' was wonderin' what anybody was doin' down here with a wagon, or where you might be headed."

"Doesn't this lead us anywhere?" she asked.

"Ma'am," Dusty replied, "if you're lookin' for a settlement, there ain't none thisaway in less'n a hundred miles. There's a sort of town then, place they call Pie Town."

"But where did you come from?" Her eyes were wide and dark. If she was fixed up, he reflected, she would be right pretty.

"Place they call Jarilla," he said, "but I reckon this was a better way if you're travelin' alone. Jarilla's a Hickman town, an' they sure are a no-account lot."

"My father died," she told him, putting the gun in a holster hung to the wagon bed, "back there. Billy an' I buried him."

"You come across the basin alone?" He was incredulous.

"Yes. Father died in the mountains on the other side. That was three days ago."

Dusty removed his hat and began to strip the saddle and bridle from the stallion while the girl bent over her cooking. He found a hunk of bacon in his saddle pockets. "Got plenty of bacon?" he asked. "I 'most generally pack a mite along."

She looked up, brushing a strand of hair away from her face. She was flushed from the fire. "We haven't had any bacon for a week." She looked away quickly, and her chin quivered a little and then became stubborn. "Nor much of anything else, but you're welcome to join us."

He seated himself on the ground and leaned back on his saddle while she dished up the food. It wasn't much. A few dry beans and some cornbread. "You got some relatives out here somewhere?"

"No." She handed him a plate, but he was too thirsty to eat more than a few mouthfuls. "Father had a place out here. His lungs were bad and they told him the dry air would be good for him. My mother died when Billy was born, so there was nothing to keep us back in Missouri. We just headed West."

"You say your father had a place? Where is it?"

"I'm not sure. Father loaned some man some money, or, rather, he provided him with money with which to buy stock. The man was to come West and settle on a place, stock it, and then send for Dad."

Dusty ate slowly, thinking that over. "Got anything to show for it?"

"Yes, Father had an agreement that was drawn up and notarized. It's in a leather wallet. He gave the man five thousand dollars. It was all we had."

When they had eaten, the girl and boy went to sleep in the wagon box while Dusty stretched out on the ground nearby. *What a mess!* he told himself. *Those kids comin' away out here, all by themselves now, an' the chances are that money was blowed in over a faro layout long ago!*

In the morning, Dusty hitched up the mules for them. "You foller me," he advised, and turned the stallion up the trail to the north.

It was almost noon before he saw the thumb-like butte that marked the entrance to Gallo Gap. He turned toward it, riding ahead to scout the best trail, and at times dismounting to roll rocks aside so the wagon could get through.

Surmounting the crest of a low hill, he looked suddenly into Gallo Gap. His red-rimmed eyes stared greedily at the green grass and trees. The stallion smelled water and wanted to keep going, so waving the wagon on, he rode down into the gap.

Probably there were no more than 200 acres here, but it was waist deep in rich green grass, and the towering yellow pines were tall and very old. It was like riding from desolation into a beautiful park. He found the spring by the sound of running water, crystal clear and beautiful, the water rippling over the rocks to fall into a clear pond at least an acre in extent. Nearby, space had been cleared for a cabin, and then abandoned.

Dusty turned in the saddle as his horse stood knee deep in the water. The wagon pulled up. "This is a little bit of heaven!" he said, grinning at the girl. "Say, what's your name, anyway?"

"Ruth Grant," she said shyly.

All the weariness seemed to have fled from her face at the sight of the water and trees. She smiled gaily, and a few minutes later, as he walked toward the trees with a rifle in the crook of his elbow, he heard laughter and then her voice, singing. He stopped suddenly, watching some deer feeding a short distance off, and listening to her voice. It made a lump of loneliness rise in his throat.

That night, after they had eaten steaks from a fat buck he'd killed, their first good meal in days, he looked across the fire at her. "Ruth," he said, "I think I'll locate me a home right here. I've been lookin' for a place of my own. I reckon what we better do is for you-all to stay here with me until you get rested up. I'll build a cabin, and those mules of yours can get some meat on their bones again. Then I'll ride on down to Pie Town and locate this *hombre* your father had dealin's with an' see how things look."

That was the way they left it, but in the days that followed Dusty Barron had never been happier. He felled trees on the mountainside and built a cabin, and in working around he found ways of doing things he had never tried before. Ruth was full of suggestions about the house, sensible, knowing things that helped a lot. He worked the mules a little, using only one at a time and taking them turnabout.

He hunted a good deal for food. Nearby he found a salt lick and shot an occasional antelope, and several times, using a shotgun from the wagon, he killed blue grouse. In a grove of trees he found some ripe black cherries similar to those growing wild in the Guadalupe Mountains of West Texas. There was also some Mexican plum.

When the cabin was up and there was plenty of meat on hand, he got his gear in shape. Then he carefully oiled and cleaned his guns.

Ruth noticed them, and her face paled a little. "You believe there will be trouble?" she asked quickly. "I don't want you to. . . ."

"Forget it," he interrupted. "I've got troubles of my own." He explained about the killing of Dan Hickman and the long-standing feud between the families.

He left at daybreak. In his pocket he carried the leather wallet containing the agreement Roger Grant had made with Dick Lowe. It was a good day's ride from Gallo Gap to Aimless Creek, where Dusty camped the first night. The following day he rode on into Pie Town. From his talks with Ruth he knew something of Lowe and enough of the probable location of the ranch, if there was one.

A cowhand with sandy hair and crossed eyes was

seated on the top rail of the corral. Dusty reined in and leaned his forearm on the saddle horn and dug for the makings. After he had rolled a smoke, he passed them on to the cross-eyed rider.

"Know anything about an' *hombre* name of Dick Lowe?" he asked.

"Reckon so." They shared a match and, looking at each other through the smoke, decided they were men of a kind. "He's up there in the Spur Saloon now."

Dusty made no move. After a few drags on the cigarette, he glanced at the fire end. "What kind of *hombre* is he?"

"Salty." The cowhand puffed for a moment on his cigarette. "Salty an' mean. Plumb poison with a shootin' iron, an', when you ride for him, he pays you what he wants to when you quit. If you don't think you got a square deal, you can always tell him so, but when you do, you better reach."

"Like that, huh?"

"Like that." He smoked quietly for a few minutes. "Four *hombres* haven't liked what he paid 'em. He buried all four of 'em in his own personal boothill, off to the north of the ranch house."

"Sounds bad. Do all his own work or does he have help?"

"He's got help. Cat McQuill an' Bugle Nose Bender. Only nobody calls him Bugle Nose to his face."

"What about the ranch? Nice place?"

"Best around here. He come in here with money, had near five thousand dollars. He bought plenty of cattle an' stocked his range well." The cross-eyed cowhand looked at him, squinting through the smoke. "My name's Blue Riddle. I rode for him once."

"I take it you didn't argue none," Barron said, grinning.

"My maw never raised no foolish children," Riddle replied wryly. "They had me in a cross fire. Been Lowe alone, I'd maybe've took a chance, but as it was, they would have cut me down quick. So I come away, but I'm stickin' around, just waiting. I told him I aimed to have my money, an' he just laughed."

Dusty dropped his hand back and loosened his left-hand gun. Then he swung his leg back over the saddle and thrust his toe in the stirrup. "Well," he said, "I got papers here that say I speak for a gal that owns half his layout. I'm goin' up an' lay claim to it for her."

Riddle looked up cynically. "Why not shoot yourself and save the trouble? They'll gun you down." Then he sized Barron up again. "What did you say your name was?"

Dusty grinned. "I didn't say, but its Dusty Barron."

Blue Riddle slid off the corral rail. "One of the Barrons from Castle Rock?" He grinned again. "This I gotta see!"

Dusty was looking for a big man, but Dick Lowe, who he spotted at once on entering the saloon, was only a bit larger than himself, and he was the only small man among the Barrons.

Lowe turned to look at him as he entered. The man's

features were sharp, and his quick eyes glanced from Dusty Barron to Riddle, and then back again. Dusty walked to the bar, and Riddle loitered near the door.

The man standing beside Lowe at the bar must be Cat McQuill. The reason for the nickname was obvious, for there was something feline about the man's facial appearance.

"Lowe?" Dusty inquired.

"That's right." Lowe turned toward him slowly. "Something you want?"

"Yeah." Dusty leaned nonchalantly on the bar and ordered a drink. "I'm representin' your partner."

Dick Lowe's face blanched, and then turned hard as stone. His eyes glinted. However, he managed a smile with his thin lips. "Partner? I have no partner."

Dusty leaned on the bar watching his drink poured. He took his time.

Lowe watched him, slowly growing more and more angry. "Well," he said sharply, "if you've got something to say, say it!"

Dusty looked around, simulating surprise. "Why, I was just givin' you time to remember, Lowe. You can't tell me you can draw up an agreement with a man, have it properly notarized, and then take five thousand dollars of his money to stock a ranch, and not remember it!"

Dusty was pointedly speaking loudly, and the fact angered Lowe. "You have such an agreement?" Lowe demanded.

"Sure I got it."

"Where's the party this supposed agreement belongs to? Why doesn't he speak for himself?"

"He's dead. He was a lunger an' died on his way West."

Lowe's relief was evident. "I'm afraid," he said, "that this is all too obvious an attempt to get some money out of me. It won't work."

"It's nothing of the kind. Grant's dead, but he left a daughter and a son. I aim to see they get what belongs to 'em, Mister Lowe. I hope we can do it right peaceable."

Lowe's face tightened, but he forced a smile. He was aware he had enemies in Pie Town and did not relish their overhearing this conversation. He was also aware that it was pretty generally known that he had come into Pie Town with $5,000 in cash and bought cattle when everyone on the range was impoverished.

"I reckon this'll be easy settled," he said. "You bring the agreement to the ranch, an', if it's all legal, I reckon we can make a deal."

"Sure," Dusty agreed. "See you tomorrow."

On the plank steps of the hotel he waited until Riddle caught up with him. "You ain't actually goin' out there, are you?" Blue demanded. "That's just askin' for trouble!"

"I'm goin' out," Dusty agreed. "I want a look at the ranch myself. If I can ride out there, I can get an idea what kind of stock he's got and what shape the ranch is in. I've got a hunch, if we make a cash settlement, Lowe isn't goin' to give us much more chance to look around if he can help it. Besides, I've talked in front o' the folks here in town, and rough as some of them may be, they ain't goin' to see no orphans get gypped. No Western crowd would stand for that unless it's some outlaws like Lowe and his two pals."

Riddle walked slowly away, shaking his head with doubt. Dusty watched him go, and then went on inside.

He was throwing a saddle on the steel-dust next morning when he heard a low groan. Gun in hand he walked around the corner of the corral. Beyond a pile of poles he saw Blue Riddle pulling himself off the ground. "What happened?" Dusty demanded.

"Bender an' McQuill. They gave me my walkin' papers. Said I'd been in town too long, which didn't bother Lowe none till I took up with you. They gave me till daybreak to pull my freight." He staggered erect, holding a hand to his head. "Then Bender bent a gun over my noggin."

Barron's eyes narrowed. "Play rough, don't they?" He looked at Riddle. "What are you goin to do?"

"You don't see me out there runnin' down the road, do you?" Riddle said. "I'm sittin' tight!"

"Wash your face off, then," Dusty suggested, "an' we'll eat!"

"You go ahead," Riddle replied. "I'll be along."

Dusty glanced back over his shoulder as he left and saw Blue Riddle hiking toward the Indian huts that clustered outside of Pie Town.

. . .

When he rode out of town an hour later, Dusty Barron was not feeling overly optimistic. Riddle had stayed behind only at Dusty's insistence, but now that Dusty was headed toward Lowe's ranch, he no longer felt so confident. Dick Lowe was not a man to give up easily, nor to yield his ranch or any part of it without a fight. The pistol-whipping of Riddle had been ample evidence of the lengths to which he was prepared to go.

The range through which Dusty rode was good. This was what he had wanted to see. How they might have bargained in town he was not sure. He doubted if anyone there would interfere if a deal was made by him. It was his own problem to see that Ruth and Billy Grant got a fair deal, and that could not be done unless he knew something, at least, of the ranch and the stock.

Dusty was quite sure now that Lowe had never expected the consumptive Roger Grant to come West and claim his piece of the ranch. Nor had he planned to give it to him if he had. He knew very well that he himself was riding into the lion's mouth, but felt he could depend on his own abilities and that Lowe would not go too far after his talk before the bystanders who had been in the saloon. By now Lowe would know that the story would be known to all his enemies in Pie Town.

Cat McQuill was loafing on the steps when Dusty rode up, and the gunman's eyes gleamed with triumph at seeing him. "Howdy," he said affably. "Come on in. The boss is waitin' for you."

Bugle Nose Bender was leaning against the fireplace and Lowe was seated at his desk. "Here he is, boss!" McQuill said as they entered.

Lowe glanced up sharply. "Where's the agreement?" he asked, holding out his hand.

Barron handed it to him, and the rancher opened it, took a quick look, and then glanced up. "This is it, Cat!"

Too late Dusty heard the slide of gun on leather and whirled to face McQuill, but the pistol barrel crashed down over the side of his head and he hit the floor. Even as he fell, he realized what a fool he had been, yet he had been so sure they would talk a little, at least, that Lowe would try to run a blazer or to buy him off cheap.

Bender lunged toward him and kicked him in the ribs. Then Lowe reached over and, jerking him to his knees, struck him three times in the face. The pistol barrel descended again and drove him down into a sea of blackness.

How long they had pounded him, he had no idea. When he opened his eves, he struggled, fighting his way to a realization of where he was. It took him several minutes to understand that he was almost standing on his head in the road, one foot caught in the stallion's stirrup!

The steel-dust, true to his training, was standing rigidly in the road, his head turned to look at his master. "Easy boy," Dusty groaned. "Easy does it." Twisting his foot in the stirrup, he tried to free it, but to no avail.

He realized what they had planned. After beating him, they had brought him out here, wedged his foot in the stirrup, struck the horse, and, when he started to move, ridden hastily away before they could be seen. Most horses, frightened by the unfamiliar burden in the stirrup, would have raced away over the desert and dragged him to death. It had happened to more than one unwary cowhand.

They had reckoned without the steel-dust. The stallion had been reared by Dusty Barron from a tiny colt, and the two had never been long apart. The big horse had known instantly that something was radically wrong and had gone only a little way, and then stopped. His long training told him to stand, and he stood stockstill.

Dusty twisted his foot again but couldn't get loose. Nor could he pull himself up and get hold of the stirrup and so into the saddle. He was still trying this when hoof beats sounded on the road.

He looked around wildly, fearful of Lowe's return. Then a wave of relief went over him. It was Blue Riddle!

"Hey!" Blue exclaimed. "What the heck happened?" He swung down from his horse and hastily extricated Dusty from his predicament.

Barron explained. "They wanted me killed, so it would look like I was dragged to death. Lucky they got away from here in a hurry, afraid they might be seen."

"But they got the agreement!" Riddle protested.

"Uhn-uh." Barron grinned, and then gasped as his bruised face twinged with pain. "That was a copy. I put the agreement down an' traced over it. He took a quick look and thought it was the real thing. Now we got to get to town before he realizes what happened."

Despite his battered and bruised body and the throbbing of his face, Dusty crawled into the saddle and they raced up the road to Pie Town.

Two men were standing on the hotel porch as they rode up. One of them glanced at Dusty Barron. "Howdy. Young woman inside wants to see you."

Dusty rushed into the lobby and stopped in surprise. Facing him was Ruth Grant, holding Billy by the hand, but her smile fled when she saw his face. "Oh!" she cried. "What's happened to you?"

Briefly he explained. Then he demanded: "How'd you get here?"

"After you left," Ruth told him, "I was worried. After Father's death and the trouble we had before you came, there was no time to think of anything, and I had to always be thinking of where we would go and what we would do. Then I remembered a comment Father made once. You see, Mister Lowe left a trunk with us to bring West or send to him later. It wasn't quite full, so Father opened it to pack some other things in it. He found something there that worried him a great deal, and he told me several times that he was afraid he might have trouble when we got out here. From all he said I had an idea what he found, so after you were gone, we searched through the trunk and found some letters and a handbill offering a five-thousand-dollar reward for Lowe. Why he kept them I can't imagine, but the sheriff says some criminals are very vain and often keep such things about themselves."

"And then you rode on here?"

She nodded. "We met two men who were trailing you, and, as they had extra horses with them so they could travel fast, we joined them."

Dusty's face tightened. "Men looking for me?"

Riddle interrupted. "Dick Lowe's ridin' into town now!"

Dusty Barron turned, loosening his guns. He started for the door.

"I'm in on this, too!" Riddle said, trailing him.

They walked out on the porch and stepped down into the street, spreading apart. Dick Lowe and his two henchmen had dismounted and were starting into the saloon when something made them glance up the street.

"Lowe!" Dusty yelled. "You tried to kill me, an' I'm comin' for you!"

Dick Lowe's hard face twisted with fury as he wheeled, stepping down into the dust.

He stopped in the street, and Cat McQuill and Bender moved out to either side.

Dusty Barron walked steadily down the street, his eyes on Dick Lowe. All three men were dangerous, but Lowe was the man he wanted, and Lowe was the man he intended to get first.

"This man's an outlaw!" he said, speaking to Bender and McQuill. "He's wanted for murder in Saint Louis! If you want out, get out now!"

"You're lying!" Bender snarled.

Dusty Barron walked on. The sun was bright in the street, and little puffs of dust arose at every step. There were five horses tied to the hitch rail behind the three men. He found himself hoping none of them would be hit by a stray shot. To his right was Blue Riddle, walking even with him, his big hands hovering over his guns.

His eyes clung to Dick Lowe, riveted there as though he alone lived in the world. He could see the man drop into a half crouch, noticed the bulge of the tobacco sack in his breast pocket, the buttons down the two sides of his shirt. Under the brim of the hat he could see the straight bar of the man's eyebrows and the hard gleam of the eyes beneath, and then suddenly the whole tableau dissolved into flaming, shattering action.

Lowe's hand flashed for his gun and Dusty's beat him by a hair's breadth, but Dusty held his fire, lifting the gun slowly. Lowe's quick shot flamed by his ear, and he winced inwardly at the proximity of death. Then the gunman fired again and the bullet tugged impatiently at his vest. He drew a long breath and squeezed off a shot, then another.

Lowe rose on tiptoes, opened his mouth widely as if to gasp for breath, seemed to hold himself there for a long moment, and then pitched over into the street.

Dusty's gun swung with his eyes and he saw Bender was down on his knees, and so he opened up on McQuill. The cat man jerked convulsively, and then began to back away, his mouth working and his gun hammering. The man's gun stopped firing, and he stared at it, pulled the trigger again, and then reached for a cartridge from his belt.

Barron stood, spraddle-legged, in the street and saw Cat's hand fumble at his belt. The fingers came out with a cartridge and moved toward the gun, and then his eyes glazed and he dropped his iron. Turning, as though the whole affair had slipped his mind, he started for the saloon. He made three steps, and then lifted his foot, seemed to feel for the saloon step, and fell like a log across the rough board porch.

Blue Riddle was on his knees, blood staining a trouser leg. Bender was sprawled out in the dust, a darkening pool forming beneath him.

Suddenly the street was filled with people. Ruth ran up to Dusty and he slid his arm around her. With a shock, he remembered. "You said two men were looking for me. Who?"

"Only us."

He turned, staring. Two big men were facing him, grinning. "Buck and Ben! How in tarnation did you two find me?"

Buck Barron grinned. "We was wonderin' what happened to you. We come to town and had a mite of a ruckus with the Hickmans. What was left of them headed for El Paso in a mighty hurry . . . both of 'em. Then an Injun kid come ridin' up on a beat-up hoss and said you-all was in a sight of trouble, so we figgered we'd come along and see how you made out."

"An Injun?" Dusty was puzzled.

"Yeah," Riddle told him, "that was my doin'. I figgered you was headed for trouble, so I sent an Injun kid off after your brothers. Heck, if I'd knowed what you was like with a six-gun, I'd never have sent for 'em!"

Ben Barron grinned and rubbed at the stubble of whiskers. "An' if we'd knowed there was on'y three, we'd never have come!" He looked from Dusty to Ruth. "Don't look like you'll be comin' home right soon with that place at Gallo Gap an' what you've got your arm around. But what'll we tell Allie?"

"Allie?" Ruth drew away from him, eyes wide. "Who's Allie? You didn't tell me you had a girl!"

Dusty winked at his brothers. "Allie? She's war chief of the Barron tribe. Allie's my ma." He turned to Riddle. "Blue, how's about you sort of keepin' an eye on that gap place for me for a week or so? I reckon I'd better take Ruth home for a spell. Allie, she sure sets a sight of store by weddin's."

Ruth's answering pressure on his arm was all the answer he needed.

McQueen of the Tumbling K

Ward McQueen reined in the strawberry roan and squinted his eyes against the sun. Salty sweat made his eyes smart, and he dabbed at them with the end of a bandanna. Kim Sartain was hazing a couple of rambunctious steers back into line. Bud Fox was walking his horse up the slope to where Ward waited, watching the drive.

Fox drew up alongside him and said: "Ward, d'you remember that old brindle *ladino* with the scarred hide? This here is his range, but we haven't seen hide nor hair of him."

"That's one old mossyhorn I won't forget in a hurry. He's probably hiding back in one of the cañons. Have you cleaned them out yet?"

"Uhn-huh, we surely have. Baldy an' me both worked 'em, and no sign of him. Makes a body mighty curious."

"Yeah, I suppose you've got a point. It ain't like him to be away from the action. He'd surely be down there makin' trouble." He paused, suddenly thoughtful. "Missed any other stock since I've been gone?"

Fox shrugged. "If there's any missin', it can't be more than a few head, but you can bet if that old crow-bait is gone, some others went with him. He ramrods a good-sized herd all by himself."

Baldy Jackson joined them on the slope. He jerked his head to indicate a nearby cañon mouth. "Seen some mighty queer tracks over yonder," he said, "like a man afoot."

"We'll go have a look," McQueen said. "A man afoot in this country? It isn't likely."

He started the roan across the narrow valley, with Baldy and Bud following.

The cañon was narrow and high-walled. Parts of it were choked with brush and fallen rock, with only the winding watercourse to offer a trail. In the spreading fan of sand where the wash emptied into the valley, Baldy drew up.

Ward looked down at the tracks Baldy indicated. "Yes, they do look odd," said Ward. "Fixed him some homemade footgear. Wonder if that's his blood or some critter?" Leading the roan, he followed the tracks up the dry streambed.

After a few minutes, he halted. "He's been hurt. Look at the tracks headed this way. Fairly long, steady stride. I'd guess he's a tall man. But see here? Goin' back, the steps are shorter an' he's staggerin'. He stopped twice in twenty yards, each time to lean against something."

"Reckon we'd better follow him?" Baldy looked at the jumble of boulders and crowded brush. "If he doesn't aim to be ketched, he could make us a powerful lot of trouble."

"We'll follow him anyway. Baldy, you go back an' help the boys. Tell Kim an' Tennessee where we're at. Bud will stay with me. Maybe we can track him down, an' he should be grateful. It looks like he's hurt bad."

They moved along cautiously for another 100 yards. Bud Fox stopped, mopping his face. "He doesn't figure on bein' followed. He's makin' a try at losin' his trail. Even tried to wipe out a spot of blood."

Ward McQueen paused and looked up the water-course with keen, probing eyes. There was something wrong about all this. He had been riding this range for months now and believed he knew it well, yet he remembered no such man as this must be, and had seen no such tracks. Obviously the man was injured. Just as obviously he was trying, even in his weakened condition, to obliterate his trail. That meant that he expected to be followed and that those who followed were enemies.

Pausing to study the terrain, he ran over in his mind the possibilities from among those who he knew. Who might the injured man be? And who did he fear?

They moved on, working out the trail in the close, hot air of the cañon. The tracks split suddenly and disappeared on a wide ledge of stone where the cañon divided into two.

"We're stuck," Fox said. "He won't leave tracks with those makeshift shoes of his, and there's nowhere he can go up the cañons."

The right-hand branch ended in a steep, rocky slide, impossible to climb without hours of struggle, and the left branch ended against the sheer face of a cliff against whose base lay a heaped-up pile of boulders and rocky débris.

"He may have doubled back or hidden in the brush," Fox added.

Ward shrugged. "Let's go back. He doesn't want to be found, but hurt like he is, he's apt to die out here without care."

Deliberately he had spoken loudly. Turning their mounts, they rode back down the cañon to rejoin the herd.

Ruth Kermitt was waiting on the steps when they left the grassy bottom and rode up to the bunkhouse. With her was a slender, narrow-faced man in a black frock coat. As Ward drew up, the man's all-encompassing glance took him in, then slid away.

"Ward, this is Jim Yount. He's buying cattle and wants to look at the herd you just brought in."

"Howdy," Ward said agreeably. He glanced at Yount's horse, and then at the tied-down gun.

Two more men sat on the steps of the bunkhouse. A big man in a checkered shirt and a slim redhead with a rifle across his knees.

"We're looking to buy five hundred to a thousand head," Yount commented. "We heard you had good stock."

"Beef?"

"No, breeding stock, mostly. We're stockin' a ranch. I'm locatin' the other side of Newton's place."

Ward commented: "We have some cattle. Or rather, Miss Kermitt has. I'm just the foreman."

"Oh?" Yount looked around at Ruth with a quick,

flashing smile. "Miss, is it? Or are you a widow?"

"Miss. My brother and I came here together, but he was killed."

"Hard for a young woman to run a ranch alone, isn't it?" His smile was sympathetic.

"Miss Kermitt does very well," Ward replied coolly, "and she isn't exactly alone."

"Oh?" Yount glanced at McQueen, one eyebrow lifted. "No," he said after a minute, "I don't expect you could say she was alone as long as she had cattle on the place, and cowhands."

Ruth got up quickly, not liking the look on Ward's face. "Mister Yount? Wouldn't you like some coffee? Then we can talk business."

When they had gone inside, Ward McQueen turned on his heel and walked to the bunkhouse, leading his horse. He was mad and he didn't care who knew it. The thin-faced redhead looked at him as he drew near.

"What's the matter, friend? Somebody steal your girl?"

Ward McQueen halted and turned slowly. Baldy Jackson got up quickly and moved out of line. The move put him at the corner of the bunkhouse, leaving Yount's riders at the apex of a triangle of which McQueen and himself formed the two corners.

"Miss Kermitt"—McQueen's tone was cold—"is my boss. She is also a lady. Don't get any funny notions."

The redhead chuckled. "Yeah, and our boss is a ladies' man. He knows how to handle 'em." Deliberately he turned his back on Baldy. "Ever been foreman on a place like this, Dodson. Maybe you or me will have a new job."

Ward walked into the bunkhouse. Bud Fox was loitering beside the window. He, too, had been watching the pair.

"Don't seem the friendly type," Bud commented, pouring warm water into the tin wash basin. "Almost like they wanted trouble."

"What would be the idea of that?" Ward inquired.

Bud was splashing in the basin and made no reply, but Ward wondered. Certainly their attitude was not typical. He glanced toward the house, and his lips tightened. Jim Yount was a slick-talking sort and probably a woman would think him good-looking.

Out beyond the ranch house was a distant light, which would be Gelvin's store in Mannerhouse. Gelvin had ranched the country beyond Newton's. Suddenly McQueen made up his mind. After chow he would ride into Mannerhouse and have a little talk with Gelvin.

Supper was served in the ranch house as always and was a quiet meal but for Ruth and Jim Yount, who laughed and talked at the head of the table.

Ward, seated opposite Yount, had little to say. Baldy, Bud, and Tennessee sat in strict silence. Only Red Lund, seated beside Pete Dodson, occasionally ventured a remark. At the foot of the table, lean, wiry Kim Sartain let his eyes rove from face to face.

When supper was over, Ward moved outside into the

moonlight and Kim followed. "What goes on?" Kim whispered. "I never did see anybody so quiet."

Ward explained, adding: "Yount may be a cattle buyer, but the two riders with him are no average cow-punchers. Red Lund is a gun hand if I ever saw one, and Dodson's right off the Owlhoot Trail or I miss my guess." He hitched his belt. "I'm ridin' into town. Keep an eye on things, will you?"

"I'll do that." He lowered his tone. "That Lund now? I don't cotton to him. Nor Yount," he added.

Gelvin's store was closed but McQueen knew where to find him. Swinging down from the saddle, he tied his horse and pushed through the batwing doors. Abel was polishing glasses behind the bar, and Gelvin was at a table with Dave Cormack, Logan Keane, and a tall, lean-bodied stranger. They were playing poker.

Two other strangers lounged at the bar. They turned to look at him as he came in.

"Howdy, Ward! How's things at the Tumblin' K?"

The two men at the bar turned abruptly and looked at Ward again, quick, searching glances. He had started to speak to Gelvin, but something warned him and instead he walked to the bar.

"Pretty good," he replied. "Diggin' some stuff out of the breaks today. Tough work. All right for a brush-popper, but I like open country."

He tossed off his drink, watching the two men in the bar mirror. "They tell me there's good range beyond Newton's. I think I'll ride over and see if there's any lyin' around loose."

Gelvin glanced up. He was a short, rather handsome man with a keen, intelligent face.

"There's plenty that you can have for the taking. That country is going back to desert as fast as it can. Sand moving in, streams drying up. You can ride a hundred miles and never find a drink. Why"—he picked up the cards and began to shuffle them—"old Coyote Benny Chait came in two or three weeks ago. He was heading out of the country. He got euchred out of his ranch by some slick card handler. He was laughin' at the man who won it, said he'd get enough of the country in a hurry."

The two men at the bar had turned and were listening to Gelvin. One of them started to speak and the other put a cautioning hand on his arm.

"Who was it won the ranch? Did he say?"

"Sure." Gelvin began to deal. "Some driftin' card-sharp by the name of. . . ."

"You talk too much!" The larger of the two men at the bar stepped toward the card table. "What d'you know about the country beyond Newton's?"

Startled by the unprovoked attack, Gelvin turned in his chair. His eyes went from one to the other of the two men. Ward McQueen had picked up the bottle.

"What is this?" Gelvin asked, keeping his tone even. These men did not seem to be drunk, yet he was experienced enough to know he was in trouble, serious trouble. "What did I say? I was just commenting on the country beyond Newton's."

"You lied!" The big man's hand was near his gun.

"You lied! That country ain't goin' back! It's as good as it ever was!"

Gelvin was a stubborn man. This man was trying to provoke a fight, but Gelvin had no intention of being killed over a trifle. "I did not lie," he replied coolly. "I lived in that country for ten years. I came in with the first white men, and I've talked with the Indians who were there earlier. I know of what I speak."

"Then you're sayin' I'm a liar?" The big man's hand spread over his gun.

Ward McQueen turned in one swift movement. His right hand knocked the bottle spinning toward the second man and he kept swinging around, his right hand grabbing the big man by the belt. With a heave he swung the big man off balance and whirled him, staggering, into the smaller man who had sprung back to avoid the bottle.

The big man staggered again, fell, and then came up with a grunt of fury. Reaching his feet, his hand went to his gun, then froze. He was looking into a gun in Ward McQueen's hand.

"That was a private conversation," Ward said mildly. "In this town we don't interfere. Understand?"

"If you didn't have the drop on me, you wouldn't be talkin' so big!"

Ward dropped his six-gun into its holster. "All right, now you've got an even break."

The two men faced him, and suddenly neither liked what they saw. This was no time for bravery, they decided.

"We ain't lookin' for trouble," the smaller man said. "We just rode into town for a drink."

"Then ride out," Ward replied. "And don't butt into conversations that don't concern you."

"Hollier 'n' me . . . ," the big man started to speak, but then suddenly stopped and started for the door.

Ward stepped back toward the bar. "Thanks, Gelvin. You told me something I needed to know."

"I don't get it," Gelvin protested. "What made them mad?"

"That card shark you mentioned? His name wouldn't be Jim Yount, would it?"

"Of course! How did you know?"

The tall stranger playing cards with Gelvin glanced up and their eyes met. "You wouldn't be the Ward McQueen from down Texas way, would you?"

"That's where I'm from. Why?"

The man smiled pleasantly. "You cut a wide swath down thataway. I heard about your run-in with the Maravillas Cañon outfit."

McQueen was cautious when he took the trail to the Tumbling K, but he saw nothing of the two men in the saloon. Hollier—he was the smaller one. There had been a Hollier who escaped from a lynch mob down Uvalde way a few years back. He had trailed around with a man called Packer, and the larger of these two men had a P burned on his holster with a branding iron.

What was Jim Yount's game? Obviously the two

70

men from the saloon were connected with him somehow. They had seemed anxious Yount's name not be spoken, and they seemed eager to quiet any talk about the range beyond Newton's.

The available facts were few. Yount had won a ranch in a poker game. Gelvin implied the game was crooked. The ranch he won was going back to desert. In other words, he had won nothing but trouble. What came next?

The logical thing for a man of Yount's stamp was to shrug off the whole affair and go on about his business. He was not doing that, which implied some sort of a plan. Lund and Dodson would make likely companions to Packer and Hollier. Yount was talking of buying cattle, but he was not the sort to throw good money after bad. Did they plan to rustle the cattle?

One thing was sure. It was time he got back to the ranch to alert the boys for trouble. It would be coming sooner, perhaps, because of what happened tonight. But what about Ruth? Was she taken with Yount? Or simply talking business and being polite? Did he dare express his doubts to her?

The Tumbling K foreman was riding into the ranch yard when the shot rang out. Something had struck a wicked blow on his head, and he was already falling when he heard the shot.

His head felt constricted, as if a tight band had been drawn around his temples. Slowly, fighting every inch of the way, he battled his way to consciousness. His

lids fluttered, then closed, too weak to force themselves open. He struggled against the heaviness and
finally got his eyes open. He was lying on his back in
a vague half light. The air felt damp, cool.

Awareness came. He was in a cave or mine tunnel.
Turning his head carefully, he looked around. He was
lying on a crude pallet on a sandy floor. Some twenty
feet away was a narrow shaft of light. Nearby his gun
belt hung on a peg driven into the wall and his rifle
leaned against the wall.

The rift of light was blotted out and someone
crawled into the cave. A man came up and threw down
an armful of wood. Then he lighted a lantern and
glanced at McQueen.

"Come out of it, did you? Man, I thought you never
would."

He was lean and old, with twinkling blue eyes and
almost white hair. He was long and tall. Ward noted
the footgear suddenly. This was the man they had
trailed up the cañon!

"Who are you?" he demanded.

The man smiled and squatted on his heels. "Charlie
Quayle's the name. Used to ride for Chait, over
beyond Newton's."

"You're the one we trailed up the cañon the other
day. Yesterday, I believe it was."

"I'm the man, all right, but it wasn't yesterday.
You've been lyin' here all of two weeks, delirious
most of the time. I was beginning to believe you'd
never come out of it."

"Two weeks?" McQueen struggled to sit up, but the effort was too much. He sank back. "Two weeks? They'll figure I'm dead back at the ranch. Why did you bring me here? Who shot me?"

"Hold your horses. I've got to wash up and fix some grub." He poured water in a basin and began to wash his face and hands. As he dried his hands, he explained. "You was shot, and I ain't sure who done it. Two of them rustlin' hands of Yount's packed you to the cañon and dropped you into the wash. Then they caved sand over you and some brush. But they weren't about to do more than need be, so figurin' you were sure enough dead, they rode off. I was almighty curious to know who'd been killed, so I pulled the brush away and dug into the pile and found you was still alive. I packed you up here, and mister, it took some packin'. You're a mighty heavy man."

"Were you trailin' them when they shot me?"

"No. To tell you the truth, I was scoutin' the layout at the ranch, figurin' to steal some coffee when I heard the shot. Then I saw them carry you off, so I follered." Quayle lighted his pipe. "There's been some changes," he added. "You friend Sartain has been fired. So have Fox and that bald-headed gent. Tennessee had a run-in with Lund and Lund killed him. Picked a fight, and then beat him to the draw. Yount is real friendly with Ruth Kermitt, and he's runnin' the ranch. One or more of those tough gunmen of his is there all the time."

Ward lay back on his pallet. Kim Sartain fired! It

didn't seem reasonable. Kim had been with Ruth Kermitt longer than any of them. He had been with them when Ruth and her brother came over the trail from Montana. Kim had been with her through all that trouble at Pilot Range when Ward himself had first joined them. Kim had always ridden for the brand. Now he had been fired, run off the place. And Tennessee killed!

What sort of girl was Ruth Kermitt? She had fired her oldest and most loyal hands and taken on a bunch of rustlers with a tinhorn gambler for boss. And to think he had been getting soft on her! He'd actually been thinking she was the girl for him, and the only reason he'd held off was because he had no money, nothing to offer a woman. Well, this showed what a fool he would have been.

"You've got a hard head," Quayle was saying, "or you'd be dead by now. That bullet hit right over your eye and skidded around your skull under the skin. Laid your scalp open. You had a concussion, too. I know the signs. And you lost blood."

"I've got to get out of here," Ward said. "I've got to see Ruth Kermitt."

"You'd be better off to sit tight and get well. Right now she's right busy with that there Yount. Rides all over the range with him, holdin' hands more'n half the time. Everybody's seen 'em. And if she fired all the rest of her hands, you can be sure she doesn't want her foreman back."

He was right, of course. What good would it do even

to talk to a woman who would fire such loyal hands as she'd had?

"Where d' you fit into all this?"

Quayle sliced bacon into a frying pan. "Like I told you. I rode for Chait. Yount rooked him out of his ranch, but as a matter of fact Chait was glad to get shut of it. When Yount found what he'd won, he was sore. Me, I'd saved me nigh on a year's wages an' was fixin' to set up for myself. One of those hands of Yount's, he seen the money and trailed me down, said it was ranch money. We had us a fight and they got some lead into me. I got away an' holed up in this here cañon."

All day McQueen rested in the cave, his mind busy with the problem. But what could he do? If Ruth Kermitt had made her choice, it was no longer any business of his. The best thing he could do was to get his horse and ride out of there, just drop the whole thing.

It was well after dark before Quayle returned, but he had news and was eager to talk.

"That Yount is takin' over the country! He went into Mannerhouse last night, huntin' Gelvin, but Gelvin had gone off with that stranger friend of his that he plays poker with all the time. Yount had words with Dave Cormack and killed him. They say this Yount is greased lightning with a gun. Then Lund an' Pete Dodson pistol-whipped Logan Keane. Yount told them he was runnin' the Tumblin' K and was going to marry Ruth Kermitt, and he was fed up with the talk about him and his men. He thinks he's got that town treed, an' maybe he has. Takes some folks a long time to get riled."

Ruth to marry Jim Yount! Ward felt a sharp pang. He realized suddenly that he was in love with Ruth. Now that he realized it, he knew he had been in love with her for a long time. And she was to marry Yount.

"Did you see anything of Kim Sartain?"

"No," Quayle replied, "but I heard the three of them rode over into the range beyond Newton's."

Ward McQueen was up at daybreak. He rolled out of his blankets, and, although his head ached, he felt better. No matter. It was time to be up and doing. His long period of illness had at least given him rest, and his strength was such that he recovered rapidly. He oiled his guns and reloaded them. Quayle watched him preparing to travel but said nothing until he pulled on his boots. "Better wait until sundown if you're huntin' trouble," he said. "I got a hoss for you. Stashed him down in the brush."

"A horse? Good for you! I'm going to have a look at the ranch. This deal doesn't figure right to me."

"Nor me." Quayle knocked the ash from his pipe. "I seen that girl's face today. They rid past as I lay in the brush. She surely didn't look like a happy woman. Not like she was ridin' with a man she loved. Maybe she ain't willin'."

"I don't like to think she'd take up with a man like Yount. Well, tonight I ride."

"We ride," Quayle insisted. "I didn't like gettin' shot up any more than you-all. I'm in this fight, too."

"I can use the help, but what I'd really like you to do is hunt down Kim Sartain and the others. I can use their help. Get them back here for a showdown. Warn them it won't be pretty."

Where Quayle had found the quick-stepping buckskin Ward neither knew nor cared. He needed a horse desperately, and the buckskin was not only a horse but a very good one.

Whatever Yount's game was he had been fast and thorough. He had moved in on the Tumbling K, had Ward McQueen dry-gulched, had Ruth Kermitt fire her old hands, replaced them with his own men, and then rode into Mannerhouse and quieted all outward opposition by killing Dave Cormack and beating another man. If there was to have been opposition, it would have been Cormack and Keane who would have led it. Tennessee, too, had been killed, but Tennessee was not known in town, and that might be passed off as a simple dispute between cowhands. Yount had proved to be fast, ruthless, and quick of decision. As he acted with the real or apparent consent of Ruth Kermitt, there was nothing to be done by the townspeople in the village of Mannerhouse.

Probably, with Cormack and Keane out of the picture and Gelvin off God knew where, they were not inclined to do anything. None of them was suffering any personal loss, and nothing was to be gained by bucking a man already proven to be dangerous. Obviously the gambler was in control. He had erred in only two things. He had failed to kill Charlie Quayle and to make sure that McQueen was dead.

The buckskin had a liking for the trail and moved out fast. Ward rode toward the Tumbling K, keeping out of sight. Quayle had ridden off earlier in the day to find Kim, Baldy, and Bud Fox. The latter two were good cowhands and trustworthy, but the slim, dark-faced youngster, Kim Sartain, was one of the fastest men with a gun Ward had ever seen.

"With him," Ward told the buckskin, "I'd tackle an army."

He left the buckskin in a clump of willows near the stream, and then crossed on stepping-stones, working his way through the brush toward the Tumbling K ranch house.

He had no plan of action, or anything on which to base a plan. If he could find Ruth and talk to her, or if he could figure out what it was that Yount was trying to accomplish, it would be a beginning.

The windows were brightly lit. For a time he lay in the brush studying the situation. An error now would be fatal, if not to him, at least to their plans.

There would be someone around, he was sure. Quayle had said one of the gunmen was always on the ranch, for the gambler was a careful man.

A cigarette glowed suddenly from the steps of the bunkhouse. Evidently the man had just turned toward him. Had he inadvertently made a sound? At least he knew that somebody was there, on guard.

Ward eased off to the left until the house was between himself and the guard. Then he crossed swiftly to the side of the house. He eased a window a little higher. It was a warm night and the window had been open at the bottom.

Jim Yount was playing solitaire at the dining room table. Red Lund was oiling a pistol. Packer was leaning his elbows on the table and smoking, watching Yount's cards.

"I always wanted a ranch," Yount was saying, "and this is it. No use gallivanting around the country when a man can live in style. I'd have had it over beyond Newton's if that damned sand bed I got from Chait had been any good. Then I saw this place. It was too good to be true."

"You worked fast," Packer said, "but you had a streak of luck when Hollier an' me got McQueen. From what I hear, he was nobody to fool around with."

Yount shrugged. "Maybe so, but all sorts of stories get started and half of them aren't true. He might be fast with a gun, but he had no brains, and it takes brains to win in this kind of game." He glanced at Lund. "Look, that Logan Keane outfit lies south of Hosstail Creek, and it joins onto this one. Nice piece of country, thousands of acres with good water, running right up to the edge of town. Keane's scared now. Once me and Ruth Kermitt are married so our title to this ranch is cinched, we'll go to work on Keane. We'll rustle his stock, run off his hands, and force him to sell. I figure the whole job shouldn't take more than a month, at the outside."

Red glanced up from his pistol. "You get the ranches, what do we get?"

Yount smiled. "You don't want a ranch, and I do, but I happen to know that Ruth has ten thousand dollars cached. You boys"—for a moment his eyes held those of Red Lund—"can split that among you. You can work out some way of dividing it even up all around."

Lund's eyes showed his understanding, and McQueen glanced at Packer, but the big horse thief showed no sign of having seen the exchange of glances. Ward could see how the split would be made; it would be done with Red Lund's six-shooter. They would get the lead; he'd take the cash. It had the added advantage to Jim Yount of leaving only one witness to his treachery.

Crouched below the window, Ward McQueen calculated his chances. Jim Yount was reputed to be a fast man with a gun. Red Lund had already proved his skill. Packer would, also, be good, even if not an artist like the others. Three to one made the odds much too long, and at the bunkhouse would be Hollier and Pete Dodson, neither a man to be trifled with.

A *clatter* of horses' hoofs on the hard-packed trail, and a horseman showed briefly in the door and was ushered into the room. It was the lean stranger who had played poker with Gelvin and Keane.

"You Jim Yount? Just riding by and wanted to tell you there's an express package at the station for Miss

Kermitt. She can drop in tomorrow to pick it up if she likes."

"Express package? Why didn't you bring it out?"

"Wouldn't let me. Seems like its money or something like that. A package of *dinero* that's payment for some property in Wyoming. She's got to sign for it herself. They won't let anybody else have it."

Yount nodded. "All right. She's asleep, I think, but come morning I'll tell her."

The rider went out, and a few minutes later Ward heard his horse's hoofs on the trail.

"More money?" Packer grinned. "Not bad, boss! She can pick it up for us and we'll split it."

Red Lund was wiping off his pistol. "I don't like it," he spoke suddenly. "Looks like a move to get us off the ranch and the girl into town."

Yount shrugged. "I doubt it, but suppose that's it? Who in town has the guts or the skill to tackle us? Personally I believe it's the truth, but if it ain't, why worry? We'll send Packer in ahead to scout. If there's any strangers around, he can warn us. I think it's all right. We'll ride in tomorrow."

An hour later, and far back on a brush-covered hillside, Ward McQueen bedded down for the night. From where he lay, he could see anybody who arrived at or left the ranch. One thing he knew. Tomorrow was the pay-off. Ruth Kermitt would not be returning to the ranch.

At daylight he was awake and watching, his buck-

81

skin saddled and ready. It had been a damp, uncomfortable night, and he stretched, trying to get the chill from his muscles. The sunshine caught reflected light from the window. Hollier emerged and began roping horses in the corral. He saddled his own, Ruth's brown mare, and Yount's big gray.

Ward McQueen tried to foresee what would happen. He was convinced, as was Red Lund, that the package was a trick. There were only nine buildings on the town's main street, scarcely more than two dozen houses scattered about. The express and stage office was next to the saloon. Gelvin's store was across the street.

Whatever happened, Ruth would be in danger. She would be with Yount, closely surrounded by the others. To fire on them was to endanger her.

And where did that young rider stand? He had been called Rip, and he had known of McQueen's gun battle in Maravillas Cañon. Ward was sure he was not the aimless drifter he was supposed to be. His face was too keen, his eyes too sharp. If he had baited a trap with money, he had used the only bait to which these men would rise. But what was he hoping to accomplish?

There were no men in Mannerhouse who could draw a gun in the same league with Yount or Lund. Gelvin would try, if he was there, but Gelvin had only courage, and no particular skill with a handgun, and courage alone was not enough.

It was an hour after daylight when Packer mounted

his paint gelding and started for town. Ward watched him go, speculating on what must follow. He had resolved upon his own course of action. His was no elaborate plan. He intended to slip into town and at the right moment kill Jim Yount and, if possible, Red Lund.

The only law in Mannerhouse was old John Binns, a thoroughly good man of some seventy years who had been given the job largely in lieu of a pension. He had been a hardworking man who owned his home and a few acres of ground, and he had a wife only a few years younger.

Mannerhouse had never been on the route of trail drives, land booms, or mining discoveries, and in consequence the town had few disturbances or characters likely to cause them. The jail had been used but once, when the town first came into being, and few citizens could remember the occasion. John Binns's enforcement of the law usually was a quiet suggestion to be a little less noisy or to go home and sleep it off.

Ward McQueen, a law-abiding man, found himself faced with a situation where right, justice, and the simple rules of civilized society were being pushed aside by men who did not hesitate to kill. One prominent citizen had been murdered, another pistol-whipped. Their stated intention was to do more of the same, to say nothing of Jim Yount's plan to marry Ruth, and his implication had been that it was simply a means to seize her land. Once they had won what they wished, there was no reason to believe the violence would cease. Gangrene had infected the area, and the only solution open to Ward McQueen was to amputate.

Yet he was no fool. He knew something of the gun skills of the men he would face. Even if he was killed himself, he must eliminate them. The townspeople could take care of such as Hollier and Packer. If he succeeded, Kim Sartain could handle the rest of it, and would. That was Kim's way.

Mounting the buckskin, he started down the trail toward Mannerhouse, only a few miles away. When he had ridden but a few hundred yards, he saw from his vantage point above the ranch that three riders were also headed for town. Jim Yount, Ruth, and, a few yards behind, Red Lund.

Pete Dodson, riding a sorrel horse, was also headed for town but by another route. Jim Yount was taking no chances.

The dusty main street of Mannerhouse lay warm under the morning sun. On the steps of the express office Rip was sunning himself. Abel, behind his bar, watched nervously both his window and his door. He was on edge and aware, aware as a wild animal is when a strange creature nears its lair. Trouble was in the wind.

Gelvin's store was closed, unusual for this time of day. Abel glanced at Rip, and his brow furrowed. Rip was wearing two tied-down guns this morning, unusual for him.

Abel finished polishing the glass and put it down, glancing nervously at Packer. Suddenly Packer downed the drink and got to his feet. Walking to the door, he glanced up and down the street. All was quiet, yet the big man was worried. A man left the post office and walked along the boardwalk to the barbershop, and entered. The sound of the closing door was the only sound. A hen pecked at something in the mouth of the alley near Gelvin's store. As he watched, he saw Pete Dodson stop his horse behind Gelvin's. Pete was carrying a rifle. Packer glanced over at Rip, noting the guns.

Packer turned suddenly, glaring at Abel. "Give me that scatter-gun you got under the bar!"

"Huh?" Abel was frightened. "I ain't got. . . ."

"Don't give me that! I want that gun!"

There was an instant when Abel considered covering Packer or even shooting him, but the big man frightened him and he put the shotgun on the bar. Packer picked it up and tiptoed to the window and put the gun down beside it. Careful to make no sound, he eased the window up a few inches. His position now covered Rip's side and back.

Abel cringed at what he had done. He liked Rip. The lean, easygoing, friendly young man might now be killed because of him. He'd been a coward. He should have refused, covered Packer, and called Rip inside. And he could have done that. If he wasn't such a coward. Now, because of him, a good man might be murdered, shot in the back. What was going on, anyway? This had been such a quiet little town.

Jim Yount rode up the street with Ruth beside him. Her face was pale and strained, and her eyes seemed unnaturally large.

Red Lund trailed a few yards behind. He drew up, and tied his horse across the street.

From the saloon Abel could see it all. Jim Yount and Ruth Kermitt were approaching Rip from the west. North and west was Red Lund. Due north and in the shadow of Gelvin's was Pete Dodson. In the saloon was Packer. Rip was very neatly boxed, signed, and sealed. All but delivered.

Jim Keane, Logan's much older brother, was the express agent. He saw Jim Yount come, saw Red Lund across the street.

Rip got up lazily, smiling at Ruth.

"Come for your package, Miss Kermitt?" he asked politely. "While you're here, would you mind answering some questions?"

"By whose authority?" Yount demanded sharply.

Ward McQueen, crouched behind the saloon, heard the reply clearly. "The state of Texas, Yount," Rip replied. "I'm a Texas Ranger."

Jim Yount's short laugh held no humor. "This ain't Texas, and she answers no questions."

Ward McQueen opened the back door of the saloon and stepped inside.

Packer, intent on the scene before him, heard the door open. Startled and angry, he whirled around. Ward McQueen, who he had buried, was standing just inside the door. The shotgun was resting on the windowsill behind Rip. Packer went for his six-gun, but even as he reached, he knew it was hopeless. He saw the stab of flame, felt the solid blow of the bullet, and felt his knees turn to butter under him. He pitched forward on his face.

Outside all hell broke loose. Ruth Kermitt, seeing Rip's situation, spurred her horse to bump Yount's, throwing him out of position. Instantly she slid from the saddle and threw herself to the ground near the edge of the walk.

All seemed to have begun firing at once. Yount, cursing bitterly, fired at Rip. He in turn was firing at Red Lund. Ward stepped suddenly from the saloon and saw himself facing Yount, who had brought his mount under control. He fired at Yount, and a bullet from Dodson's rifle knocked splinters from the post in front of his face.

Yount's gun was coming into line and McQueen fired an instant sooner. Yount fired and they both missed. Ward's second shot hit Yount, who grabbed for the pommel. Ward walked a step forward, but something hit him and he went to his knee. Red Lund loomed from somewhere, and Ward got off another shot. Lund's face was covered with blood.

There was firing from the stage station and from Gelvin's store. There was a thunder of hoofs, and a blood-red horse came charging down the street, its rider hung low like an Indian, shooting under the horse's neck.

Yount was down, crawling on his belly in the dust. He had lost hold of his six-shooter, but his right hand held a knife and he was crawling toward Ruth. McQueen's six-shooter *clicked* on an empty chamber. How many shots were left in his other gun? He lifted it with his left hand. Something was suddenly wrong with his right. He rarely shot with his left hand, but now. . . .

Yount was closer. Ruth was staring across the street, unaware. McQueen shot past Ruth, squeezing off the shot with his left hand. He saw Yount contract sharply as the bullet struck. McQueen fired again, and the gambler rolled over on his side and the knife slipped from his fingers.

Abel ran from the saloon with a shotgun, and Gelvin from his store with a rifle. Then Ruth was running toward him, and he saw Kim Sartain coming back up the street, walking the red horse. Ward tried to rise to meet Ruth, but his knees gave way and he went over on his face, thinking how weak she must think him. He started to rise again, and blacked out.

When he could see again Ruth was beside him. Kim was squatting on his heels. "Come on, Ward!" he said. "You've only been hit twice and neither of 'em bad. Can't you handle lead any more?"

"What happened?"

"Clean sweep, looks like. Charlie Quayle got to us and we hightailed it to the ranch. Hollier wanted to give us trouble, but we smoked him out. I believe there were others around, but if there were, they skipped the country. Whilst they were cleanin' up, I took it on the run for town. Halfway here, I thought I heard a shot, and, when I hit the street, everybody in town was shootin', or that's what it looked like. Reg'lar Fourth of July celebration! Pete Dodson is dead, and Red Lund's dying with four bullets in him. Yount's alive, but he won't make it, either. Packer's dead."

Ward's head was aching and he felt weak and sick, but he did not want to move, even to get out of the street. He just wanted to sit, to forget all that had taken place. With fumbling fingers, from long habit, he started to reload his pistols. Oddly he found one of them contained three live shells. Somehow he must have reloaded, but he had no memory of it.

Rip came over. "My name's Coker, Ward. I couldn't figure any way to bust up Yount's operation without getting Ruth Kermitt away from him first, so I faked that package to get them into town, hoping I could get her away from them. I didn't figure they'd gang up on me like they did."

They helped Ward up and into the saloon. Gelvin brought the doctor in. "Yount just died," Gelvin said, "cussing you and everybody concerned."

He sat back in a chair while the doctor patched him up. Again he had lost blood. "I've got to find a bed," he said to Kim. "There must be a hotel in town."

"You're coming back to the ranch," Ruth said. "We need you there. They told me you left me, Ward. Jim

Yount said you pulled out and Kim with you. I hadn't seen him, and Yount said he'd manage the ranch until I found someone. Then he brought his own men in and fired Kim, who I hadn't seen, and I was surrounded and scared. If you had been there, or if I'd even known you were around, I. . . ."

"Don't worry about it." Ward leaned his head back. All he wanted was rest.

Baldy Jackson helped him into a buckboard, Bud Fox driving. "You know that old brindle longhorn who turned up missin'? Well, I found him. He's got about thirty head with him, holed up in the prettiest little valley you ever did see. Looks like he's there to stay."

"He's like me," Ward commented, "so used to his range he wouldn't be happy anywhere else."

"Then why think of anywhere else?" Ruth said. "I want you to stay."

A Man Called Trent

I

Smoke lifted wistfully from the charred timbers of the house, and smoke lifted from the shed that had been Moffitt's barn. The corral bars were down and the saddle stock run off, and, where Dick Moffitt's homestead had been in the morning, there was now only desolation, emptiness, and death.

Dick Moffitt himself lay sprawled on the ground. The dust was scratched deeply where his fingers had dug in the agony of death. Even from where he sat on the long-legged buckskin, the man known as Trent could see he had been shot six times. Three of those bullets had gone in from the front. The other three had been fired directly into his back by a man who stood over him. And Dick Moffitt wore no gun.

The little green valley was still in the late afternoon sun. It was warm, and there was still a faint heat emanating from the charred timber of the house.

The man who called himself Trent rode his horse around the house. Four or five men had come here. One of them riding a horse with a split right rear hoof. They had shot Moffitt down and then burned his layout.

What about the kids? What about Sally Crane, who was sixteen? And young Jack Moffitt, who was fourteen? Whatever had happened, there was no evidence of them here. He hesitated, looking down the trail. Had they been taken away by the killers? Sally, perhaps, but not Jack. If the killers had found the two, Jack would have been dead.

Thoughtfully Trent turned away. The buckskin knew the way was toward home, and he quickened his pace. There were five miles to go, five miles of mountains and heavy woods, and no clear trails.

This could be it. Always, he had been sure it would come. Even when happiest, the knowledge that sooner or later he must sling his gun belts on his hips had been ever present in the back of his mind. Sooner or later there would be trouble, and he had seen it coming here along the rimrock.

Slightly more than a year ago he had built his cabin and squatted in the lush green valley among the peaks. No cattle ranged this high. No wandering cowpunchers drifted up here. Only the other nesters had found homes, the Hatfields, O'Hara, Smithers, Moffitt, and the rest.

Below, in the vicinity of Cedar Bluff, there was one ranch—one and only one. On the ranch and in the town, one man ruled supreme. He rode with majesty, and, when he walked, he strode with the step of kings. He never went unattended. He allowed no man to address him unless he spoke first, he issued orders and bestowed favor like an Eastern potentate, and, if there were some who disputed his authority, he put them down, crushed them.

King Bill Hale had come West as a boy, and he had

had money even then. In Texas he had driven cattle over the trails and had learned to fight and sling a gun, and to drive a bargain that was tight and cruel. Then he had come farther West, moved into the town of Cedar Bluff, built the Castle, and drove out the cattle rustlers who had used the valley as a hide-out. The one other honest rancher in the valley he bought out, and, when that man had refused to sell, Hale had told him to sell, or else. And he had cut the offered price in half. The man sold.

Cedar Bluff and Cedar Valley lived under the eye of King Bill. A strong man and an able one, Hale had slowly become power mad. The valley was cut off from both New Mexico and Arizona. In his own world he could not be touched. His will was law. He owned the Mecca, a saloon and gambling house. He owned the stage station, the stage line itself, and the freight company that hauled supplies in and produce out. He owned the Cedar Hotel, the town's one decent rooming house. He owned 60,000 acres of good grazing land and controlled 100,000 more. His cattle were numbered in the tens of thousands, and two men rode beside him when he went among his other men. One was rough, hard-scaled Pete Shaw, and the other was his younger son, Cub Hale. Behind him trailed the gold-dust twins, Dunn and Ravitz, both gunmen.

The man who called himself Trent rarely visited Cedar Bluff. Sooner or later, he knew, there would be someone from the outside, someone who knew him, someone who would recognize him for what and who he was, and then the word would go out.

"That's Kilkenny!"

Men would turn to look, for the story of the strange, drifting gunman was known to all in the West, even though there were few men anywhere who knew him by sight, few who could describe him or knew the way he lived.

Mysterious, solitary, and shadowy, the gunman called Kilkenny had been everywhere. He drifted in and out of towns and cow camps, and sometimes there would be a brief and bloody gun battle, and then Kilkenny would be gone again, and only the body of the man who had dared to try Kilkenny remained.

So Kilkenny had taken the name of Trent, and in the high peaks he had found the lush green valley where he built his cabin and ran a few head of cows and broke wild horses. It was a lonely life, but when he was there, he hung his guns on a peg and carried only his rifle, and that for game or for wolves.

Rarely, not over a dozen times in the year, he went down to Cedar Bluff for supplies, packed them back, and stayed in the hills until he was running short again. He stayed away from the Mecca, and most of all he avoided the Crystal Palace, the new and splendid dance hall and gambling house owned by the woman, Nita Riordan.

The cabin in the pines was touched with the red glow of a sun setting beyond the notch, and he swung down from the buckskin and slapped the horse cheerfully on the shoulder.

"Home again, Buck! It's a good feeling, isn't it?"

He stripped the saddle and bridle from the horse and carried them into the log barn, then he turned the buckskin into the corral, and forked over a lot of fresh green grass.

It was a lonely life, yet he was content. Only at times did he find himself looking long at the stars and thinking about the girl in Cedar Bluff. Did she know he was here? Remembering Nita from the Live Oak country, he decided she did. Nita Riordan knew all that was going on; she always had.

He went about the business of preparing a meal, and thought of Parson Hatfield and his tall sons. What would the mountaineer do now? Yet, need he ask that question? Could he suspect, even for a moment, that the Hatfields would do anything but fight? They were the type. They were men who had always built with their hands and who were beholden to no man. They were not gunfighters, but they were lean, hard-faced men, tall and stooped a little, who carried their rifles as if they were part of them. And big Dan O'Hara, the talkative, friendly Irishman who always acted as though campaigning for public office—could he believe that Dan would do other than fight?

War was coming to the high peaks, and Trent's face grew somber as he thought of it. War meant that he would once more be shooting, killing. He could, of course, mount in the morning and ride away. He could give up this place in the highlands and go once more, but even as the thought came to him, he did not recognize it as even a remote possibility. Like O'Hara and the Hatfields, he would fight.

There were other things to consider. The last time he had been to Cedar Bluff, there had been a letter from Lee Hall, the Ranger.

We're getting along all right here, but I thought you would like to know: Cain Brockman is out. He swears he will hunt you down and kill you for killing his brother and whipping him with your fists. And he'll try, so be careful.

He dropped four slices of bacon into the frying pan, humming softly to himself. Then he put on some coffee water and sat watching the bacon. When it was ready, he took it out of the pan and put it on a tin plate. He was reaching for the coffee when he heard a muffled movement.

Instantly he froze in position. His eyes fastened on the blanket that separated his bedroom from the living room of the two-room cottage. His guns were hanging from a peg near the cupboard. He would have to cross the room to them. His rifle was nearer.

Rising, he went about the business of fixing the coffee, and, when close to the rifle, he dropped his hand to it. Then, swinging it hip high, he crossed the room with a bound, and jerked back the blanket.

Two youngsters sat on the edge of his homemade

bed, a slender, wide-eyed girl of sixteen and a boy with a face thickly sprinkled with freckles. They sat tightly together, frightened and pale.

Slowly he let the gun butt down to the floor. "Well, I'll be . . . ! Say, how did you youngsters get here?"

The girl swallowed and stood up, trying to curtsey. Her hair, which was very lovely, hung in two thick blonde braids. Her dress was cheap and cotton and now, after rough treatment, was torn and dirty. "We're . . . I mean, I'm Sally Crane, and this is Jackie Moffitt."

"They burned us out!" Jackie cried out, his face twisted and pale. "Them Hales done it! An' they kilt Pappy!"

"I know." Trent looked at them gravely. "I came by that way. Come on out here an' we'll eat. Then you can tell me about it."

"They come in about sunup this mornin'," Jack said. "They told Pap he had two hours to get loaded an' movin'. Pap, he allowed he wasn't movin'. This was government land an' he was settled legal, an' he was standin' on his rights."

"What happened?" Trent asked. He sliced more bacon and dropped it in the pan.

"The young 'un, he shot Pap. Shot him three times afore he could move. Then after he fell, he emptied his gun into him."

Something sank within Trent, for he could sense the fight that was coming. The "young 'un" would probably be Cub Hale. He remembered that slim, erect, panther-like young man in white buckskins and riding

97

his white horse, that young, handsome man who loved to kill. Here it was, and there was no way a man could duck it. But, no. It wasn't his fight. Not yet, it wasn't.

"How'd you kids happen to come here?" he asked kindly.

"We had to get away. Sally was gettin' wood for the house, an', when I met her, we started back. Then we heard the shootin', an', when I looked through the brush, I seen the young 'un finishin' Pap. I wanted to fight, but I ain't got no gun."

"Did they look for you?" Trent asked.

"Uhn-huh. We heard one of 'em say he wanted Sally!" Jackie glanced at the girl, whose face was white, her eyes wide. "They allowed there wasn't no use killin' her . . . yet!"

"You had horses?" Trent asked.

"Uhn-huh. We done left them in the brush. We wasn't sure but what they'd come here, too. But we come here because Pap, he done said if anythin' ever happened to him, we was to come here first. He said you was a good man, an' he figgered you was some shakes with a gun."

"All right." Trent dished them out some food. "You kids can stay here tonight. I got blankets enough. Then in the mornin' I'll take you down to Parson's."

"Let me fix that," Sally pleaded, reaching for the skillet. "I can cook."

"She sure can," Jackie declared admiringly. "She cooked for us all the time."

A horse's hoof *clicked* on a stone, and Trent doused

the light instantly. "Get down," he whispered hoarsely. "On the floor. Let's see who this is."

He could hear the horses coming closer, two of them from the sound. Then a voice rang out sharply.

"Halloo, the house! Step out here!"

From inside the door, Trent replied shortly: "Who is it? What d' you want?"

"It don't make a damn who it is! Trent, we're givin' you till noon tomorrow to hit the trail! You're campin' on Hale range! We're movin' everybody off!"

Trent laughed harshly. "That's right amusin', friend," he said dryly. "You go back an' tell King Bill Hale that I'm stayin' right where I am. This is government land, filed on all fittin' an' proper." He glimpsed the light on a gun barrel and spoke sharply. "Don't try it, Dunn. I know you're there by your voice. If you've got a lick of sense, you know you're outlined against the sky. A blind man could get you both at this range."

Dunn cursed bitterly. Then he shouted: "You won't get away with this, Trent!"

"Go back an' tell Hale I like it here, an' I'm plannin' to stay!"

When they had gone, Trent turned to the youngsters. "We'll have a little time now. Sally, you take the bed in the other room, Jackie an' me, we'll bunk out here."

"But . . . ?" Sally protested.

"Go ahead. You'll need all the sleep you can get. I think the trouble has just started. But don't be afraid. Everything is goin' to be all right."

"I'm not afraid." Sally Crane looked at him with large, serious eyes. "You'll take care of us, I know."

He stood there a long minute staring after her. It was a strange feeling to be trusted, and trusted so implicitly. The childish sincerity of the girl moved him as nothing had ever moved him before. He recognized the feeling for what it was, the need within him to protect and care for something beyond himself. It was that, in part, that during these past years had led him to fight so many fights that were not his. And yet, was not the cause of human liberty and freedom always every man's trust?

Jackie was going about the business of making a bed on the floor as though he had spent his life at it. He seemed pleased with this opportunity to show some skill, some ability to do things.

Trent reached up and took down his guns and checked them as he had every night of the entire year in which they had hung from the peg. For a minute after he completed the check, he held them. He liked the feel of them, even when he hated what they meant. Slowly he replaced them on the peg.

II

The early morning sun was just turning the dew-drenched grass into settings for diamonds when Trent was out of his pallet and roping some horses. Yet, early as it was when he returned to the cabin, the fire was going and Sally was preparing breakfast. She smiled at him, but her eyes were red and he could see she had been crying.

Jackie, beginning to realize now the full meaning of the tragedy, was showing his grief through his anger, but was very quiet. Trent was less worried about Jackie than about Sally. Only six years before, according to what Dick Moffitt had told him, Sally Crane had been found hiding in the bushes. Her father's wagons had been burned and her parents murdered by renegades posing as Indians. Since then, Dick had cared for her. Dick's wife had died scarcely a year before, and the girl had tried to take over the household duties, yet even to a Western girl, hardened to a rough life, two such tragedies, each driving her from a home, might be enough to upset her life.

When breakfast was over, he took them out to the saddled horses. Then he walked back to the cabin alone, and, when he returned, he carried an old Sharps rifle. He looked at it a moment, and then he glanced up at Jackie. The boy's eyes were widening, unbelieving, yet bright with hope.

"Jackie," Trent said quietly, "when I was fourteen, I was a man. Had to be. Well, it looks like your pappy dyin' has made you a man, too. I'm goin' to give you this Sharps. She's an old gun, but she can shoot. But Jackie, I'm not givin' this gun to a boy. I'm givin' it to a man. I'm givin' it to Jackie Moffitt, an' he's already showed himself pretty much of a man. A man, Jackie, he don't ever use a gun unless he has to. He don't go around shootin' heedless-like. He shoots only when he has to, an' then he don't miss. This gun's a present, Jackie, an' there's no strings attached, but it carries a responsibility, an' that is never to use it against a man unless it's in defense of your life or the lives or homes of those you love. You're to keep it loaded always. A gun ain't no good to a man unless it's loaded, an', if it's seen settin' around, people won't be handlin' it careless. They'll say 'that's Jackie Moffitt's gun, an' it's always loaded.' It's always guns people think are empty that kill people by accident."

"Gosh!" Jackie stared in admiration at the battered old Sharps. "That's a weapon, man!" Then he looked up at Trent, and his eyes were filled with tears of sincerity. "Mister Trent, I sure do promise! I'll never use no gun unless I have to!"

Trent swung into the saddle and watched the others mount. He carried his own Winchester, one of the new 1873 models that were replacing the old Sharps on the frontier. He was under no illusions. If King Bill Hale had decided to put an end to the nesters among the high peaks, he would probably succeed. But Hale was so impressed with his own power that he was not reckoning with the Hatfields, O'Hara, or himself.

"Y'know, Jackie," Trent said thoughtfully, "there's a clause in the Constitution that says the right of an American to keep and bear arms shall not be abridged. They put that in there so a man would always have a gun to defend his home or his liberty. Right now there's a man in this valley who is tryin' to take the liberty an' freedom of some men away from 'em.

When a man starts that, and when there isn't any law to help, you got to fight. I've killed men, Jackie, an' it ain't a good thing, no way. But I never killed a man unless he deserved killin' an' unless he forced me to a corner where it was me or him. This here country is big enough for all, but some men get greedy for money or power, an', when they do, the little men have to fight to keep what they got. Your pappy died in a war for freedom just as much as if he was killed on a battlefield somewheres. Whenever a brave man dies for what he believes, he wins more'n he loses. Maybe not for him, but for men like him that want to live honest an' true."

The trail narrowed and grew rougher, and Trent felt a quick excitement within him, as he always did when he rode up to this windy plateau. They went up through the tall pines toward the knife-like ridges that crested the divide, and, when they finally reached the plateau, he reined in, as he always did when he reached that spot.

Off over the vast distance that was Cedar Valley lay the blue haze that deepened to purple against the far-distant mountains. Here the air was fresh and clear, crisp with the crispness of the high peaks and the sense of limitless distance.

Skirting the rim, Trent led on and finally came to the second place he loved, a place he not only loved but which was a challenge to all that was in him. For here the divide, with its skyscraping ridges, was truly a divide. It drew a ragged, mountainous line between the lush beauty of Cedar Valley and the awful waste of the scarred and tortured Smoky Desert.

Always there seemed a haze of dust or smoke hanging in the sky over Smoky Desert, and what lay below it, no man could say, for no known trail led down the steep cañon to the waste below. An Indian had once told him his fathers knew of a trail to the bottom, but no living man knew it, and no man seemed to care, nobody but Trent, drawn by his own loneliness to the vaster loneliness below. Far away were ragged mountains, red, black, and broken like the jagged stumps of broken teeth gnawing at the sky. It was, he believed, the far edge of what was actually an enormous crater, greater than any other of its kind on earth.

"Someday," he told his companions, "I'm goin' down there. It looks like the mouth of hell itself, but I'm goin' down."

Parson Hatfield and his four tall sons were all in sight when the three rode up to the cabin. All were carrying their long Kentucky rifles.

"Alight, Trent," Parson drawled, widening his gash of a mouth into a smile. "We was expectin' 'most anybody else. Been some ructions down to the valley."

"Yeah." Trent swung down. "They killed Dick Moffitt. These are his kids, Parson. I figgered maybe you could make a place for 'em."

"You thought right, son. The good Lord takes care of His own, but we have to help. There's always room for another beneath the roof of a Hatfield."

Quincy Hatfield, oldest of the lean, raw-boned Kentucky boys, joined them. "Howdy," he said. "Did Pap tell you all about Leathers?"

"Leathers?" Trent frowned in quick apprehension. "What about him?"

"He ain't a-goin' to sell anything to us no more." The tall young man spat and shifted his rifle to the hollow of his arm. "That makes the closest store over at Blazer, an' that's three days across the mountains."

Trent shrugged, frowning. "Aims to freeze us out or kill us off." He glanced at Parson speculatively. "What are you plannin'?"

Hatfield shook his head. "Nothin' so far. We sort of figgered we might get together with the rest of the nesters an' try to figger out somethin'. I had Jake ride down to get O'Hara, Smithers, an' young Bartram. We got to have us a confab." Parson Hatfield rubbed his long, grizzled jaw and stared at Trent. His gray eyes were inquisitive, sly. "Y'know, Trent, I always had me an idea you was some shakes of a battler yourself. Maybe, if you'd wear some guns, you'd make some of them gun-slick *hombres* of Hale's back down cold."

Trent smiled. "Why, Parson, I reckon you guess wrong. Me, I'm a peace-lovin' *hombre*. I like the hills, an' all I ask is to be let alone."

"An' if they don't let alone?" Parson stared at him shrewdly, chewing his tobacco slowly and watching Trent with his keen gray eyes.

"If they don't let me alone? An' if they start killin' my friends?" Trent turned to look at Hatfield. "Why,

Parson, I reckon I'd take my guns down from that peg. I reckon I'd fight."

Hatfield nodded. "That's all I wanted to know, Trent. I ain't spent my life a-feudin' without knowin' a fightin' man when I see one. O'Hara an' young Bartram will fight. Smithers, too, but he don't stack up like no fightin' man. My young 'uns, they cut their teeth on a rifle stock, so I reckon when the fightin' begins I'll be bloodin' the two young 'uns like I did the two older back in Kentucky."

Trent kicked his toe into the dust. "Don't you reckon we better get the womenfolks off to Blazer? There ain't many of us, Parson, an' Hale must have fifty riders. We better get them out while the gettin' is good."

"Hale's got more'n fifty riders, but the women'll stay, Trent. Ma, she ain't for goin'. You ain't got no woman of your own, Trent, so I don't reckon you know how unpossible ornery they can be, but Ma, she'd be fit to be tied if it was said she was goin' to go to Blazer while we had us a scrap. Ma loaded rifles for me in Kentucky when she was a gal, an' she loaded 'em for me crossin' the plains, an' she done her share of shootin'. Trent, I'd rather face all them Hales than Ma if we tried to send her away. She always says her place is with her menfolks, an' there she'll stay. I reckon Quince's wife feels the same, an' so does Jesse's woman."

Trent nodded. "Parson, we got us an argument when the rest of them get here. They've got to leave their places an' come up here. Together, we could make a pretty stiff fight of it. Scattered, they'd cut us down one by one." He swung into the saddle. "I'm goin' down to Cedar Bluff. I'm goin' to see Leathers."

Without waiting for a reply, Trent swung the buckskin away and loped down the trail. He knew very well he was taking a chance. The killing had started. Dick Moffitt was down. They had burned his place, and within no time at all the Hale riders would be carrying fire and blood through the high hills, wiping out the nesters. If he could but see King Bill, there might be a chance.

Watching him go, Parson Hatfield shook his head doubtfully and then turned to his eldest. "Quince, you rope yourself a horse, boy, an' you an' Jesse follow him into Cedar Bluff. He may get hisself into trouble."

A few minutes later the two tall, loose-limbed mountain men started down the trail on their flea-bitten mustangs. They were solemn, dry young men who chewed tobacco and talked slowly, but they had grown up in the hard school of the Kentucky mountains, and they had come West across the plains.

III

Unknowing, Trent rode rapidly. He knew what he had to do, yet, even as he rode, his thoughts were on the Hatfields. He liked them. Hardworking, honest, opinionated, they were fierce to resent any intrusion on their personal liberty, their women's honor, or their pride.

They were the kind of men to ride the river with. It was such men who had been the backbone of America, the fence-corner soldier, the man who carried his rifle in the hollow of his arm, but the kind of men who knew that fighting was not a complicated business but simply a matter of killing and keeping from being killed. They were men of the blood of Dan Boone, Kit Carson, Jim Bridger, the Green Mountain Boys, Dan Freeman, and those who whipped the cream of the British regulars at Concord, Bunker Hill, and New Orleans. They knew nothing of Prussian methods of close-order drill. They did nothing by the numbers. Many of them had flat feet and many had few teeth. But they fought from cover and they made every shot count—and they lived while the enemy died.

The Hale Ranch was a tremendous power, and it had many riders, and they were men hired for their ability with guns as well as with ropes and cattle. King Bill Hale, wise as he was, was grown confident, and he did not know the caliber of such men as the Hatfields. The numbers Hale had might lead to victory, but not until many men had died.

O'Hara? The big Irishman was blunt and hard. He was not the shrewd fighter the Hatfields were, but he was courageous, and he knew not the meaning of retreat. Himself? Trent's eyes narrowed. He had no illusions about himself. As much as he avoided trouble, he knew that within him there was something that held a fierce resentment for abuse of power, for tyranny. There was something in him that loved battle, too. He could not dodge the fact. He would avoid trouble, but when it came, he would go into it with a fierce love of battle for battle's sake. Someday, he knew, he would ride back to the cattle in the high meadows, back to the cabin in the pines, and he would take down his guns and buckle them on, and then Kilkenny would ride again.

The trail skirted deep cañons and led down toward the flat bottom land of the valley. King Bill, he knew, was learning what he should have known long ago, that the flatlands, while rich, became hot and dry in the summer weather, while the high meadows remained green and lush, and there cattle could graze and grow fat. And King Bill was moving to take back what he had missed so long ago. Had the man been less blinded by his own power and strength, he would have hesitated over the Hatfields. One and all, they were fighting men.

Riding into Cedar Bluff would be dangerous now. Changes were coming to the West, and Trent had hoped to leave his reputation in Texas. He could see the old days of violence were nearing an end. Billy the Kid had been killed by Pat Garrett. King Fisher and Ben Thompson were heard of much less; one and all, the gunmen were beginning to taper off. Names that had once been mighty in the West were already drifting into legend. As for himself, few men could describe him. He had come and gone like a shadow, and where he was now no man could say, and only one woman.

King Bill even owned the law in Cedar Bluff. He had called an election to choose a sheriff and a judge. Yet there had been no fairness in that election. It was true that no unfair practices had been tolerated, but the few nesters and small ranchers had no chance against the fifty-odd riders from the Hale Ranch and the townspeople who needed the Hale business or who worked for him. Trent had voted himself. He had voted for O'Hara. There had been scarcely a dozen votes for O'Hara. One of those votes had been that of Jim Hale, King Bill's oldest son. Another, he knew, had been the one person in Cedar Bluff who he had studiously avoided, the half-Spanish, half-Irish girl, Nita Riordan. Trent had avoided Nita Riordan because the beautiful girl from the Texas-Mexican border was the one person who knew him for what he was—who knew him as Kilkenny, the gunfighter.

Whenever Trent thought of the trouble in Cedar Bluff, he thought less of King Bill but more of Cub Hale. The older man was huge and powerful physically, but he was not a killer. It was true that he was responsible for deaths, but they were of men who he believed to be his enemies or to be trespassing on his land. But Cub Hale was a killer. Two days after Trent had first come to Cedar Bluff he had seen Cub Hale kill a man. It was a drunken miner, a burly, quarrelsome fellow who could have done with a pistol barrel

110

alongside the head, but needed nothing more. Yet Cub Hale had shot him down ruthlessly, heedlessly.

Then there had been the case of Jack Lindsay, a known gunman, and Cub had killed him in a fair, stand-up fight, with an even break all around. Lindsay's gun had barely cleared its holster when the first of three shots hit him. Trent had walked over to the man's body to see for himself. You could have put a playing card over those three holes. That was shooting. There had been other stories of which Trent had only heard. Cub had caught two rustlers, red-handed, and killed them both. He had killed a Mexican sheepherder in Magdalena. He had killed a gun-fighter in Fort Sumner, and gut shot another one near Socorro, leaving him to die slowly on the desert.

Besides Cub, there were Dunn and Ravitz. Both were graduates of the Lincoln County War. Both had been in Trail City and had left California just ahead of a posse. Both were familiar names among the dark brotherhood that lived by the gun. They were strictly cash-and-carry warriors, men whose guns were for hire.

"Buck," Trent told his horse thoughtfully, "if war starts in the Cedar hills, there'll be a power of killin'. I got to see King Bill. I got to talk reason into him."

Cedar Bluff could have been any cow town. Two things set it off from the others. One was the stone stage station, which also contained the main office of the Hale Ranch; the other was the huge and sprawling Crystal Palace, belonging to Nita Riordan.

Trent loped the yellow horse down the dusty street and swung down in front of Leathers's General Store. He walked into the cool interior. The lace smelled of leather and dry-goods. At the rear, where they dispensed food and other supplies, he halted.

Bert Leathers looked up from his customer as Trent walked in, and Trent saw his face change. Leathers wet his lips and kept his eyes away from Trent. At the same time, Trent heard a slight movement, and, glancing casually around, he saw a heavy-set cowhand wearing a tied-down gun lounging against a rack of saddles. The fellow took his cigarette from his lips and stared at Trent from shrewd, calculating eyes.

"Need a few things, Leathers," Trent said casually. "Got a list here."

The man Leathers was serving stepped aside. He was a townsman, and he looked worried.

"Sorry, Trent," Leathers said abruptly, "I can't help you. All you nesters have been ordered off the Hale range. I can't sell you anything."

"Lickin' Hale's boots, are you?" Trent asked quietly. "I heard you were, Leathers, but doubted it. I figgered a man with nerve enough to come West an' set up for himself would be his own man."

"I am my own man!" Leathers snapped, his pride stung. "I just don't want your business!"

"I'll remember that, Leathers," Trent said quietly. "When all this is over, I'll remember that. You're forgettin' something. This is America, an' here the people always win. Maybe not at first, but they always win in the end. When this is over, if the people win, you'd better leave . . . understand?"

Leathers looked up, his face white and yet angry. He looked uncertain.

"You all better grab yourself some air," a cool voice suggested.

Trent turned, and he saw the gun hand standing with his thumbs in his belt, grinning at him. "Better slide, Trent. What the man says is true. King Bill's takin' over. I'm here to see Leathers doesn't have no trouble with nesters."

"All right," Trent said quietly, "I'm a quiet man myself. I expect that rightly I should take the gun away from you an' shove it down your throat. But Leathers is probably gun shy, an' there might be some shootin', so I'll take a walk."

"My name's Dan Cooper," the gun hand suggested mildly. "Any time you really get on the prod about shovin' this gun down my throat, look me up."

Trent smiled. "I'll do that, Cooper, an', if you stay with King Bill, I'm afraid you're going to have a heavy diet of lead. He's cuttin' a wide swath."

"Uhn-huh." Cooper was cheerful and tough. "But he's got a blade that cuts 'em off short."

"Ever see the Hatfields shoot?" Trent suggested. "Take a tip, old son, an', when those long Kentucky rifles open up, you be somewhere else."

Dan Cooper nodded sagely. "You got somethin' there, pardner. You really have. That Parson's got him a cold eye."

Trent turned and started for the street, but Cooper's voice halted him. The gun hand had followed him to the door.

"Say," Cooper's voice was curious. "Was you ever in Dodge?"

Trent smiled. "Maybe. Maybe I was. You think that one over, Cooper." He looked at the gun hand thoughtfully. "I like you," he said bluntly, "so I'm givin' you a tip. Get on your horse an' ride. King Bill's got the men, but he ain't goin' to win. Ride, because I always hate to kill a good man."

Trent turned and walked down the street. Behind him, he could feel Dan Cooper's eyes on his back.

The gunman was scowling. "Now, who the hell . . . ?" he muttered. "That *hombre*'s salty, plumb salty."

Three more attempts to buy supplies proved to Trent he was frozen out in Cedar Bluff. Worried now, he started back to his horse. The nesters could not buy in Cedar Bluff, and that meant their only supplies must come by the long wagon trip across country from Blazer. Trent felt grave doubts that Hale would let the wagons proceed unmolested, and their little party was so small they could not spare men to guard the wagons on the three-day trek over desert and mountains.

"Trent!" He turned slowly and found himself facing Price Dixon, a dealer from the Crystal Palace. "Nita wants to see you. Asked me to find you and ask if you'd come to see her."

For a long moment, Trent hesitated. Then he

shrugged. "All right," he said, "but it won't do any good to have her seen with me. We nesters aren't looked upon with much favor these days."

Dixon nodded, sober faced. "Looks like a shoot-out. I'm afraid you boys are on the short end of it."

"Maybe."

Dixon glanced at him out of the corner of his eyes. "Don't you wear a gun? They'll kill you someday."

"Without a gun you don't have many fights."

"It wouldn't stop Cub Hale. When he decides to shoot, he does. He won't care whether you are packin' a gun or not."

"No. It wouldn't matter to him."

Price Dixon studied him thoughtfully. "Who are you, Trent?" he asked softly.

"I'm Trent, a nester. Who else?"

"That's what I'm wondering. I'm dry behind the ears. I've been dealing cards in the West ever since the War Between the States. I've seen men who packed guns, and I know the breed. You're not Wes Hardin, and you're not Hickok, and you're not one of the Earps. You never drink much, so you can't be Thompson. Whoever you are, you've packed a gun."

"Don't lose any sleep over it."

Dixon shrugged. "I won't. I'm not taking sides in this fight or any other. If I guess, I won't say. You're a friend of Nita's, and that's enough for me. Besides, Jaime Brigo likes you." He glanced at Trent. "What do you think of him?"

"Brigo?" Trent said thoughtfully. "Brigo is part

Yaqui, part devil, and all loyal, but I'd sooner tackle three King Bill Hales than him. He's poison."

Dixon nodded. "I think you're right. He sits there by her door night after night, apparently asleep, yet he knows more about what goes on in this town than any five other men."

"Dixon, you should talk Nita into selling out. Good chance of getting the place burned out or shot up if she stays. It's going to be a long fight."

"Hale doesn't think so."

"Parson Hatfield does."

"I've seen Hatfield. He looks like something I'd leave alone." Dixon paused. "I was in Kentucky once, a long time ago. The Hatfields have had three feuds. Somehow, there's always Hatfields left."

"Well, Price"—Trent threw his cigarette into the dust—"I've seen a few fighting men, too, and I'm glad the Hatfields are on my side, an' particularly the Parson."

IV

The Crystal Palace was one of those places that made the Western frontier what it was. Wherever there was money to spend, gambling joints could be found, and some became ornate palaces of drinking and gambling like this one. They had them in Abilene and Dodge, but not so much farther West.

Cedar Bluff had the highly paid riders of the Hale Ranch. It also drew miners from Rock Creek. The

116

Palace was all gilt and glass, and there were plenty of games going, including roulette, faro, and dice. Around the room at scattered tables were at least a dozen poker games.

Nita Riordan, Trent decided, was doing all right. This place was making money and lots of it. Trent knew a lot about gambling houses, enough to know what a rake-off these games would be turning in to the house. There was no necessity for crooked games. The percentage was entirely adequate.

They crossed the room, and Trent saw Jaime Brigo sitting on a chair against the wall as he always sat. The sombrero on the floor was gray and new. He wore dark, tailored trousers and a short velvet jacket, also black. The shirt under it was silk and blue. He wore, as always, two guns.

He looked up as Trent approached, and his lips parted over even white teeth. *"Buenos días, señor,"* he said.

Price stopped and nodded his head toward the door. "She's in there."

Trent faced the door, drew a deep breath, and stepped inside. His heart was pounding, and his mouth was dry. No woman ever stirred him so deeply or made him realize so much what he was missing in his lonely life.

It was a quiet room, utterly different from the garish display of the gambling hall behind him. It was a room to live in, the room of one who loved comfort and peace. On a ledge by the window were several potted plants; on the table lay an open book. These things he absorbed rather than observed, for all his attention was centered upon Nita Riordan.

She stood across the table, taller than most women, with a slender yet voluptuous body that made a pulse pound in his throat. She was dressed for evening, an evening walking among the tables of the gambling room, and she was wearing a black and spangled gown, utterly different from the room in which she stood. Her eyes were wide now, her full lips parted a little, and, as he stopped across the table, he could see the lift of her bosom as she took a deep breath.

"Nita," he said softly. "You've not changed. You're the same."

"I'm older, Lance," she said softly, "more than a year older."

"Has it been only a year? It seems so much longer." He looked at her thoughtfully. "And you are lovely, as always. I think you could never be anything but lovely and desirable."

"And yet," she reminded him, "when you could have had me, you rode away. Lance, do you live all alone in that cabin of yours? Without anyone?"

He nodded. "Except for memories. Except for the thinking, I do. And the thinking only makes it worse, for, whenever I think of you, and all that could be, I remember the Brockmans, Bert Polti, and all those others back down the trail. Then I start wondering how long it will be before I fall in the dust myself."

"That's why I sent for you," Nita told him. Her eyes were serious and worried. She came around the table and took his hands. "Lance, you've got to go. Leave here, now. I can hold your place for you, if that's what you want. If that doesn't matter, say so, and I'll go with you. I'll go with you anywhere, but we must leave here."

"Why?" It was like him to be direct. She looked up into his dark, unsmiling face. "Why, Nita? Why do you want me to go?"

"Because they are going to kill you!" she exclaimed. She caught his arm. "Lance, they are cruel, ruthless, vicious. It isn't King Bill. He's their leader, but what he does he believes to be right. It's Cub. He loves to kill. I've seen him. Last week he killed a boy in the street in front of my place. He shot him down, and then emptied his gun into him with slow, methodical shots. He's a fiend!"

Lance shook his head. "I'll stay, no matter."

"But listen, Lance," she protested. "I've heard them talking here. They are sure you'll fight. I don't know why they think so, but they do. They've decided you must die, and soon. They won't give you a chance. I know that."

"I can't, Nita. These people in the high meadows are my friends. They depend upon me to stand by them. I won't be the first to break and run, or the last. I'm staying. I'm going to fight it out here, Nita, and we'll see who is to win, the people or a man of power and greed."

"I was afraid you'd say that." Nita looked at him seriously. "Hale is out to win, Lance. He's got men. They don't know you're Lance Kilkenny. I've heard them talking, and they do suspect that you're something more than a nester named Trent. But Hale is sure he is right, and he'll fight to the end."

Trent nodded. "I know. When a man thinks he is right, he will fight all the harder. Has anybody tried to talk to him?"

"You can't. You can't even address him. He lives in a world of his own. In his way, I think he is a little insane, Lance, but he does have ability, and he has strength. He's a fighter, too."

Trent studied her thoughtfully. "You seem to know him. Has he made you any trouble?"

"Why do you ask that?" Nita asked quickly.

"I want to know."

"He wants to marry me, Lance."

Trent tightened and then stared at her. "I see," he said slowly. "And you?"

"I don't know." She hesitated, looking away. "Lance, can't you see? I'm lonely. Dreadfully, frighteningly lonely. I have no life here, just a business. I know no women but those of the dance hall. I see no one who feels as I do, thinks as I do. King Bill is strong. He knows how to appeal to a woman. He has a lot to offer. He has a son as old as I, but he's only forty, and he's a powerful man, Lance. A man a woman could be proud of. I don't like what he's doing, but he does think he's right. No," she said finally, "I won't marry him. I'll admit, I've been tempted. He's a little insane, I think. Drunk with power. He got too much and got it too easily, and he believes he is better than other men because he has succeeded. But whatever you do, Lance, don't underrate him. He's a fighter."

"You mean he'll have his men fight?" Trent asked.

"No. I mean *he* is a fighter. By any method. With his fists, if he has to. He told me once in such a flat, ordinary voice that it startled me that he could whip any man he ever saw with his hands."

"I see."

"Shaw, his foreman, tells a story about King Bill beating a man to death in El Paso. He killed another one with his fists on the ranch."

"I've got to see him today. I've got to convince him that we must be left alone."

"He won't talk to you, Lance." Nita looked at him with grave, troubled eyes. "I know him. He'll just turn you over to his cowhands, and they'll beat you up or kill you."

"He'll talk to me."

"Don't go down there, Lance. Please don't."

"Has he ever made any trouble for you?"

"No." She shook her head. "So far, he has listened to me and has talked very quietly and very well. No one has made any trouble yet, but largely because they know he is interested in me. Some men tried to hold me up one night, but Jaime took care of that. He killed them both, and that started some talk. But if King Bill decides he wants this place . . . or me . . . he'll stop at nothing."

"Well,"—he turned—"I've got to see him, Nita. I've got to make one attempt to stop this before anyone else is killed."

"And if you fail . . . ?"

He hesitated, and his shoulders drooped. Then he looked up, and he smiled slowly. "If I fail, Nita, I'll buckle on my guns, and they won't have to wait for war. I'll bring it to Cedar Bluff myself!"

He stopped in the outer room and watched Price Dixon dealing cards, but his mind wasn't on the game. He was thinking of King Bill.

Hale was a man who fought to win. In this little corner of the West, there was no law but that of the gun. Actually there were but two trails in and out of Cedar Valley. What news left the valley would depend on Hale. The echoes of the war to come need never be heard beyond these hills. Only one trail led into Cedar Bluff, and one led out. Most of the traffic went in and out on the same route. The other trail, the little-used route to Blazer, was rough and bad. Yet in Blazer, too, Hale owned the livery stable, and he had his spies there as all around.

Hale himself lived in the Castle, two miles from Cedar Bluff. He rode into town once each day and stopped in at the Mecca for a drink and again at the Crystal Palace. Then he rode out of town. He went nowhere without his gunmen around him. Thinking of that, Trent decided on the Mecca. There would be trouble unless everything happened just right. He didn't want the trouble close to Nita.

He knew what Nita meant when she said she was lonely. There had never been a time when he hadn't been lonely. He had been born on the frontier in Dakota, but his father had been killed in a gun battle, and he had gone to live with an uncle in New York, and later in Virginia.

Trent walked out on the street. It was late now, and the sun was already gone. It would soon be dark. He walked down to the buckskin and led him to a watering trough. Then he gave him a bundle of hay and left him tied at the hitching rail.

There were few people around. Dan Cooper had left the store and was sitting on the steps in front now. He watched Trent thoughtfully. Finally he got up and walked slowly down the walk. He stopped near the buckskin.

"If I was you, Trent," he said slowly, "I'd get on that horse an' hit the trail. You ain't among friends."

"Thanks." Trent looked up at Cooper. "I think that's friendly, Cooper. But I've got business. I don't want a war in Cedar Bluff, Cooper. I want to make one more stab at stopping it."

"An' if you don't?" Cooper studied him quizzically.

"If I don't?" Trent stepped up on the boardwalk. "Well, I'll tell you like I've told others. If I don't, I'm going to buckle on my guns and come to town."

Dan Cooper began to roll a cigarette. "You sound all-fired sure of yourself. Who are you?"

"Like I said, old son, I'm a nester, name of Trent."

He turned and strolled down the walk toward the Mecca, and, even as he walked, he saw a small cavalcade of horsemen come up the road from the Castle. Four men, and the big man on the bay would be King Bill Hale.

Hale got down, and strode through the doors. Cub followed. Ravitz tied King Bill's horse, and Dunn stood for a moment, staring at Trent, who he could not quite make out in the gathering gloom. Then he and Ravitz walked inside.

V

Walking up, Trent pushed open the swinging doors. He stopped for an instant inside the door. The place was jammed with Hale cowhands. At the bar, King Bill was standing, his back to the room. He was big— no taller than Trent, and perhaps an inch shorter than Trent's six one, but much heavier. He was broad and powerful, with thick shoulders and a massive chest. His head was a block set upon the thick column of a muscular neck. The man's jaw was broad, his face brown and hard. He was a bull. Looking at him, Trent could guess that the stories of his killing men with his fists were only the truth.

Beside him, in white buckskin, was the slender, cat-like Cub Hale. And on either side of the two stood the gunmen, Dunn and Ravitz.

Trent walked slowly to the bar and ordered a

drink. Dunn, hearing his voice, turned his head slowly. As his eyes met Trent's, the glass slipped from his fingers and crashed on the bar, scattering rye whiskey.

"Seem nervous, Dunn," Trent said quietly. "Let me buy you a drink."

"I'll be hanged if I will!" Dunn shouted. "What do you want here?"

Trent smiled. All the room was listening, and he knew that many of the townspeople, some of whom might still be on the fence, were present.

"Why, I just thought I'd ride down an' have a talk with King Bill," he said quietly. "It seems there's a lot of war talk, an' somebody killed a harmless nester the other day. It seemed a man like King Bill Hale wouldn't want such things goin' on."

"Get out!" Dunn's hand hovered above a gun. "Get out or be carried out!"

"No use you makin' motions toward that gun," Trent said quietly. "I'm not heeled. Look for yourself, I'm makin' peace talk, an' I'm talkin' to King Bill."

"I said . . . get out!" Dunn shouted.

Trent stood with his hands on his hips, smiling. Suddenly Dunn's hand streaked for his gun, and instantly Trent moved.

One hand dropped to Dunn's gun wrist, while his right whipped up in a short, wicked arc and exploded on Dunn's chin. The gunman sagged, and Trent released his gun hand and shoved him away so hard he fell headlong into a table. The table crashed over, and among the scattered cards and chips Bing Dunn lay, out cold.

In the silence that followed, Trent stepped quickly up to King Bill.

"Hale," he said abruptly, "some of your men killed Dick Moffitt, shot him down in cold blood, and then burned him out. Those same men warned me to move out. I thought I'd come to you. I've heard you're a fair man."

King Bill did not move. He held his glass in his fingers and stared thoughtfully into the mirror back of the bar, giving no indication that he heard. Cub Hale moved out from the bar, his head thrust forward, his eyes eager.

"Hale," Trent said sharply, "this is between you an' me. Call off your dogs! I'm talkin' to you, not anybody else. We want peace, but if we have to fight to keep our land, we'll fight! If we fight, we'll win. You're buckin' the United States government now."

Cub had stepped out, and now his lips curled back in a wolfish snarl as his hand hovered over his gun.

"What's the matter, Hale?" Trent persisted. "Making a hired killer of your son because you're afraid to talk?"

Hale turned deliberately. "Cub, get back. I'll handle this!"

Cub hesitated, his eyes alive with eagerness and disappointment.

"I said," Hale repeated, "to get back." He turned. "As for you, you squatted on my land. Now you're gettin' off, all of you. If you don't get off, some of you may die. That's final!"

"No!" Trent's voice rang out sharply. "It's not final, Hale! We took those claims legal. You never made any claim to them until now. You got more land now than you can handle, and we're stayin'. I filed my claim with the United States, so did the others. If we don't get justice, we'll get a United States marshal in here to see why."

"Justice!" Hale sneered. "You blasted nesters'll get all the justice you get from me. I'm givin' you time to leave . . . now get!"

Trent stood his ground. He could see the fury bolted up in Hale, could see the man was relentless. Well, maybe. . . . Suddenly Trent smiled. "Hale," he said slowly, "I've heard you're a fightin' man. I hope that ain't a lie. I'm callin' you now. We fight, man to man, right here in this barroom, no holds barred, an', if I win, you leave the nesters alone. If you win, we all leave."

King Bill wheeled, his eyes bulging. "You challenge *me?* You dirty-necked, nestin' renegade. No! I bargain with no man. You nesters get movin' or suffer the consequences."

"What's the matter, Bill?" Trent said slowly. "Afraid?"

For a long moment, there was deathly stillness in the room, while Hale's face grew darker and darker. Slowly, then, he unbuckled his gun belt. "You asked for it, nester," he sneered. "Now you get it."

He rushed. Trent had been watching, and, as Hale rushed, he side-stepped quickly. Hale's rush missed, and Trent faced him, smiling.

"What's the matter, King. I'm right here!"

Hale rushed, and Trent stepped in with a left jab that split Hale's lips and showered him with blood. In a fury, Hale closed in and caught Trent with a powerful right swing that sent him staggering back on his heels. Blood staining his gray shirt, King Bill leaped at Trent, swinging with both hands. Trent crashed to the floor, rolled over, and got up. Another swing caught him, and he went down again, his head roaring with sound.

King Bill rushed in, aiming a vicious kick, but Trent rolled out of the way and scrambled up, groggy and hurt. Hale rushed, and Trent weaved inside of a swing and smashed a right and left to that massive body. Hale grabbed Trent and hurled him into the bar with terrific power, and then sprang close, swinging both fists to Trent's head. Trent slipped the first punch, but took the other one, and started to sag. King Bill set himself, a cold sneer on his face, and measured Trent with a left, aiming a ponderous right, but Trent pushed the left aside and smashed a wicked left uppercut to Hale's wind.

The bigger man gasped and missed a right, and Trent stabbed another left to the bleeding mouth. Hale landed a right and knocked Trent rolling on the floor. Somebody kicked him wickedly in the ribs as he rolled against the feet of the crowd, and he came up staggering as Hale closed in. Hurt, gasping with pain, Trent clinched desperately and hung on.

Hale tore him loose, smashed a left to his head that split his cheek bone wide open, and then smashed him on the jaw with a powerful right. Again Trent stabbed that left to the mouth, ducked under a right, and bored in, slamming away with both hands at close quarters. Hale grabbed him and threw him, and then rushed upon him, but, even as he jumped at him, Trent caught Hale with a toe in the pit of the stomach and pitched him over on his head and shoulders.

King Bill staggered up, visibly shaken. Then Trent walked in. His face was streaming blood and his head was buzzing, but he could see Hale's face weaving before him. He walked in, deliberately lanced that bleeding mouth with a left, and then crossed a right that ripped the flesh over Hale's eye.

Dunn started forward, and with an oath Hale waved him back. He put up his hands and walked in, his face twisted with hatred. Trent let him come, feinted, and then dropped a right under the big man's heart. Hale staggered, and Trent walked in, stabbed another left into the blood-covered face, and smashed another right to the wind.

Then he stood there and began to swing. Hale was swinging, too, but his power was gone. Trent bored in, his head clearing, and he slammed punch after punch into the face and body of the tottering rancher. He was getting his second wind now, although he was hurt, and blood dripped from his face to his shirt. He brushed Hale's hands aside and crossed a driving right to the chin. Hale's knees buckled, but, before he could fall, Trent hit him twice more, left and right to the chin. Then Hale crashed to the floor.

In the instant of silence that followed the fall of the King, a voice rang out. "You all just hold to where you're standin' now. I ain't a-wantin' to shoot nobody, but sure as my name's Quince Hatfield, the one to make the first move dies!"

The long rifle stared through the open window at them, and on the next window sill they saw another. Nobody in the room moved.

In three steps, Trent was out of the room. The buckskin was standing at the edge of the walk with the other horses. Swinging into the saddle, he wrenched the rifle from the boot and with two quick shots sent the chandelier crashing to the floor, plunging the Mecca into darkness. Then, the Hatfields at his side, he raced the buckskin toward the edge of town. When they slowed down, a mile out of town, Quince looked at him, grinning in the moonlight.

"I reckon you all sure busted things wide open now."

Trent nodded soberly. "I tried to make peace talk. When he wouldn't, I thought a good lickin' might show the townspeople the fight wasn't all on one side. We're goin' to need friends."

"You done a good job!" Jesse said. "Parson'll sure wish he'd been along. He always said what Hale needed was a good whuppin'. Well, he sho' nuff had it tonight."

Nothing, Trent realized, had been solved by the fight. Taking to the brush, they used every stratagem to ward off pursuit, although they knew it was exceedingly doubtful if any pursuit would be started against three armed men who were skilled woodsmen. Following them in the dark would be impossible and scarcely wise.

Three hours later, they swung down at the Hatfield cabin. A tall young man with broad shoulders stepped out of the darkness.

"It's us, Saul," Jesse said, "an' Trent done whipped King Bill Hale with his fists!"

Saul Hatfield strode up, smiling. "I reckon Paw will sure like to hear that!"

"They gone to bed?"

"Uhn-huh. Lijah was on guard till a few minutes back. He just turned in to catch hisself some sleep afore mornin'."

"O'Hara get here?" Quince asked softly.

"Yeah. Him an' Smithers an' Bartram are here. Havin' a big confab, come mornin'."

VI

The morning sun was lifting over the pines when the men gathered around the long table in the Hatfield home. Breakfast was over, and the women were at work. Trent sat quietly at the foot of the table, thoughtfully looking at the men around him. Yet even as he looked, he could not but wonder how many would be alive to enjoy the fruits of the victory, if victory it was to be.

The five Hatfields were all there. Big O'Hara was there, too, a huge man with great shoulders and mighty hands, a bull for strength and a good shot. Bartram, young, good-looking, and keen, would fight. He believed in what he was fighting for, and he had youth and energy enough to be looking forward to the struggle. Smithers was middle-aged, quiet, a man who had lived a peaceful life, avoiding trouble, yet fearless. He was a small man, precise, and an excellent farmer, probably the best farmer of the lot.

Two more horsemen rode in while they were sitting down. Jackson Hight was a wild-horse hunter, former cowhand, and buffalo hunter; Steven Runyon was a former miner.

Parson Hatfield straightened up slowly. "I reckon this here meetin' better get started. Them Hales ain't a-goin' to wait on us to get organized. I reckon they's a few things we got to do. We got to pick us a leader, an' we got to think of gettin' some food."

Trent spoke up. "Parson, if you'll let me have a word. We all better leave our places an' come here to yours. We better bring all the food an' horses we got up here."

"Leave our places?" Smithers objected. "Why, man, they'd burn us out if we aren't there to defend 'em. They'd ruin our crops."

"He's right," O'Hara said. "If we ain't on hand to defend 'em, they sure won't last long."

"Which of you feel qualified to stand off Hale's riders?" Trent asked dryly. "What man here could hold off ten or twenty men? I don't feel I could. I don't think the Parson could, alone. We've got to get together. Suppose they burn us out. We can build again, if we're alive to do it, an' we can band together and help each other build back. If you ain't alive, you ain't goin' to build very much."

"Thet strikes me as bein' plumb sense," Hight said, leaning forward. "Looks to me like we got to sink or swim together. Hale's got too much power, an' we're too scattered. He ain't plannin' on us gettin' together. He's plannin' on wipin' us out one at a time. Together, we got us a chance."

"Maybe you're right," O'Hara said slowly. "Dick Moffitt didn't do very well alone."

"This place can be defended," Trent said. "Aside from my own place, this is the easiest to defend of them all. Then, the house is the biggest and strongest. If we have to fall back from the rocks, the house can hold out."

"What about a leader?" Bartram asked. "We'd better get that settled. How about you, Parson?"

"No." Parson drew himself up. "I'm right flattered, right pleased. But I ain't your man. I move we choose Trent, here."

There was a moment's silence, and then O'Hara spoke up. "I second that motion. Trent's good for me. He whipped old King Bill."

Runyon looked thoughtfully at Trent. "I don't know this gent," he said slowly. "I ain't got any objections to him. But how do we know he's our man? You've done a power of feudin', Parson. You should know this kind of fightin'."

"I do," Parson drawled. "But I ain't got the savvy Trent has. First, lemme say this here. I ain't been here all my life. I was a sharpshooter with the Confederate Army, an' later I rid with Jeb Stuart. Well, we was only whipped once, an' that was by a youngster of a Union officer. He whipped our socks off with half as many men . . . an' that officer was Trent here."

Trent's eyes turned slowly to Parson, who sat there staring at him, his eyes twinkling.

"I reckon," Hatfield went on, "Trent is some surprised. I ain't said nothin' to him about knowin' him, specially when his name wasn't Trent, but I knowed him from the first time I seen him."

"That's good enough for me," Runyon said flatly. "You say he's got the savvy, I'll take your word for it."

Trent leaned over the table. "All right. All of you mount up and go home. Watch your trail carefully. When you get home, load up and get back. Those of you who can, ride together. Get back here with everything you want to save, but especially with all the grub you've got. But get back, and quick." He got to his feet. "We're goin' to let Hale make the first move, but we're goin' to have a Hatfield watchin' the town. When Hale moves, we're goin' to move, too. We've got twelve men. . . ."

"Twelve?" Smithers looked around. "I count eleven."

"Jackie Moffitt's the twelfth," Trent said quietly. "I gave him a Sharps. He's fourteen. Many of you at fourteen did a man's job. I'll stake my saddle that Jackie Moffitt will do his part. He can hit squirrels with that gun, an' a man's not so big. He'll do. Like I say, we've got twelve men. Six of them can hold this place. With the other six, or maybe with four, we'll strike back. I don't know how you feel, but I feel no man ever won a war by sittin' on his royal American tail, an' we're not a-goin' to."

"That's good talk," Smithers said quietly. "I'm not a war-like man, but I don't want to think of my place being burned when they go scotfree. I'm for striking back, but we've got to think of food."

"I've thought of that. Lije an' Saul Hatfield are goin' out today after some deer. They know where they are, an' neither of them is goin' to miss any shots. With the food we have, we can get by a few days. Then I'm goin' after some myself!"

"You?" O'Hara stated. "Where you figger on gettin' this grub?"

"Blazer." He looked down at his hands on the table, and then looked up. "I'm not goin' to spend three days, either. I'm goin' through Smoky Desert."

There was dead silence. Runyon leaned forward, starting to speak, but then he sat back, shaking his head. It was Smithers who broke the silence.

"I'll go with you," he said quietly.

"But, man!" Hight protested. "There ain't no way through that desert, an', if there was. . . ."

"The Indians used to go through," Trent said quietly, "and I think I know how. If it can be done, I could reach Blazer in a little over a day an' start back the same night." He looked over at Jesse Hatfield. "You want to watch Cedar Bluff? I reckon you know how to Indian. Don't take any chances, but keep an eye on 'em. You take that chestnut of mine. He's a racer. You take that horse, an', when they move, you take the back trails for here."

Jesse Hatfield got up and slipped from the room.

Then Trent said: "All right, start rolling. Get back here when you can."

He walked outside and saddled the buckskin. Jackie sauntered up, the Sharps in the hollow of his arm.

"Jackie," Trent said, "you get up there in the eye, an' keep a lookout on the Cedar trail." Mounting, he rode out of the hollow at a lope and swung into the trail toward his own cabin.

He knew what they were facing, but already in his mind the plan of campaign was taking shape. If they sat still, sooner or later they must be wiped out, and sooner or later his own men would lose heart. They must strike back. Hale must be made to learn that he could not win all the time, that he must lose, too.

All was quiet and green around the little cabin, and he rode up, swinging down. He stepped through, hurriedly put his grub into sacks, and hung it on a pack horse. Then he hesitated. Slowly he walked across to the peg on the cupboard. For a long minute he looked at the guns hanging there. Then he reached up and took them down. He buckled them on, heavy-hearted and feeling lost and empty.

It was sundown when he hazed his little band of carefully selected horses through the notch into the Hatfield hollow and, with Jackie's help, put them in the corral. All the men were back, and the women were working around, laughing, pleasant. They were true women of the West, and most of them had been through Indian fights before this.

Hight was the last one in. He came riding through the notch on a spent horse, his face drawn and hard.

"They burned me out," he said hoarsely, sweat streaking his face. "They hit me just as I was a-packin'. I didn't get off with nothin'. I winged one of 'em, though."

Even as he spoke, Smithers caught Trent's arm. "Look!" he urged, and pointed. In the sky they could see a red glow from reflected fire. "O'Hara's place," he said. "Maybe they got him, too."

"No." O'Hara walked up, scowling. "They didn't get me. I got here twenty minutes ago. They'll pay for this, the wolves."

Jesse Hatfield on the chestnut suddenly materialized in the gloom. "Two bunches ridin'," he said, "an' they aim to get here about sunup. I heard 'em talkin'."

Trent nodded. "Get some sleep, Jesse. You, too, Jackie. Parson, you an' Smithers better keep watch. Quince, I want you an' Bartram to ride with me."

"Where you all goin'?" Saul demanded.

"Why, Saul"—Trent smiled in the darkness—"I reckon we're goin' to town after groceries. We're goin' to call on Leathers, an' we'll just load up while we're there. If he ain't willin', we may have to take him along, anyway."

"Count me in," Saul said. "I sure want to be in on that."

"You'd better rest," Trent suggested. "You got three antelope today, you an' Lije."

"I reckon I ain't so wearied I'd miss that ride, Captain, if you all say I can go."

"We can use you."

Suddenly there was a burst of flame to the south. "There goes my place!" Smithers exclaimed bitterly. "I spent two years a-buildin' that place. Had some onions comin' up, too, an' a good crop of potatoes in."

Trent had started away, but he stopped and turned. "Smithers," he said quietly, "you'll dig those potatoes yourself. I promise you . . . if I have to wipe out Hales personally so's you can do it."

Smithers stared after him as he walked away. "Y'know," he remarked thoughtfully to the big Irishman, "I believe he would do it. O'Hara, maybe we can win this fight after all."

VII

Cedar Bluff lay, dark and still, when the four horsemen rode slowly down the path behind the town. Trent, peering through the darkness, studied the town carefully. Taking the trail might have been undue precaution, for there was small chance the road would be watched. There had been, of course, the possibility that some late cowpuncher might have spotted them on the trail.

It was after three, and the Crystal Palace and the Mecca had closed their doors over an hour earlier. Trent reined in on the edge of the town and studied the situation. King Bill, secure in his power even after the beating he had taken, would never expect the nesters to approach the town. He would be expecting them to try the overland route to Blazer for supplies, and in his monumental conceit he would never dream that they would come right to the heart of his domain.

"Bartram," Trent whispered, "you an' Saul take the pack horses behind the store. Keep 'em quiet. Don't try to get in or do anything. Just hold 'em there." He turned to the older Hatfield. "Quince, we're goin' to get Leathers."

"Why not just bust in?" Saul protested. "Why bother with him? We can find what we need."

"No," Trent said flatly. "He's goin' to wait on us, an' we're goin' to pay him. We ain't thieves, an' we're goin' to stick to the legal way. I may hold him up an' bring him down there, but we're goin' to pay him, cash on the barrel head, for everything we take."

Leaving their horses with the others behind the store, Trent took Quince and soft-footed it toward the storekeeper's home, about 100 yards from the store. Walking along the dark street, Trent looked around from time to time to see Quince. The long, lean Hatfield, six foot three in his socks, could move like an Indian. Unless Trent had looked, he would never have dreamed there was another man so close.

Trent stopped by the garden gate. There was a faint scent of lilacs in the air, and of some other flowers. Gently he pushed open the gate. It creaked on rusty hinges, and for an instant they froze. All remained dark and still, so Trent moved on, and Quince deftly took the gate from him and eased it slowly shut.

The air was heavy with lilac now, and the smell of damp grass. Trent stopped at the edge of the shadow and motioned to Quince to stand by. Ever so gently, he lifted one foot and put it down on the first step. Lifting himself by the muscles of his leg, he put down the other foot. Carefully, inch by inch, he worked his way across the porch to the house.

Two people slept inside. Leathers and his wife. His wife was a fat, comfortable woman, one of those in the town who idolized King Bill Hale and held him up as an example of all the West should be and all a man should be. King Bill's swagger and his grandiose manner impressed her. He was, she was convinced, a great man. Once, shortly after he had first come to

Cedar Bluff, Trent had been in this house. He had come to get Leathers to buy supplies after the store had been closed. He remembered vaguely the layout of the rooms.

The door he was now opening gently gave access to the kitchen. From it, there were two doors, one to a living room, rarely used, and one to the bedroom. In that bedroom, Leathers would be sleeping with his wife.

Once inside the kitchen he stood very still. He could hear the breathing of two people in the next room, the slow, heavy breathing of Elsa Leathers and the more jerky, erratic breathing of the storekeeper. The kitchen smelled faintly of onions and of homemade soap.

Drawing a large handkerchief from his pocket, he tied it across his face under his eyes. Then he slid his six-gun into his hand and tiptoed through the door into the bedroom. For a moment, Elsa Leathers's breathing caught, hesitated, and then went on. He heaved a sigh of relief. If she awakened, she was almost certain to start screaming.

Alongside the bed, he stooped and put the cold muzzle of his gun under the storekeeper's nose. Almost instantly the man's eyes opened. Even in the darkness of the room, Trent could see them slowly turn upward toward him. He leaned down, almost breathing the words.

"Get up quietly."

Very carefully, Leathers eased out of bed. Trent gestured for him to put on his pants, and, as the man drew them on, Trent watched him like a hawk. Then Trent gestured toward the door, and Leathers tiptoed outside.

"What's the matter?" he whispered, his voice hoarse and shaking. "What do you want me for?"

"Just a little matter of some groceries," Trent replied. "You open your store an' give us what we want, an' you won't have any trouble. Make one squawk an' I'll bend this gun over your noggin."

"I ain't sayin' anythin'," Leathers protested. He buckled his belt and hurried toward the store with Trent at his heels. Quince Hatfield sauntered along behind, stopping only to pluck a blue cornflower and stick it in an empty buttonhole of his shirt.

Leathers fumbled for the lock on the door. "If my wife wakes up an' finds me gone, mister," he said grumpily, "I ain't responsible for what happens."

"Don't you worry about that," Trent assured him dryly, "you just fill this order an' don't make us any trouble."

He motioned to Saul, who came forward. "As soon as you get four horses loaded, you let Bartram take 'em back to the trail an' hold 'em there. Then, if anything happens, he can take off with that much grub."

As fast as Leathers piled out the groceries, Saul and Quince hurried to carry them out to the horses. Trent stood by, gun in hand.

"You ain't goin' to get away with this," Leathers stated finally. "When Hale finds out, he's a-goin' to make somebody sweat."

"Yeah," Trent said quietly, "maybe he will. From all I hear, he'd better wait until he gets over one beatin' afore he starts huntin' another. An', while we're talkin', you better make up your mind, too. When this war is over, if Hale doesn't win, what d'you suppose happens to you?"

"Huh?" Leathers straightened, his face a shade whiter. "What d'you mean?"

"I mean, brother," Trent said harshly, "that you've taken sides in this fuss. An' if Hale loses, you're goin' out of town . . . but fast!"

"He ain't a-goin' to lose!" Leathers brought out a sack of flour and put it down on the floor. "Hale's got the money, an' he's got the men. Look what happened to Smithers's place today, an' O'Hara's. An' look what happened to. . . ."

"To Dick Moffitt?" Trent's voice was cold. "That was murder."

Quince stepped into the door. "Somebody's comin'," he hissed. "Watch it."

"Let 'em come in," Trent said softly, "but no shootin' unless they shoot first."

Trent thrust a gun against Leathers. "If they come in," he whispered, "you talk right, see? Answer any questions, but answer 'em like I tell you, because if there is any shootin', Elsa Leathers is goin' to be a widow, but quick."

Two men walked up to the door, and one tried the knob. Then, as the door opened, he thrust his head in.

"Who's there?" he demanded.

143

"It's me," Leathers said, and as Trent prodded him with the gun barrel, "fixin' up an order that has to get out early."

The two men pushed on inside. "I never knew you to work this late afore. Why, man, it must be nearly four o'clock."

"Right," Quince stepped up with a six-gun. "You *hombres* invited yourself to this party, now pick up them sacks an' cart 'em outside."

"Huh?" The two men stared stupidly. "Why . . . ?"

"Get movin'!" Quince snapped. "Get them sacks out there before I bend this over your head!" The man hesitated and then obeyed, and the other followed a moment later.

It was growing gray in the east when the orders were completed. Quickly they tied up the two men while Leathers stood by. Then, at a motion from Trent, Saul grabbed Leathers and he was bound and gagged. Carrying him very carefully, Trent took him back into his cottage and placed him in bed, drawing the blankets over him. Elsa Leathers sighed heavily, and turned in her sleep. Trent stood very still, waiting. Then her breathing became even once more, and he tiptoed from the house.

Quince was standing in the shadow of the store, holding both horses. "They've started up the trail," he said. Then he grinned. "Gosh a'mighty, I'll bet old Leathers is some sore."

"There'll be a chase, most likely," Trent said. "We'd better hang back a little in case."

Bartram was ahead, keeping the horses at a stiff trot. He was a tough, wiry young farmer and woodsman who had spent three years convoying wagon trains over the Overland Trail before he came south. He knew how to handle a pack train, and he showed it now. Swinging the line of pack horses from the trail, he led them into the shallow water of Cedar Branch and walked them very rapidly through the water. Twice he stopped to give them a breather, but kept moving at a good pace, Saul riding behind the string, his long Kentucky rifle across his saddle.

"You pay Leathers?" Quince asked, riding close.

"Yeah." Trent nodded. "I stuck it down between him an' his wife after I put him in bed. He'll be some surprised."

Using every trick they knew to camouflage their trail, they worked steadily back up into the hills. They were still five miles or more from the Hatfield place when they heard shots in the distance.

Quince reined in, his features sharpened. "Looks like they've done attacked the place," he said. "What d'you think, Trent? Should we leave this to Saul an' ride up there?"

Trent hesitated, and then shook his head. "No. They can hold 'em for a while. We want to make sure this food is safe." Suddenly he reined in. "Somebody's comin' up our back trail. Go ahead, Saul. But don't run into the attackin' party."

Saul nodded grimly, and Trent, taking a quick look around, indicated a bunch of boulders above the trail.

They rode up and swung down, and Quince gave an exclamation of satisfaction as he noted the deep arroyo behind the boulders—a good place for their horses and good for a getaway, if need be.

The horsemen were coming fast now. Lying behind the boulders, they could see the dust rising above them as they wound their way through the cedars and huge rocks that bordered the narrow trail. Only yards away they broke into the open.

"Dust 'em!" Trent said, and fired.

Their two rifles went off with the same sound and two puffs of dust went up in front of the nearest horse. The horse reared sharply and spun halfway around. Trent lowered his rifle to note the effect of their shots, and then aimed high at the second horseman and saw his sombrero lift from his head and sail into the brush. The men wheeled and whipped their horses back into the brush.

Quince chuckled and bit off a chew. "That'll make 'em think a mite . . . say!" He nodded toward a nest of rocks on the other side. "What'll you bet one of them rannies ain't a-shinnyin' up into that nest of rocks about now?"

There was a notch in the rocks and a boulder beyond, not four feet beyond by the look of it. Quince Hatfield lifted his Kentucky rifle, took careful aim, and then fired. There was a startled yell, and then curses.

Quince chuckled a little. "Dusted him with granite off that boulder," he said. "They won't hurry to get up there again."

Trent thought swiftly. If he took the arroyo and circled back, he could then get higher up on the mountain. With careful fire, he could still cover the open spot and so give Quince a chance to retreat while he held them. Swiftly he told Hatfield. The big mountaineer nodded.

"Go ahead. They won't move none till you get there."

It took Trent ten minutes to work his way out of the arroyo and up the mountain. As distance went, he wasn't so far, being not more than 400 yards away. He signaled his presence to Quince Hatfield by letting go with three shots into the shelter taken by their pursuers. From above, that shelter was scarcely more than concealment and not at all cover.

In a few minutes Quince joined him. They each let go with two shots, and then, mounting, rode swiftly away, out of view of the men in the brush below.

"They'll be slow about showin' themselves, I reckon," Quince said, "so we'll be nigh to home afore they get nerve enough to move."

When they had ridden four miles, Quince reined in sharply. "Horses ahead," he advised. "Maybe they're ours."

Approaching cautiously, they saw Bartram with the eight pack horses. He was sitting with his rifle in his hands, watching the brush ahead. He glanced around at their approach, and then with a wave of the hand, motioned them on.

"Firing up ahead. Saul's gone up. He'll be back pretty soon."

Low voiced, Trent told him what had happened. Then, as they talked, they saw Saul Hatfield coming through the brush on foot. He walked up to them and caught his horse by the bridle.

"They got 'em stopped outside the cup," he said. "I think only one man of theirs is down. He's a-lyin' on his face in the open not far from the boulders where O'Hara is. There must be about a dozen of them, no more."

"Is there a way into the cup with these horses?" Trent asked.

Saul nodded. "Yeah, I reckon if they was busy over yonder for a few minutes, we could run 'em all in."

"We'll make 'em busy, eh, Quince?" Trent suggested. "Bart, you an' Saul whip 'em in there fast as soon as we open up." He had reloaded his rifle, and the two turned their horses and started skirting the rocks to outflank the attackers.

Trent could see what had happened. The Hatfield place lay in a cup-like depression surrounded on three sides by high, rocky walls and on the other by scattered boulders. Through the cliffs, there were two ways of getting into the cup. One of these, now about to be attempted, lay partly across an open space before the cut was entered. The attackers were mostly among the scattered boulders, but had been stopped and pinned down by O'Hara and someone else. Two men there could hold that ground against thirty. Obviously some of the others were up in the cliffs above the cup, waiting for any attack.

Approaching as they were, Trent and Quince were

coming down from the south toward the west end of the cup, where the scattered boulders lay. By working up close there, they could find and dislodge the attackers, or at least keep them so busy the pack animals could get across the open to the cup.

About three acres of land lay in the bottom of the cup. There was a fine, cold spring, the barn, horse corrals, and adequate protection. The cliffs were ringed with scattered cedar and rocks, so men there could protect the approach to the boulder. However, if a rifleman got into those rocks on the edge of the cup, he could render movement in the cup impossible until he could be driven out. It was the weak spot of the stronghold.

When they had ridden several hundred yards, the two men reined in and dismounted. Slipping through the cedars, Indian fashion, they soon came to the edge of the woods overlooking the valley of boulders. Not fifty yards away, two men lay behind boulders facing toward the Hatfield cup.

Trent lifted his Winchester and let go with three fast shots. One, aimed at the nearest man's feet, clipped a heel from his boot; the others threw dust in his face, and with a yell the fellow scrambled out of there. Trent followed him with two more shots, and the man tumbled into a gully and started to run.

The other man started to get up, and Quince Hatfield made him leap like a wild man with a well-placed shot that burned the inside of his leg. Scattering their shots, the two had the rest of the attackers scattering for better cover.

VIII

Parson Hatfield walked out to meet them as they rode in. He grinned through his yellowed handlebar mustache.

"Well, I reckon we win the first round." He chuckled. "Sure was a sight to see them 'punchers dustin' out of there when you all opened up on 'em!"

"Who was the man we saw down?" Trent asked.

"Gun hand they called Indian Joe. A killer. He wouldn't stop comin', so O'Hara let him have it. Dead center."

They walked back to the cabin.

"We got grub to keep us for a few days, but we got a passel of folks here," Parson said, squatting on his haunches, "an' I don't reckon you're goin' to be able to hit Cedar Bluff again."

Trent nodded agreement. "We've got to get to Blazer," he said. "There isn't any two ways about it. I wish I knew what they'd do now. If we had a couple of days' leeway. . . ."

"You know anythin' about the celebration Hale's figurin' on down to Cedar Bluff? They's been talk about it. He's been there ten years, an' he figures that's reason to celebrate."

"What's happenin'?" Trent asked.

"Horse races, horseshoe pitchin', wrestlin', footraces, an' a prize fight. King Bill's bringing in a prize fighter. Big feller, they called him Tombull Turner."

150

Trent whistled. "Say, he is good! Big, too. He fought over in Abilene when I was there. A regular bruiser."

"That may keep 'em busy," Quince said. He had a big chunk of corn pone in his hand. "Maybe we'll get some time to get grub."

Trent got up. "Me, I'm goin' to sleep," he said. "I'm fairly dead on my feet. You'd better, too," he added to Quince Hatfield.

It was growing dusk when Trent awakened. He rubbed his hand over his face and got to his feet. He had been dead tired, and no sooner had he lain down on the grass under the trees than he had fallen asleep.

Walking over to the spring, he drew a bucket of water and plunged his head into it. Then he dried himself on a rough towel Sally handed him.

"Two more men came in," Sally told him. "Tot Wilson from down in the breaks by the box cañon, and Jody Miller, a neighbor of his."

Saul looked up as he walked into the house. "Wilson an' Miller were both burned out. They done killed Wilson's partner. Shot him down when he went out to rope him a horse."

"Hi." Miller looked up at Trent. "I've seen you afore."

"Could be." Trent looked away.

This was it. He could tell by the way Miller looked at him and said: "I'd have knowed you even if it wasn't for that *hombre* down to the Mecca."

"What *hombre?*" Trent demanded.

"Big feller, bigger'n you. He come in there about sundown yesterday, askin' about a man fittin' your description. Wants you pretty bad."

"Flat face? Deep scar over one eye?"

"That's him. Looks like he'd been in a lot of fights, bad ones."

"He was in one," Trent said dryly. "One was enough."

Cain Brockman! Even before he'd heard from Lee Hall, he had known this would come sooner or later. All that was almost two years behind him, but Cain wasn't a man to forget. He had been one of the hard-riding, fast-shooting duo, the Brockman twins. In a fight at Cottonwood, down in the Live Oak country, Trent, then known by his real name, had killed Abel. Later, in a hand-to-hand fight, he had beaten Cain Brockman into a staggering, punch-drunk hulk. Now Brockman was here. As if it weren't enough to have the fight with King Bill Hale on his hands!

Parson Hatfield was staring at Trent. Then he glanced at Miller. "You say you know this feller?" He gestured at Trent. "I'd like to . . . myself!"

"The name," Trent said slowly, "is Lance Kilkenny."

"Kilkenny!" Bartram dropped his plate. "You're Kilkenny."

"Uhn-huh." He turned and walked outside and stood there with his hands on his hips, staring out toward the scattered boulders at the entrance to the Hatfield cup. He was Kilkenny. The name had come back again. He dropped his hands, and almost by magic the big guns leaped into them, and he stood there, staring at them. Slowly, thoughtfully he replaced them.

Cain Brockman was here. The thought made him suddenly weary. It meant, sooner or later, that he must shoot it out with Cain. In his reluctance to fight the big man there was something more than his hatred of killing. He had whipped Cain Brockman with his hands; he had killed Abel. It should be enough. If there was to be any killing—his thoughts skipped Dunn and Ravitz, and he found himself looking again into the blazing white eyes of a trim young man in buckskin, Cub Hale.

He shook his head to clear it and walked toward the spring. What would King Bill do next? He had whipped Hale. Knowing what he had done to the big man, he knew he would still be under cover. Also, Hale's pride would be hurt badly by his beating. Also, it was not only that he had taken a licking. He had burned out a few helpless nesters, only to have those nesters band together and fight off his raiding party, and in the meantime they had ridden into his own town and taken a load of supplies, supplies he had refused them.

The power of any man is built largely on the belief of others in that power. To maintain leadership, he must win victories, and King Bill had been whipped and his plans had been thwarted. The answer to that seemed plain—King Bill must do something to retrieve his losses. But what would he do? Despite the victories the nesters had won, King Bill was still in the driver's seat. He knew how many men they had. He knew about what supplies they had taken from the store, and he knew the number they had at the Hatfields' could not survive for long without more food. Hale could, if he wished, withdraw all his men and just sit tight across the trail to Blazer and wait until the nesters had to move or starve. He might do that. Or he might strike again, and in greater force.

Kilkenny—it seemed strange to be thinking of himself as Kilkenny again, he had been Trent so long—ruled out the quick strike. By now Hale would know that the Hatfields were strongly entrenched. The main trail to Blazer led through Cedar Bluff. There was a trail, only occasionally used, from the Hatfields' to the Blazer mountain trail, but Hale knew that, and would be covering it. There was a chance they might slip through. Yet even as he thought of that, he found himself thinking again of the vast crater that was the Smoky Desert. That was still a possibility.

O'Hara walked out to where he was standing under the trees. "Runyon an' Wilson want to try the mountain trail to Blazer," he told him. "What do you think?"

"I don't think much of it," Kilkenny said truthfully, "yet we've got to have grub."

"Parson told 'em what you said about Smoky Desert. Wilson says it can't be done. He said he done tried it."

Jackson Hight, Miller, and Wilson walked out. "We're all for tryin' the mountain trail," Wilson said.

"I don't believe Hale will have it watched this far up. What do you say, Kilkenny?"

Kilkenny looked at his boot toe thoughtfully. They wanted to go, and they might get through. After all, the Smoky Desert seemed an impossible dream, and even more so to them than to him. "It's up to you," he said finally. "I won't send a man over that trail, but if you want to try it, go ahead."

It was almost midnight when the wagon pulled out of the cup. Miller was driving, with Wilson, Jackson Hight, and Lije Hatfield riding escort. Kilkenny was up to watch them go, and, when the sound of the wagon died away, he returned to his pallet and turned in.

Twice during the night he awakened with a start, to lie there listening in the stillness, his body tense, his mind fraught with worry, but despite his expectations there were no sounds of shots, nothing.

When daybreak came, he ate a hurried breakfast and swung into the saddle. He left the cup on a lope and followed the dim trail of the wagon. He followed it past the charred ruins of his own cabin and past those of Moffitt's cabin, yet, as he neared the Blazer trail, he slowed down, walking the buckskin and stopping frequently to listen. He could see by the tracks that Lije and Hight had been riding ahead, scouting the way. Sometimes they were as much as a half mile ahead, and he found several places where they had sat their horses, waiting.

Suddenly the hills seemed to fall away and he saw

the dim trail that led to Blazer, more than forty miles away. Such a short distance, yet the trail was so bad that fifteen miles a day was considered good. There was no sign of the wagon or of the men. There were no tracks visible, and that in itself was a good thing. It meant that someone, probably Lije, was remembering they must leave no trail.

He turned the buckskin then and rode back over the trail. He took his time, and it was the middle of the afternoon before he reached the ledge where he could look down into the awful haze that hung over the Smoky Desert. Once, in his first trip up over this route, it had been clearer below, and he had thought he saw a ruined wagon far below. Kilkenny found the place where he had stood that other day, for long since he had marked the spot with a cairn of stones. Then slowly and with great pains he began to seek. Time and again he was turned back by sheer drops of hundreds of feet, and nowhere could he find even the suggestion of a trail.

Four hours later, with long fingers of darkness reaching out from the tall pines, he mounted the buckskin and started down toward the cup. Jackson Hight could be correct. Possibly he was mistaken and the Indians were wrong, and there was no trail down to the valley below and across that wasteland. In his long search he had found nothing.

Parson met him as he rode through the notch. Ma Hatfield had come to the door and was shading her eyes toward him.

"They got through to the trail," Kilkenny said. "Maybe they'll make it."

Sally was working over the fireplace when he walked inside. Young Bartram was sitting close by, watching her. Kilkenny glanced at them and smiled grimly. Sally caught his eye and flushed painfully, so he walked outside again and sat down against the house.

Quince had gone after deer into the high meadows, and Saul was on guard. Runyon was sleeping on the grass under the trees, and Jesse Hatfield was up on the cliffs somewhere. Kilkenny sat for a long time against the house, and then he took his blankets over to the grass, rolled up, and went to sleep.

Shortly after daybreak he roped a black horse from his string, saddled up, and with a couple of sandwiches headed back toward the Smoky Desert. There must be a route. There had to be one.

When he reached the rim of the cliff again, he dismounted and studied the terrain thoughtfully. He stood on a wide ledge that thrust itself out into space. The desert below was partially obscured, as always, by clouds of dust or smoke, yet the rim itself was visible for some distance.

Actually, studying the rim, he could see that it bore less resemblance to the crater he had previously imagined than to a great sink. In fact, it looked as though some internal upheaval had caused the earth to subside at this point, breaking off the rock of the ledge and sinking the plateau several hundred feet. For the

157

most part the cliffs below the rim were jagged but almost sheer, yet at places the rim had caved away into steep rock slides that led, or seemed to lead, to the bottom. This great rift in the plateau led for miles, causing the trail to Blazer to swing in a wide semi-circle to get around it. Actually, as best he could figure, Blazer was almost straight across from the ledge where he now stood.

Again he began to work with painstaking care along the rim. The Indians had said it could be crossed, that there was a way down, and Lance Kilkenny had lived in the West long enough to know that what the Indians said was usually right.

It was almost noon before he found the path. It was scarcely three feet wide, so he left his horse standing under the cedars and started walking. The path dipped through some gigantic slabs of ragged-edged rock and then ran out to the very edge of the cliff itself. When it seemed he was about to step right off into space, the path turned sharply to the right and ran along the face of the cliff.

He hesitated, taking off his hat and mopping his brow. The path led right along the face of the cliff, and at times it seemed almost broken away, but then it continued on. One thing he knew—this was useless for his purpose, for no man could take a horse, not even such a sure-footed mountain horse as the buck-skin, along this path. Yet he walked on.

The end was abrupt. He started to work his way around a thread of path that clung to the precipice, but when he could see around the corner, he saw the trail had ended. An hour of walking had brought him to a dead-end. Clinging to the rock, he looked slowly around. Then his eyes riveted. There, over 300 feet below, on what even at this distance was obviously a trail, he could see a wagon wheel.

Leaning out with a precarious handhold on a root, he could distinguish the half-buried wagon from which the wheel had been broken. Of the rest of the trail, he could see nothing. It vanished from sight under the bulge of the cliff. He drew back, sweating.

The trail was there. The wagon was there. Obviously someone, at some time, had taken a wagon or wagons over that trail. But where was the beginning? Had the shelf upon which it ran broken off and ruined the trail for use?

Taking a point of gray rock for a landmark, he retraced his steps along the path. By the time he reached the buckskin again, his feet hurt from walking over the rough rock in his riding boots, and he was tired, dead tired. He had walked about six miles, and that was an impossible distance to a horseman.

IX

When he rode into the cup that night, Parson looked up from the rifle that he was cleaning. "Howdy, son! You look done up!"

Kilkenny nodded and stopped beside the older man. He was tired, and his shirt stuck to his back with sweat. For the first time he wondered if they would win. For the first time, he doubted. Without food they were helpless. They could neither escape nor resist. He doubted now if Hale would ever let them go, if he would ever give them any chance of escape.

They ate short rations that night. He knew there was still a good deal of food, yet fourteen men, if he included those who were gone, and six women had to eat there. And there were nine children. Yet there was no word of complaint, and only on the faces of those women who had men with the food wagon could he distinguish the thin gray lines of worry.

"Any sign from Hale?" he asked O'Hara.

The Irishman shook his head. "Not any. He's got men out in the rocks. They ain't tryin' to shoot nobody. Just a-watchin'. But they're there."

"I don't think he'll try anything now until after the celebration," Bartram said. "He's plannin' on makin' a lot of friends with that celebration. It means a lot to him, anyway."

Jesse Hatfield pushed back his torn felt hat. "I took me a ride today," he said. "Done slipped out through the brush. I got clean to Cedar Bluff without bein' seen. I edged up close to town, an' I could see a lot of workin' around. They got 'em a ring set up out in front of the livery stable near the horse corral. Ropes an' everythin'. Lots of talk around, an' the big wonder is who's goin' to fight Tombull Turner."

Kilkenny listened absently, not caring. His thoughts were back on that ragged rim, working along each notch and crevice, wondering where that road reached the top of the plateau.

"This here Dan Cooper was there, an' he done some talkin'. He looked powerful wise, an' he says Turner ain't been brought here by accident. He's been brought to whip one man . . . Kilkenny!"

"Did he say Kilkenny?" Kilkenny looked around to ask. "Do they know who I am?"

"He said Trent," Jesse drawled. "I don't reckon they know."

Tombull Turner to beat him? Kilkenny remembered the bullet head, the knotted cauliflower ears, the flat nose and hard, battered face of the big bare-knuckle fighter. Tombull was a fighter. He was more; he was a brute. He was an American who had fought much in England, and against the best on both continents. He had even met Joe Goss and Paddy Ryan. While he, Kilkenny, was no prize fighter.

An idle rumor. It could be no more, for he was not in Cedar Bluff, nor was he likely to be. Studying the faces of the men around him, he could see what was on their minds. Despite their avoidance of the subject, he knew they were all thinking of the wagon on the road to Blazer.

The food was necessary, but four men were out there, four men they all knew, men who had shared their work, their trials, and even the long trip West from their lands in Kentucky, Pennsylvania, and Missouri. Lije Hatfield was gone, and, knowing the family, Kilkenny knew that, if he were killed, no Hat-

161

field would stop until all the Hales were dead or the Hatfields wiped out.

Knowing the route, he could picture the wagon rolling slowly along over the rocky road, horsemen to the front and rear, watching, hoping, fearing. They, too, if still alive and free, would have their worries. They would know that back here men and women were getting close to the end of their food supply, that those men and women were depending on them.

On the morning of the third day, Kilkenny mounted again and started for the rim. He saw Parson Hatfield staring after him, but the old man said nothing.

This time Kilkenny had a plan. He was going back where he had been the day before, and by some means he was going down the face of the cliff to the wagon. Then he would backtrack. If there was no trail back, he would have to come up the cliff. Well, that was a bridge to be crossed later. Somewhere in that jumble of broken cliffs, great slabs of jagged rock, and towering shoulders of stone, there must be a trail down which that wagon had gone.

It was almost seven o'clock in the morning before he found himself, two ropes in his hands, at the tapering edge of the trail along the face of the cliff. Lying flat, he peered over the edge. The rock on which he lay was a bulge that thrust out over the face of the cliff, and, if he dropped over here, he must use the rope purely as a safety precaution and work down with his hands. There were cracks and knobs that could be used. The depth below was sickening, but partially obscured by the strange thickness of the air.

A gnarled cedar grew from the face of the rock, and he tested it for strength. The thing seemed as immovable as the rocks themselves. Making his first rope fast to the cedar, Kilkenny knotted the other end in a bowline around himself. Then he turned himself around and backed over the edge, feeling with his feet for a toehold.

For a time, he knew, he would be almost upside down like a fly on a ceiling. Unless he could find handholds where he could get a good grip and, if necessary, hang by them, there was small chance of making it. But there were, he had noticed, a number of roots, probably of rock cedar, thrusting out through the rock below.

Forcing himself to think of nothing but the task at hand, he lowered himself over the edge, and, when he got the merest toehold, he swung one hand down and felt around until he could grasp one of the roots. Then he let go with his left hand and let himself down until he was half upside down, clinging by a precarious toehold and his grip on the root.

Finding another hold for his left hand, he took a firm grasp, and then pulled out his left toe and felt downward. He found a crack, tested it with his toe, and then set the foot solidly. Carefully he released a handhold and lowered his hand to another root, lower down. Then, sweating profusely, he lowered his weight to the lower foot.

He resolutely kept his thoughts away from the awful

depths below. He had a chance, but a very slim one. Slowly and with great care he shifted himself down the bulging overhang. Every time he moved a foot or hand, his life seemed about to end. He was, he knew, wringing with perspiration, his breath was coming painfully, and he swung himself precariously toward the sheer cliff below. Even that great height of straight up and down cliff seemed a haven to this bulge of the overhang.

Clinging to a huge root and pressing himself as tightly to the face as he could, he turned his head right, and then left, searching the face of the bulge. There were handholds enough here. The roots of the cedars that had grown on the ledge above thrust through the bulge. Yet that very fact seemed to indicate that at some time in the past huge chunks of rock had given way, leaving these roots exposed. It had happened once, and it could happen again.

Far out in the blue sky a buzzard whirled in great, slow circles. His fingers ached with gripping, and he lowered himself away from the face of the cliff and looked down between his legs. A notch showed in the rock, and he worked his toe loose, and then lowered it with care until he could test the notch. He tried it.

Solid. Slowly, carefully he began to settle weight on the ball of his foot. There was a sudden sag beneath his foot and then a rattle of stones, and the notch gave way under him, forcing him to grip hard with his hands to catch the additional weight.

His right foot hung free. Carefully he began to feel

with his toe for another foothold. He found it, tried, and rested his weight again, and the stone took it. Slowly he shifted hands again, and then lowered himself down a little more.

Glancing down again, he found himself looking at a stretch of rock at least fifteen feet across that was absolutely smooth. No single crack or crevice showed, no projection of stone, no root. His muscles desperate with weariness, he stared, unbelieving—to come this far and fail.

Forcing himself to think, he studied the face of the cliff. There was, some twenty feet below and almost that far to the left, a gnarled and twisted rock cedar growing out of the mountainside. It was too far to the right, and there was no way of reaching it. Yet, as he stared, he could see that a crevice, deep enough for a good foothold, ran off at an angle from the cedar. If he could reach it—but how?

There was a way. It hit him almost at once. If he released his grip on the roots, he would instantly swing free. As he had worked himself far to the right of the cedar to which his lariat was tied, his release would swing him far out from the cliff, and then, as he swung back, for an instant he would be above the clump of cedar. On each succeeding swing he would fall shorter and shorter, until finally he was suspended in mid-air, hanging like a great pendulum from the cedar above.

Then all his efforts would be vain, for he would have to catch the rope over his head and go up it, hand over hand, to the cedar above, and he would have failed. On the other hand, if he could release himself above the cedar, he would fall into it, and unless some sharp branch injured him, the chances were the limbs would cushion his fall.

He had his knife, and it was razor sharp. Even as these thoughts flitted through his mind, he was drawing the knife. Luckily, before leaving his horse, he had tied a rawhide thong over each six-shooter, so his guns were secure. Yet the rope was rawhide and tough. Could he slash through at one blow?

The answer to that was simple. He had to. If he swung out over the void below on half or less of the strength of the lariat, there was small chance it would not break at the extreme end of the swing, and he would go shooting out over the deadly waste of the Smoky Desert to fall, and fall—over and over into that murky cloud that obscured the depths.

He let go and shoved hard with both feet and hands. His body swept out in a long swing over the breathtaking depths below. Then, hesitating but an instant as the rope tore at his sides, he swept back like a giant pendulum, rushing through the air toward the cliff! It shot toward him, and he raised his arm, and, seeing the cedar below and ahead, he cut down with a mighty slash.

He felt himself come loose, and then he was hurled forward at the cedar. He hit it, all doubled into a ball, heard a splintering crash, slipped through, and felt the branches tearing at his clothes like angry fingers. Then he brought up with a jolt and lay, trembling in every limb, clinging to the cedar.

How long he lay there, he did not know. Finally he pulled himself together and crawled out of the tree and got his feet on the narrow foothold. He worked his way along until the ledge grew wide enough for him to walk. His breath was coming with more regularity now. He felt gingerly of his arms and body where the rawhide rope had burned him.

The path, if such it might be called, slanted steeply away from him, ending in some broken slabs. He stopped when he reached them. He was, at last, on the Smoky Desert.

X

Lance Kilkenny stood on a dusty desert floor littered with jagged slabs of rock, obviously fallen from the cliff above. There was no grass here, no cedar, nothing growing at all, not even a cactus. Above him, the dark, basalt cliff lifted toward the sky, towering and ugly. Looking off over the desert, he could see only a few hundred yards, and then all became indistinct. The reason was obvious enough. The floor of the desert was dust, fine as flour, and even the lightest breeze lifted it into the air, where it hung for hours on end. A strong wind would fill the air so full of these particles as to make the air thick as a cloud, and the particles were largely silicate.

One thing he knew now. Crossing the Smoky

Desert, even if there was a trail, would be a frightful job. Unfastening the thongs that had held his guns in place, he walked on slowly. It was still, only a little murmur from the wind among the rocks, and nothing else.

The cliff lifted on his right, and off to the left stretched the awful expanse of the desert, concealed behind that curtain of dust. He stepped over the dead and bleached bones of an ancient cedar, fallen from above, and rounded a short bend in the cliff. As he walked, little puffs of dust lifted from his boot soles, and his mouth grew dry. Once he stopped and carefully wiped his guns free of dust, and then lowered them once more into the holsters.

Then he saw the white scar of the road, tracks of vehicles filled with fine white dust, and the rough, barely visible marks of what had been a fairly good road, dwindling away into the gray, dusty vagueness that was the desert. He looked up and saw the trail winding steeply up the cliff's face through a narrow draw.

Turning, he began to climb the trail. Several times he paused to roll boulders from the path. He was already thinking in terms of a wagon and a team. It could be done. That is, it could be done if there was still a way of getting a team onto this trail. That might be the catch. What lay at the end?

Sweat rolled down his face, making thin rivulets through the white dust. White dust clung to the hairs on the backs of his hands, and once, when he stopped to remove his sombrero and wipe the sweat from his brow, he saw his hat was covered with a thin gray coat of it.

He looked ahead. He could see the road for no more than 100 yards, but the cliff to his right was now growing steeper, and, glancing down, he could see the trail was already far above the valley floor. He walked, making heavy work of it in his riding boots, sweat soaking his shirt under the film of gray dust, and the draw was narrowing.

The rock under the trail sloped steeply away into a dark, shadowy cañon now over 200 feet down. He walked on, plodding wearily. For over an hour he walked, winding around and around to follow the curving walls of the cañon. Then he halted suddenly.

Ahead of him the trail ended. It ended and explained his difficulties in one instant. A gigantic pine, once perched upon the edge of the cliff, had given way, its roots evidently weakened by wind erosion. The tree had blown down and fallen across the trail. Pines had sprung up around it and around its roots until the trail was blocked by a dense thicket that gave no hint of the road that had once run beneath it.

Crawling over the pine, Kilkenny emerged from the thicket and walked back to his horse. Mounting, he rode slowly homeward, and, as he rode, he thought he had never been so utterly tired as he was now. But there was coolness in the breeze through the pines, and some of their piney fragrance seemed to get into his blood. He looked up, feeling better as he rode slowly along the grassy trail, through the mountain meadows and down through the columned trunks of the great old trees toward the Hatfield cup.

Yes, it was worth fighting for, worth fighting to keep what one had in this lonely land among the high peaks. It was such a country as a man would want, a country where a man could grow and could live, and where his sons could grow. Even as he thought of that, Kilkenny found himself remembering Nita. King Bill Hale wanted her. Well, what would be more understandable? Certainly she was beautiful, the most beautiful woman in Cedar Valley and many other valleys. And what did she think? Hale had everything to offer: strength, position, wealth. She could reign like a queen at the Castle.

And Hale himself? He was a handsome man. Cold, but yet, what man ever sees another man as a woman sees him? The side of himself that a man shows to women is often much different from that seen by men. Worry began to move through him like a drug. Nita nearby was one thing, but Nita belonging to someone else, that was another idea. He realized suddenly it was an idea he didn't like, not even a little bit. Especially he did not want her to belong to the arrogant King Bill.

Hale wanted her, and, regardless of what she thought, he could bring pressure to bear, if his own eloquence failed him. He was king in Cedar Valley. Her supplies came in over the road he controlled. He could close her business. He could even prevent her from leaving. He might. Jaime Brigo was the reason why he might not succeed. Brigo and himself, Kilkenny.

King Bill's lack of action disturbed him. Hale had been beaten in a fist fight. Knowing the arrogance of the man, Kilkenny knew he would never allow that to pass. He had refused them supplies, and they had come and taken them from under his nose. Was Hale waiting to starve them? He knew how many they were. He knew the supplies they had were not enough to last long. And he held the trail to Blazer. Did he know of the trail through the Smoky Desert? Kilkenny doubted that. Even he did not know if it were passable. The chances were Hale had never even dreamed of such a thing. Aside from the Indian to whom he had talked, Kilkenny had heard no mention of it.

Saul Hatfield walked down from among the trees as he neared the cup. "Anything happen?" Kilkenny asked.

Saul shook his head, staring curiously at the dust-covered Kilkenny. "Nope. Not any. Jesse took him a ride down to town. They sure are gettin' set for that celebration. Expectin' a big crowd. They say Hale's invited some folks down from Santa Fé, some big muckety-mucks."

"From Santa Fé?" Kilkenny's eyes narrowed. That was a neat bit of politics, a good chance to entertain the officials, and then tell them casually of the outlaws in the mountains, the men who had come in and tried to take away valuable land from King Bill. Lance knew how persuasive such a man could be. And he would entertain like royalty, and these men would go away impressed. That King Bill didn't intend to strengthen his position very much would be foolhardy to imagine. Hale would know how to play politics, how to impress these men with his influence and the power of his wealth.

The audience would all be friendly, too. They would give the visiting officials the idea that all was well in Cedar Valley. Then, when the elimination of some out-laws hiding in the mountains was revealed, if it ever was, the officials would imagine it was merely that and never inquire as to the rightness or wrongness of Hale's actions.

In that moment, Kilkenny decided. He would go to Cedar Bluff for the celebration. Yet, even as the thought occurred to him, he remembered the thick neck and beetling brow of Tombull Turner. For the first time he began to think of the prize fighter. He had seen the man fight. He was a mountain of muscle, a man with a body of muscle and iron. His jaw was like a chunk of granite. His flat nose and beetling brow were fearsome.

Kilkenny rode down into the cup and swung from his horse. Parson walked slowly toward him, Jesse and O'Hara beside him. They stared at the dust on his clothes.

"Looks like you been places, son," Parson drawled.

"I have." Kilkenny removed the saddle and threw it

on the rail. "I've been down into the Smoky Desert."

"The Smoky Desert?" O'Hara stepped forward. "You found a way?"

"Uhn-huh. Take a little axe work to clear it."

"Could a wagon get across?"

Kilkenny shrugged, looking up at the big Irishman. "Your guess is as good as mine. I know I can get a wagon into the desert. I know there used to be a trail. I could see it. There's parts of a wagon down there. Somebody has been across. Where somebody else went, we'll go."

"How about gettin' out?" Parson drawled.

"That," Kilkenny admitted, "is the point. You put your finger right on the sore spot. Maybe there's a way, maybe there isn't. There was once. But I'm a-goin'. I'm goin' over, an' with luck I'll get back. We'll have to take water. We'll have to tie cloths over our faces and over the nostrils of the horses. Otherwise that dust will fix us for good."

"When you goin'?" Jesse demanded.

"Right soon. We got to make a try. If we could make it soon enough, we might bring the others back that way. I'll start tomorrow."

"Leave us short-handed," Parson suggested.

"It will." Kilkenny nodded agreement. He looked at the old mountaineer thoughtfully. "The trouble is, Hale has time, an' we haven't. I'm bankin' that he won't try anything until after the celebration. I think this is not only his tenth anniversary but a bit of politics to get friendly with them down at Santa Fé. He'll wait until he's solid with them before he cleans us out."

"Maybe. Ain't nobody down to town goin' to tell our side of this. Not a soul," Hatfield agreed.

"There will be." Kilkenny stripped off his shirt and drew a bucket of water from the well. His powerful muscles ran like snakes beneath his tawny skin. "I'm goin' down."

"They'll kill you, man!" O'Hara declared. "They'd shoot you like a dog."

"No, not while those Santa Fé officials are there. I'll go. I hear they want me to fight Tombull Turner. Well, I'm goin' down an' fight him."

"What?" Runyon shouted. "That man's a killer. He's a ringer."

"I know." Kilkenny shrugged. "But I've seen him fight. Maybe I'm a dang fool, but I've got to get down there an' see those Santa Fé men. This is my chance."

"You think you can do any good against Hale?" Parson asked keenly. "He'll be winin' and dinin' them folks from Santa Fé. He won't let you go nowhere close to 'em."

"But they'll be at the fight," Kilkenny told him. "I'm countin' on that."

At daybreak the labor gang had reached the thicket of pines covering the entrance to the road. Axes in hand, they went to work. Other men began bucking the big fallen tree into sections to be snaked out of the way with ox teams.

174

Once, during a pause when he straightened his back from the saw, Quince looked over at Kilkenny. "They should be there today," he drawled slowly. "I sure hope they make it."

"Yeah." Lance straightened and rubbed his back. It had been a long time since he'd used a cross-cut saw. "You know Blazer?"

"Uhn-huh." Hatfield bit off a chew of tobacco. "Man there named Sodermann. Big an' fat. Mean as a wolf. He's Hale's man. Got a gunman with him name of Rye Pitkin."

"I know him. A two-bit rustler from the Pecos country. Fair hand with a six-gun."

"There's others, too. Ratcliff an' Gaddis are worst. We can expect trouble."

"We?" Kilkenny looked at him. "You volunteerin' for the trip?"

"Sure." Quince grinned at him. "I need me a change of air. Gettin' old, a-settin' around. Reckon the bore of that Kentucky rifle needs a bit of cleanin', too."

They worked on until dark, and, when they stopped, the road was open. O'Hara, who had done the work of two men with an axe, stood on the edge of the cañon in the dimming light and looked across that awful expanse toward the distance, red ridges touched now with light from a vanished sun. "It don't look good to me, Kilkenny," he said. "It sure don't look good."

XI

The wagon was loaded with water—not heavily, but three good kegs of it. With Bartram on the driver's seat, they started. Kilkenny led the way down the steep trail, Quince behind him. He reined in once and watched the wagon trundle over the first stones and past the ruin of the great tree. Then he continued on. For better or worse, they were committed now.

He led the way slowly, stopping often, for it was slow going for the wagon. He watched it coming and watched the mules. They were good mules; Hale himself had no better. They would need to be good.

At the bottom of the road he swung down, and, standing there with Quince Hatfield, he waited, listening to the strange, lonely sighing of the mysterious wind that flowed like a slow current through the dusty depths of the sink.

Bartram was a hand with mules. He brought the wagon up beside them, and Kilkenny indicated the mules. "Soak those cloths in water an' hang one over the nose of each of them. We better each wear a handkerchief over the nose and mouth, too."

He was riding the buckskin, and he got down and hung a cloth over the horse's nostrils, where it would stop part of the dust at least without impeding the breathing. Then they started on.

From here, it was guesswork. He had a compass, and, before leaving the cliff top, he had taken a sight on a distant peak. How closely the trail would hold to that course he did not know, or if any trail would be visible once they got out into the desert. Walking the buckskin, he led off into the dust. The wind did not howl. It blew gently but steadily, and the dust filled the air. Much of it, he knew, was alkali. Behind him, Quince Hatfield rode a raw-boned roan bred to the desert.

Fifteen minutes after leaving the cliff, they were out of sight of it. Overhead the sky was only a lighter space dimly visible through a hanging curtain of dust. Dust arose in clouds from their walking horses and from the wagon, fine, powdery, stifling dust. Over and around them the cloud closed in, thick and prickly when the dust settled on the flesh. Glancing at Quince during one interval, Kilkenny saw the man's face was covered with a film of dust; his eyelashes were thick with it; his hair was white.

When they had been going an hour, he reined in and dismounted. Taking a damp cloth, he sponged out the buckskin's nostrils and wiped off the horse's head and ears. Quince had drawn abreast and was doing likewise, and, when the others came up, they worked over the mules.

The dust filled the air and drew a thick veil around them, as in a blizzard. Saul drew closer. "What if the wind comes up?" he asked.

Bartram's face was stern. "I've been thinking of that," he said. "If the wind comes up, in all of this, we're sunk."

"Where are we now?" Jackie asked, standing up on the wagon.

"We should have made about three or four miles. Maybe more, maybe less. We're right on our course so far."

They rested the mules. The wagon was heavy, even though it was not carrying a load now. The dust and sand in places were a couple of feet deep, but usually the wheels sank no more than six inches into the dust. The animals would all need rest, for the air was heavy with heat, and there was no coolness here in the sink. The dust made breathing an effort.

Kilkenny swung into the saddle and moved out. The flatness of the desert floor was broken now, and it began to slant away from them toward the middle. Kilkenny scowled thoughtfully, and rode more slowly. An hour later, they paused again. This time there was no talking. All of the men were feeling the frightful pressure of the heat, and, glancing at the mules, Kilkenny could see they were breathing heavily. Streaks marred the thick whiteness of the dust on their bodies.

"We'll have to stop more often," he told Bartram, and the farmer nodded.

They rode on, and almost another hour had passed before the buckskin stopped suddenly. Lance touched him gently with a spur, but Buck would not move. Kilkenny swung down. Ahead of him—and he could see for no more than fifty feet—was an even, unbroken expanse of white. It was not even marred by the blackish upthrust of rock that had occasionally appeared along the back trail.

Quince rode up and stopped. "What's wrong?" he asked. Then he swung down and walked up.

"Don't know," Kilkenny said. "Buck won't go on, something wrong." He stepped forward and felt the earth suddenly turn to jelly under his feet. He gave a cry and tried to leap backward, but only tripped himself.

Quince helped him up. "Quicksand," he said, "an' the worst I ever see. Must be springs under."

The wagon drew up, and then Saul and Jackie. "Stay here," Lance told them. "I'll scout to the left."

"I'll go right," Quince suggested. "Might be a way around."

Kilkenny turned the buckskin and let him have his head. He walked at right angles to the course and then, at Kilkenny's urging, tried the surface. It was still soggy. They pulled back and rode on. In a half hour he reined in. There was still no way around, and the edge of the quicksand seemed to be curving back toward him. Only the sagacity of Buck had kept them out of it. He rode back.

"Any luck?" he shouted as he saw Quince waiting with the wagon.

"Uhn-huh. It ends back there about two mile. High ground, rocky."

They turned the wagon and started on once more. They would lose at least an hour more, perhaps two, in skirting the quicksand.

Hour after hour they struggled on. Weariness made their limbs leaden. The mules were beginning to weave a bit now, and Kilkenny found himself sagging in the saddle. His sweat-soaked shirt had become something very like cement with its heavy coating of white dust. They stopped oftener now, stopped for water and to sponge the nostrils of the mules and horses.

At times the trail led through acres upon acres of great, jagged black rocks that thrust up in long ledges that had to be skirted. All calculations on miles across were thrown out of kilter by this continual weaving back and forth across the desert. Time had ceased to matter, and they lived only for the quiet numbness of the halts.

All of them walked from time to time now. Time and again they had to get behind the wagon and push, or had to dig out rocks to roll them aside to clear the only possible trail. The world had become a nightmare of choking, smothering, clinging dust particles, a nightmare of sticky heat and stifling dust-filled air. Even all thought of Hale was gone. They did not think of food or of family, but only of getting across, of getting out of this hell of choking white.

Kilkenny was no longer sure of the compass. Mineral deposits might have made it err. They might be wandering in circles. His only hope was that the ground seemed to rise now, seemed to be slanting upward. Choking, coughing, they moved on into the dust blizzard, hearing the lonely sough of the wind.

Dazed with heat, dust, and weariness, they moved on. The mules were staggering now, and they moved only a few yards at a time.

The black upthrust of the cliff loomed at them suddenly, when all hope seemed gone. It loomed, black and sheer, yet here at the base the dust seemed a little less, a little thinner.

Kilkenny swung down and waited until the rest came up. "Well," he said hoarsely, "we're across. Now to get up."

They rested there under the cliff for a half hour, and then his own restlessness won over his weariness. He had never been able to stop short of a goal; there was something in him that always drove him on, regardless of weariness, trouble, or danger. It came to the surface now, and he lunged to his feet and started moving.

He had walked no more than 100 yards when he found it. He stared at the incredible fact, that through all their weaving back and forth they had held that close to their destination. The road looked rough, but it was a way up, and beyond the hills, but a little way now, lay Blazer.

It was dusk when they reached the top of the cliff and drew up under the pines. Digging a hole in the ground among some rocks, they built a fire in the bottom and warmed some food and made coffee. The hole concealed the flames, and using dry wood they would make no smoke.

Kilkenny drank the strong black coffee and found

his hand growing lax and his lids heavy. He got up, staggered to his blankets, and fell asleep. He slept like he was drugged until Saul Hatfield shook him from his slumber in the last hours of the night to take over the watch.

Lance got up and stretched. Then he walked over to the water casks, drew water, and bathed himself, washing the dust from his hair and ears. Stripping to the waist, he bathed his body in the cold water. Refreshed, he crossed to the black bulk of the rocks and seated himself.

In the darkness thoughts come easily. He sat there, his eyes open and staring restlessly from side to side, yet his thoughts wandering back to Cedar Bluff. They wanted him to fight Tombull Turner. He had decided to take the fight. Sitting here in the darkness with the wind in the pines overhead, he could think clearly. It was their only chance of getting to the Santa Fé officials. He knew how men of all sorts and kinds admire a fighting man. The Santa Fé officials, especially if one of them was Halloran, would be no exception. He would be going into the fight as the underdog. Hale wanted him whipped, but King Bill's power was destroying his shrewdness.

Halloran, or whoever came, would know about Tombull. The man had been fighting, and winning, all through the West. Any man who went against him would be the underdog, and the underdog always has the crowd with him. Kilkenny knew there was scarcely a chance that he would do anything but take a beating, yet he believed he could stay in there long enough to make some impression. And between rounds—that would be his chance.

If ever, he would have a chance to talk then. King Bill would have his guests in ringside seats. He would be expecting a quick victory. Coldly Kilkenny appraised himself. Like all fighting men, he considered himself good. He had fought many times in the rough and tumble fistfights of the frontier. As a boy he had fought many times in school. During the days when he was in the East, he had taken instruction from the great Jem Mace, the English pugilist, who was one of the cleverest of all bare-knuckle fighters. Mace was a shrewd fighter who used his head for something aside from a parking place for two thick ears.

King Bill did not know that Kilkenny had ever boxed. Neither would Tombull know that. Moreover, Kilkenny had for years lived a life in the open, a life that required hard physical condition and superb strength. He had those assets, and above all he had his knowledge of Turner, whereas Turner knew nothing of him. Turner would be overconfident. Nevertheless, in all honesty, Kilkenny could find little hope of victory. His one hope was to make a game fight of it, to win the sympathy and interest of the officials before he spoke to them, as he would.

He would rest when he returned to the cup. He would soak his hands in brine, and he would wear driving gloves in the ring. Some of the younger fighters were wearing skintight gloves now, and Mace had told him of their cutting ability.

There was no sound but the sound of the forest, and he relaxed, watching and awaiting the dawn. When it came, they ate a hurried breakfast. They were rested and felt better. Kilkenny cleaned his guns carefully, both pistols and his rifle. The others did likewise.

"Quince," Kilkenny said as he holstered his guns. "You know Blazer. What d'you think?"

Hatfield shrugged. "I reckon they won't be expectin' us from hereabouts. I been takin' some bearin's, an' I reckon we will come into town from the opposite side. We got us a good chance of gettin' in afore they know who we are."

"Good!" Kilkenny turned to Bartram. "You know the team. You stay by the wagon an' keep your gun handy. Stay on the ground where you can either mount up or take cover. Saul, you an' Jackie hustle the grub out to the wagon, an' Quince will stand by to cover you."

"How about you?" Bartram asked, looking up at him.

"I'm goin' to look around for sign of the other wagon. I want to know what happened to Lije an' them. They may be all right, but I want to know." As they mounted up, he turned in his saddle. "Quince, you ride with me. Saul an' Jackie will bring up the rear."

They started out, and less than a mile from where they had come from the desert they rode down into the trail to Blazer. As Quince Hatfield had suggested, they were coming in from the opposite side.

Two rows of ramshackle saloons, cheap dance halls, and stores made up the town of Blazer. These two rows faced each other across a river of dust that was called a street. The usual number of town loafers sat on benches in front of the Crossroads, the Temple of Chance, and the Wagon Wheel.

It was morning, and few horses stood at the hitching rail. There was a blood bay with a beautifully hand-worked saddle standing in front of the Crossroads, and two cow ponies stood three-legged before the Wagon Wheel.

XII

Lance Kilkenny rode past the Perkins General Store and swung down in front of the Wagon Wheel. Bartram stopped the wagon parallel to the hitching rail and began to fill his pipe. His rifle leaned against the seat beside him.

Saul and Jackie walked into the store, and Quince leaned against the corner of the store and lighted a cigarette. His rifle lay in the wagon, but he wore a huge Walker Colt slung to his belt.

A horseman came down the trail and swung down in front of the Wagon Wheel and walked inside. Quince straightened and stared at him, and his eyes narrowed. The man was big and had red hair and a red beard. Kilkenny stared at the man, and then, as Quince motioned with his head, he idled over toward him.

"That *hombre* was wearin' an ivory-handled Colt with a chipped ivory on the right side," Hatfield said. His narrow face was empty and his eyes bitter.

"A chipped ivory butt?" Kilkenny frowned, and then suddenly his face paled. "Why, Jody Miller had a gun like that. An' Jody was with the first wagon."

"Uhn-huh. I reckon," Hatfield said, "I better ask me a few questions."

"Wait," Kilkenny said. "I'm goin' in there. You keep your eyes open. Remember, we need the grub first. Meantime, I'll find out somethin'."

He turned and walked over to the Wagon Wheel and ambled inside. Two cowpokes sat at a table with the bartender and a man in a black coat, a huge man, enormously big and enormously fat. That, he decided, would be Sodermann.

The red-bearded man was leaning on the bar. "Come on, Shorty," he snapped. "Give us a drink! I'm dry."

"Take it easy, Gaddis," Shorty barked. He was a short, thick-set man with an unshaven face. "I'll be with you in a minute."

Kilkenny leaned against the bar and looked around. It didn't look good. If the big man was Sodermann—and there was small chance of there being two such huge men in any Western town—that placed Sodermann and Gaddis. The cowpokes might be mere cowhands, but they didn't look it. One of the men might be Ratcliff. And there was still Rye Pitkin. But he knew Rye, and the rustler was not present.

Judging by appearances, Shorty could be counted on to side Sodermann, and, if that was Jody Miller's gun, it meant that the other wagon had been stopped, and the chances were that the men who accompanied it had been wiped out.

Slow rage began to mount in Kilkenny at the thought of those honest, sincere men who asked only the right to work and build homes, being killed by such as these. He was suddenly conscious that Sodermann was watching him.

Shorty got up and sauntered behind the bar. "What'll you have?" he asked, leaning on the hardwood. His eyes slanted from Gaddis to Kilkenny.

"Rye," Gaddis said. He turned abruptly and gave Kilkenny a cool glance, a glance that suddenly quickened as he noticed the dusty clothing and the tied-down guns. He stared at Kilkenny's face, but Lance had his hat brim low, and this man had never seen him before, anyway.

"Make mine rye, too," Kilkenny said. He turned his head and looked at Sodermann. "You drinkin'?"

"Maybe." The fat man got up, and he moved his huge bulk with astonishing lightness. Kilkenny's eyes sharpened. This man could move. "Maybe I will. I always likes to know who I'm drinkin' with, howsoever."

"Not so particular where I come from," Kilkenny said softly. "A drink's a drink."

"I reckon." Sodermann nodded affably. "You appear to be a stranger hereabouts. I reckon every man who

wears a gun like you wear yours knows Doc Sodermann."

"I've heard the name." Kilkenny let his eyes drift to
the table. One of the men was sitting up straight
rolling a smoke, the other idly riffling the cards.
Either could draw fast. Red Gaddis had turned to face
them.

The whole setup was too obviously ready to spring.
He was going to have to relax them a little. He would
have to relieve this tension.

"Heard there might be a job up this way for a man,"
he said slowly, "an' I could use a job up here where
it's quiet."

"Away from the law, you mean?" Sodermann
laughed until he shook all over. Kilkenny noticed
there was no laughter in his eyes.

"Uhn-huh. Away from everythin'."

"We got law here. King Bill Hale runs this country."

"Heard of him."

"You hear a lot," Gaddis suggested. His eyes were
mean.

"Yeah." Kilkenny turned a little and let his green
eyes stare from under his hat brim at the red-headed
man. "Yeah, I make it my business to hear a lot."

"Maybe you hear too much!" Gaddis snapped.

"You want to show me how much?" Kilkenny's
voice was level. He spoke coolly, yet he was sure
there would be no shooting here, yet. He was wondering if Sodermann knew Hatfield was outside
beside the window.

Gaddis stepped away from the bar, and his jaw jutted. "Why, I think you're. . . ."

"Stop it!" Sodermann's voice was suddenly charged with anger. "You're too anxious for trouble, Gaddis. Someday you'll get yourself killed."

Gaddis relaxed slowly, his eyes ugly. Yet, watching the man, Kilkenny could sense a certain relief in him, also. Gaddis was a killer, but not a gunman in the sense that he was highly skilled. He was a paid killer, a murderer, the sort of man who would dry-gulch men around a wagon. And he wore a chipped gun.

"Your friend's right proddy," Kilkenny said softly. "He must have a killin' urge."

"Forget it," Sodermann said jovially. "He's all right. Just likes to fight, that's all."

Kilkenny stared at Gaddis. "Seems like you should be somebody I know," he drawled slowly. "I don't recognize that face, but I do know you. But then, I never remember a face, anyway. I got my own methods of knowin' a man. I look at the only thing that's important to me."

"What's that?" Sodermann asked. He was studying Kilkenny, curiosity in his eyes and some puzzlement.

"I always remember a man's gun. Each gun has its own special look, or maybe it's the way a man wears a gun. Take that one now, with that chipped ivory on the side of the butt. A man wouldn't forget a gun like that in a hurry."

Gaddis stiffened, and his face turned gray. Then the tip of his tongue touched his lips. Before he could speak, Sodermann looked straight into Kilkenny's eyes.

"An' where would you see that gun?"

"In Santa Fé," Kilkenny drawled, remembering that Miller had once lived there. "It was hangin' to a man they said was comin' West to farm. His name was Jody Miller."

"You talk too much!" Gaddis snarled, his face white and his lips thin.

"It was in Santa Fé." Kilkenny was adding a touch now that he hoped would worry Sodermann. Only a word, yet sometimes. . . . "Miller stopped off in Santa Fé to see some folks at the fort there an' to talk to Halloran an' Wallace. Seems they was old friends of his."

Sodermann's face sharpened, and he turned. His raised hand made Gaddis draw back a little.

"You're talkin' a lot, stranger," he said smoothly. "You say this Miller knowed Halloran an' Wallace?"

"Uhn-huh." Kilkenny motioned to Shorty to refill his glass. "Seems he knowed them back East. One of 'em married a sister of his, or somethin'. I heard 'em talkin' in a saloon once. Heard Halloran say he was comin' out here to visit Miller." Kilkenny glanced at Gaddis, his face expressionless. "I reckon you'll be plum glad to see him, Miller. It's mighty nice to have an official, big man like that for a friend."

Lance could have laughed if he hadn't known what he knew now, that the wagon had been waylaid and that Miller was probably dead. There would be no other reason for Gaddis's looking as he did. The man was obviously afraid. Sodermann was staring, keen-eyed, yet there was uncertainty in the big man. When that uncertainty ended, there would be danger, Kilkenny knew.

"Funny," Kilkenny said softly, "I don't remember Miller havin' red hair. Seemed to me it was black. That's what it was. Black."

"It was yel . . . !" Gaddis began.

"Yellow. That's right. It was yellow. Strange, I couldn't remember that. But you, stranger, you've got Jody Miller's gun. How d'you explain that?"

Suddenly the door behind Kilkenny opened. He felt the flesh along the back of his neck tighten. He dared not turn. He had been deliberately baiting them, hoping for more information, yet baiting them, too. Now, suddenly, there was a man behind him.

Sodermann seemed to make up his mind. Assurance returned to him, and he spoke low, almost amused. "Why, howdy, Rye! I reckon you should come in an' meet our friend, here. Says he recognizes this gun Red's a-wearin'."

Rye Pitkin walked past Kilkenny and then turned.

His jaw dropped as though he had seen a ghost, and he made an involuntary step backward, his face slowly going white. "You!" he gasped. "You!"

"Why, yes," Kilkenny said. "It's me, Pitkin. Long ways from the Pecos country, isn't it? An' a sight farther from the Brazos. Now, Pitkin, I'll tell you somethin'. I'm not real anxious to kill anybody right here an' now. If I start shootin', two of you are goin' to die.

That'll be you, Rye, and Sodermann here. I couldn't miss him. An' if I am still shootin', as I will be, I'm goin' to take care of Gaddis next. Gaddis because he killed Jody Miller. But that comes later. Right now I'm leavin', an' right now you better impress it on your friends that reachin' for an iron won't do any good."

He stepped back toward the door, and his eyes shifted under the hat brim from one face to the other. Sodermann's eyes were narrowed. Pitkin's obvious fear put doubt in the big man. Who was the stranger? Red Gaddis shifted toward the center of the room, his eyes watchful.

Rye stiffened as Red moved. "Don't, Red! That's Kilkenny!"

Gaddis stopped, and his face turned blank with mingled astonishment and fear. Then glass tinkled from the front of the room, and a long Kentucky rifle barrel slid into the room. Kilkenny stepped back to the door.

"Now, if you *hombres* are smart, you'll just hole up here for the time bein'. We don't want trouble, but we may have it!"

Kilkenny stepped through the door and glanced quickly up and down the street. Bartram was on the wagon seat, his rifle across his knees. Jackie Moffitt was standing by his horse, his rifle in his hands, and Saul was across the street. Kilkenny smiled in narrow-eyed apprehension. They were fighters, these men.

"Start the wagon," he said, "down the Cedar trail. Jackie, stay with Bartram."

He walked out and swung into the saddle, and then slid a rifle from the boot. "All right, slide!"

He wheeled the buckskin and whipped down the street. A shot rang out from behind him, and he twisted to look. Saul was mounted, but Quince had turned and thrown up his rifle. He fired. A man staggered from the shelter of the Wagon Wheel and spilled on his face in the dust. The next instant there was a fusillade of shots from the Wagon Wheel and nearby buildings. The gunmen had slipped out the back way and were getting into action.

Kilkenny reined in behind the last building and swung to the ground. Then, with careful fire, he covered the Hatfields as they raced up the street to join him.

Quince was smiling, his eyes hard. "That was Red Gaddis," he said coolly. "He won't take no more dead men's guns."

"Give the wagon a start," Kilkenny said. "We three are going to make some buzzard bait! We have to come back to this town, and we might as well let them know what the score is."

Every time a head moved, one of them fired. While they stayed where they were, no man dared enter that street, and no man dared try the back way in this direction.

Leaving the two Hatfields, Kilkenny sprinted down behind the buildings toward the Wagon Wheel. The men there were killers. He did not know what had happened to the other wagon, but he meant to find out.

It was his reason for taking the Blazer trail. He was hoping they might not all be dead. At least, he could bury those that were.

XIII

The rear door of the saloon was open, and there was no one in sight. He stood behind the next building and watched for an instant. He wanted Pitkin or Ratcliff. He would get nothing from Sodermann unless the fat man elected to tell him.

Several old boards lay on the ground behind the saloon, dry and parched. On a sudden inspiration, he moved swiftly from the shelter of the building and, holstering his gun, hurriedly piled them together. Then, using a piece of old sacking and some parched grass, he lit the fire.

It was away from the buildings, but the wind would blow the smoke into the saloon. He hoped they would think he was burning them out, the last thing he wanted to do, as they needed the town as a supply base. As the boards caught fire, he stepped back quickly.

There was a startled exclamation as the fire began to crackle and wood smoke blew in the back of the saloon. A second later a man stepped to the door, thrust his head out, and then stared at the fire. He seemed puzzled. Out of sight, Kilkenny waited.

Then the man stepped out and kicked the boards apart. "All right!" Kilkenny snapped. "Don't move!"

It was Ratcliff, and the man froze. "What's up, Kilkenny? I never done nothin' to you."

"Start this way, walk careful, an' watch your hands."

Ratcliff was a weasel-faced man with shifty eyes. He started moving, but shot a glance at the doorway. He held his hands wide. When he was six feet away, Kilkenny stopped him.

"All right, talk. I want to know what happened to that other wagon."

Ratcliff sneered. "You think I'll tell? Guess again. You don't dare shoot. If you do, they'll be out, but fast."

With one quick step, Kilkenny grabbed the man by the throat and slammed him back against the building. Then he lifted the pistol.

"Want a pistol-whipping, man?" he asked harshly. "If I start on you, you'll never look the same again!"

"Leave me be," Ratcliff pleaded, his face yellow. "I'll talk."

"Get at it then."

"They done loaded up with grub. We let 'em get out of town. Then Sodermann ambushed 'em. Had about six men, I think."

"Who was killed?"

"We lost a man. We got Miller an' Tot Wilson in the first blast. It was Hatfield got our man. Nailed him dead center between the eyes."

"What happened to Hatfield an' Hight?"

"They got Hight. I seen him go down. He was shot two, maybe three times. We got Hatfield, too. But he got up, an' he dragged Hight into some rocks. We couldn't get to 'em."

"Then what?"

A voice roared from the saloon. It was Sodermann. "Ratcliff! What in time are you doin' out there?"

"Answer me!" Kilkenny snapped. "Then what?"

"Sodermann said it'd serve 'em right. Leave 'em there to die with two men to see they didn't move out of them rocks. They been there two days now."

"On the Blazer trail?"

"Yeah, almost to the turn-off to the peaks."

With a swift movement, Kilkenny flipped Ratcliff's pistol from its holster. "All right, get goin'!" he snapped.

With a dive, Ratcliff started for the saloon door. And just at that instant, Sodermann thrust his huge bulk into the open space. He glimpsed Kilkenny as he released Ratcliff and, with a swift motion, palmed his gun and fired.

He fired from the hip, and he wasn't a good hip shot. His first bullet caught Ratcliff squarely in the chest, and the weasel-faced rider stopped dead still, and then dropped. Kilkenny's gun swept up, and, straddle-legged in the open, he fired.

Sodermann's gun went off at the same instant, but Kilkenny's bullet hit him right above the belt buckle in the middle of that vast expanse. The blow staggered Sodermann, and his bullet clipped slivers from the building above Kilkenny's head and whined angrily away into the grass back of the saloon.

The big man looked sick, and then suddenly his knees gave way and he toppled face downward upon the steps. The pistol fell from fingers that had lost their life, and rattled on the boards below.

Kilkenny walked toward the saloon, keeping his gun in his hand. Stepping up beside the door, he saw Rye Pitkin and the short bartender, rifles in hand, crouched by the front window.

"Drop 'em!" Kilkenny snapped. He stepped quickly inside. "Unbuckle your belts and let those guns down quick!"

Surprised into helplessness, the men did as they were told. "Rye, I've given you a break before. I'm givin' you one again. The same for Shorty. You two mount and ride. If I ever see either of you again, I'll kill you. I'll be back to Blazer, an' you be dog-gone sure you aren't here."

Backing them away, he scooped up the guns and then backed out the door. He hurried to the corner where the Hatfields waited. Quince was chewing on a straw. He looked at the weapons, grinned a little, and started for his horse.

"Lije may be alive," Kilkenny told him. Then he explained quickly.

Quince narrowed his eyes. "You won't be needin' us," he said. "We'll ride on."

"Go ahead," Kilkenny said, "an' luck with you."

With a rush of hoofs, Saul and Quince Hatfield swept off down the trail. Kilkenny watched them go. The Hatfields were hard to kill. Lije might be alive. It was like him to have thought of Hight, even when wounded. Those lean, wiry men were tough. He might still be alive.

He rode up to the wagon and saw Bartram's face flush with relief. Jackie was riding beside the wagon, his old Sharps ready. His face was boyishly stern.

"What is it?" Bartram asked. "What happened?"

"We've won another round," Kilkenny said. "We can come to Blazer for supplies now."

Dust devils danced over the desert, and the mules plodded slowly along the trail. The wagon rumbled and bumped over the stones in the road, and Bartram dozed on the wagon seat. To the left the mountains lifted in rocky slopes with many upthrust edges of jagged rock. To the right the ground sloped away toward Cedar Branch, which lay miles away beyond the intervening sagebrush and mesquite.

Jackie Moffitt rode silently, looking from time to time at Kilkenny. Lance knew the youngster was dying to ask him about what had happened in Blazer, and he was just as loath to speak of it. He could understand the youngster's curiosity.

He moved the buckskin over alongside the boy. "Trouble back there, Jack," he said after a minute. "Men killed back there."

"Who was it? Did you kill 'em?" Jackie asked eagerly.

"One. I had to, Jack. Didn't want to. Nobody ever likes to kill a man unless there's something wrong with him. I had to get news out of somebody. I got it from Ratcliff, and then turned him loose, but, in tryin' to get me, Sodermann shot him. Then I shot Sodermann."

"What about the others?"

"Let 'em go. I told Pitkin an' Shorty to get out of the country. I think they'll go."

"We asked 'em in the store, but they was scared. They wouldn't talk, no how. Saul, he asked 'em. They was afraid. But they was right nice with us."

They rode on through the heat. Occasionally they stopped to rest the mules. It was slower this way, as the road was longer, but there was no dust, and they had to come this way to make sure about Lije and the others.

Again and again Kilkenny found his thoughts reverting to Nita. How was she faring with Hale? Would she marry him? The thought came to him with a pang. He was in love with Nita. He had admitted that to himself long before this, but he knew too well what it would mean to be the wife of a gunman, a man who never knew when he might go down to dusty death in a lead-spattered street.

A man couldn't think only of himself. A few men seemed to be able to leave it all behind, but they were few. Of course, he could go East, but his whole life had been lived in the West, and he had no source of income in the East. He had been a gambler at times and had done well, but it was nothing to build a life upon.

His thoughts moved ahead to the Hatfields. What would they find? Would the men left behind have murdered the wounded Lije? Had Hight been dead? How many more would die before this war was settled? Why did one man see fit to push this bloody fight upon men who wanted only peace and time to till their fields? Why should one man desire power so much? There was enough in the world for all to have a quiet, comfortable living, and what more could a man desire?

The wagon rumbled over the rocks, and he lifted his eyes and let them idle over the heat-waved distance. After the fire and blood there would be peace, and men could come to this land and settle these hills. Perhaps someday there would be water, and then grass would grow where now there were only cacti and sagebrush. Cicadas whined and sang in the mesquite until the sound became almost the voice of the wastelands.

They camped that night in a hollow in the hills and pushed on at dawn toward the joining of the trails. The country was rockier now. The distance closed in, pushing the mountains nearer, and there was less breeze. The air was dead and still.

Jackie traded places with Bartram and handled the mules. Bartram rode on ahead, riding carefully. Kilkenny watched him go, liking the easy way the farmer rode, and liking his clean-cut honesty.

It was morning of the third day when Kilkenny saw a horseman drawing near. He recognized him even before he came up with him. It was Saul.

"Found 'em," Saul said briefly, "both alive. Hight's plumb riddled. Lije was hit three times, one time pretty bad. They was holed up in some rocks, more dead than alive."

"Anybody around?"

"Yeah. One man. He was dead. Lije must've got him, bad off as he was. The other took out. Lije'll live. We Hatfields are tough."

When they reached the cluster of rocks, they pulled the wagon close. Quince had both men stretched out and had rigged a shelter from the sun. Kilkenny knelt over the men. That Hight was breathing was a marvel, although all his wounds showed signs of care. Lije, wounded as he was, had cared for the other man. His wounds had been bathed and crudely bandaged. His lips seemed moist, and he had evidently not lacked for water.

Lije Hatfield was grimly conscious. There was an unrelenting look in his eyes, enough to show them that Lije meant to face death, if need be, as sternly and fearlessly as he faced life and danger.

His lips were dry and parched. Even the water that Quince had given him failed to reduce the ravages brought on by several days of thirst. Obviously, from the condition of the two men, Lije had been giving the little water they had to Jackson Hight.

The two men were lifted carefully and placed in the wagon, with groceries piled around them and sacks and blankets beneath them. Another blanket was placed over two barrels to form a crude awning over their faces. Then, with Bartram handling the mules, they started once more.

XIV

It was quiet in the Hatfield cup when the little group rode in. The Hatfield women did not cry. They gathered around, and they watched when the two men were lifted from the wagon and carried within.

Parson waited, grim-faced, for Kilkenny. "That's two more, Kilkenny. Two more good men gone, an' two that are like to die! I'm tellin' you, man, I'm a-goin' to kill Bill Hale!"

"Not now. Wait." Kilkenny kicked a toe into the dust. "Any more trouble here?"

"Smithers ain't come back."

"Where'd he go?"

"To look at his crop. He sets great store by that crop. Says he'll be back to harvest it."

"When did he leave?"

"Yesterday mornin'. Shouldn't keep him that long, no-ways. I reckon he might hole up in the hills somewhere."

Talking slowly, Lance recounted all that had transpired. He told of the bitter crossing of the Smoky Desert, of the fight at Blazer, and of the death of Gaddis and the others.

"We can cross the desert anytime unless the wind is blowin' strong," he concluded. "They can't bottle us up. It's a miserable trip, an', if a man was to try it an' get caught in a windstorm, there's a good chance you'd never hear of him again. The same if he got into that quicksand."

"I knowed that Gaddis was a bad one. Glad he's gone. The same for Sodermann."

"There's something else," Kilkenny suggested after a moment. "We've proved we could get across, an' we slipped by their guards comin' back by the Blazer trail, but it won't take them much time to figure what happened. They may try comin' in our back door by that way."

Parson nodded shrewdly. "I was thinkin' of that. We'll have to be careful."

When morning came and Lance rolled out of his blankets, he looked quickly at the house. Then he saw Saul. The tall, lean boy was walking away from the house, and he looked sick and old. They saw each other at almost the same instant.

"Saul?" Kilkenny said. "Is . . . ?"

"He's dead. Lijah's dead."

Kilkenny turned away, and for the first time something like despair welled up inside of him. One of the Hatfields had died. It seemed as though something of the mountains themselves had gone, for there was in those lean, hard-headed, raw-boned men something that lived on despite everything. And Lije had died.

O'Hara came out to him later, and the big Irishman's face was sullen and ugly. "An' that doc down to Cedar

Bluff. We sneaked in an' tried to get him to come. He wouldn't come, an' he set up a squall when we tried to take him. We was lucky to get away."

"We'll remember that," Kilkenny said quietly. "We can't use a doctor who won't come when he's called, not in this country."

Parson looked at him thoughtfully, and then he looked away. "Lance, you ever think maybe we won't win? That maybe they'll wipe us out? Suppose you can't talk to them Santa Fé men? Supposin', if you do, they won't listen?"

Kilkenny looked down at the ground, and then slowly he lifted his head. "There's a man behind this, Parson," he said slowly, "a man who's gone mad with power-cravin'. His son's a-drivin' him. Parson, I've seen men murdered because they wanted homes. There was no harm in Jody Miller, nor in Tot Wilson. They were hard-workin' men an' honest ones. Lije, well, he was a fine boy, a real man, too. He had strength, courage, an' all that it takes to make a man. There at the last, when they were holed up in the rocks, he cared for Hight when he must've been near dead himself. He must've had to drag himself to Hight's side . . . he must've had to force himself to forget his own pain. Those men are dead, an' they are dead because of one man, maybe two. Maybe I'm wrong, Parson, but if all else fails, I'm ridin' to Cedar Bluff, an' I'll kill those two men."

"An' I'll go with you," Parson stated flatly. His old face was grim and hard. "Lije was my son, he. . . ."

"No, Parson, you can't go with me. You'll have to stay here, keep this bunch together, an' see they make the most of their land. I want homes in these high meadows, Parson. Homes, an' kids around 'em, an' cattle walkin' peaceful in the evenin'. No, it'll be my job down there. We all . . . we who live by the gun . . . we all die in the end. It's better for me to go alone an' live or die by what happens then. At least, it'll be in a good cause."

He lay in the shade of a huge Norway pine, resting and thinking of what lay ahead of him, thinking of the fight with Tombull Turner. Lying there with his eyes shut, he could hear the sound of the shovels as Runyon and Jesse Hatfield dug a grave for Lije. In his mind he was taking himself back to the times when he had seen Turner fight. He was remembering, not the battered men who went down before Turner, but every move the big man made. No man was without a fault. Kilkenny had been taught well. He knew how he must plan, and he ran over and over in his mind the way the big man held his hands, the way his feet moved when he advanced or retreated, the way they moved when he punched, and what Turner did when hit with a left or right. Each fighter develops habits. A certain method of stopping or countering a punch is easy for him, so he uses that method most, even though he may know others. A smooth boxer, walking out into the ring and expecting a long fight, will feel out an opponent, find how he uses a left, how he blocks one. Then he knows what to do. If he lasted in this fight,

Kilkenny knew, he would last only because of brains, only because he could think faster, better, and more effectively than Turner or those who handled him.

Yet again and again, as he lay there thinking, his mind reverted to Nita Riordan. The dark, voluptuous beauty of the Irish and Spanish girl at the Crystal Palace was continually in his mind. There was something else, too. In the back of his mind loomed the huge, ominous Cain Brockman. On that desperate day back in Cottonwood, in the Live Oak country, he had killed Abel, and Cain had been thrown from his rearing horse and knocked unconscious. Later, in the Trail House, he had slugged it out and whipped Cain in a bitter knock-down-and-drag-out fistfight. Cain had sworn to kill him. And Cain Brockman was in Cedar Bluff.

When night came, Kilkenny threw a saddle on a slim, black horse and rode out of the cup. He was going to see Nita. Even as he rode, he admitted to himself there was little reason to see her except that he wanted to. He had no right to take chances with his life when it could mean so much to the cause he was aiding, yet he had to see Nita. Also, he could find out what Hale was doing, what he was planning.

He rode swiftly, and the black horse was eager for the trail. It wasn't Buck, but the horse was fast, with speed to spare.

It was late when he rode down to the edge of Cedar Bluff, and his thoughts went back to Leathers, aroused out of a sound sleep and made to put up groceries, and to Dan Cooper, the tough cowhand and gunman who had watched Leathers's store. Cooper was a good man on the wrong side. Leathers was a man who would be on any winning side, one of the little men who think only of immediate profits and who try to ride with the powers that be. Well, the pay-off for Leathers was coming.

Leaving his horse in the shadows of the trees beyond the Crystal Palace, Kilkenny moved up into the shadows of the stable, and his eyes watched the Palace for a long time. Finally he moved, ghost-like, across the open space back of the gambling hall. Tip-toeing along the wall, he came to the door he sought. Carefully he tried the knob. It was locked.

Ahead of him a curtain blew through an open window, waving a little, and then sagging back as the momentary breeze died. He paused beneath the window, listening. Inside, he could hear the steady rise and fall of a man's breathing. It was the only way in. Hesitating only a minute, he put his foot through the open window and stepped inside.

Almost at once there was a black shadow of move-ment, and a forearm slipped across his throat in a stranglehold. Then that forearm crushed back into his throat with tremendous power. Setting the muscles in his neck, he strained forward, agonizing pain shooting through the growing blackness in his brain. He surged forward and felt the man's feet lift from the floor. Then suddenly the hold relaxed, and he felt a hand slide down to his gun and then to the other gun. Then he was released.

"Brigo?" he said.

"*Sí, señor*," Brigo answered in a whisper. "I did not know. But only one man is so powerful as you. When you lifted me, I knew it must be you. Then I felt your guns, and I know them well."

"The *señorita* is here?"

"*Sí*." Brigo was silent for a moment. "*Señor*, I fear for her. This Hale, he wants her very much. Also, the Cub of the bear. He wants her. I fear for her. One day they will come to take her."

Kilkenny could sense the worry in the big man's voice. "But you, Brigo?"

He could almost see the Yaqui shrug. "I see the two *hombres*, Dunn an' Ravitz. They watch me always. Soon they will try to kill me. The *señorita* says I must not go out to kill them, but soon I must."

"Wait, if you can," Kilkenny said. "Then act as you must. If you feel the time has come, do not wait for the *señorita* to say. You do not kill heedlessly. If there is no other way, you are to judge."

"*Gracias, señor*," Brigo said simply. "If you will come with me?"

Kilkenny followed him through the darkness down the hall to another door, and there Brigo tapped gently. Almost at once, he heard Nita's voice. "Jaime?"

"*Sí*. The *señor* is here."

The door opened quickly, and Brigo vanished into the darkness as Kilkenny stepped in. Nita closed the door. Her long dark hair fell about her shoulders. In the vague light he could see the clinging of her night-gown, the rise and fall of her bosom beneath the thin material.

"Kilkenny, what is it?" Her voice was low, and something in its timbre made his muscles tremble. It required all the strength that was in him not to take her in his arms.

"I had to see you. You are all right?"

"*Sí.* For now. He has given me until after the cele-bration to make up my mind. After that, I shall have to marry him or run."

"That celebration," he said bitterly, "is the corner-stone of everything now." Briefly, dispassionately he told her of all that had happened. Of the trip across the Smoky Desert, of the deaths of Miller, Wilson, and Lije Hatfield, and then of the death of Sodermann and the others of Hale's men.

"Does he know of that yet?" he asked.

"I doubt it. He told me there had been an attempt to get food over the Blazer trail and that the men who made it had been wiped out. I don't think he knew more than that."

"I am going to fight Turner," he said.

She caught her breath suddenly. "Oh, no! Kilkenny, he is a brute! I have seen him around the Palace. So huge. And so strong. I have seen him bend silver dol-lars in his fingers. I have seen him squat beside a table, take the edge in his teeth, and lift it clear off the floor."

"I know, but I must fight him. It is my only chance to get close to Halloran." He explained quickly. "If we can just let them know that we aren't outlaws. If they could only realize what is happening here, that these are good men, trying only to establish homes. To fight him is my only chance."

"I heard you would. Brigo told me the word had come that you would fight him."

"What did Brigo say?" Kilkenny suddenly found he was very anxious to know. The big Yaqui had an instinct for judging the fighting abilities of men. Powerful, fierce, and ruthless himself, he knew fighting men, and he had been long in lands where men lived by courage and strength.

"He says you will win." She said it simply. "I cannot see how anyone could defeat that man, but Brigo is sure. He has made bets. And he is the only one who dares to bet against Turner."

"Nita, if there's a chance, say something to Halloran."

"There won't be. Hale will see to that. But if there is, I surely will."

"Nita, when the fight is over, I'll come for you. I'm going to take you away from this. Will you go?"

"Need you ask?" She smiled up at him in the dimness. "You know I will go, Kilkenny. Wherever you go, I will go, Kilkenny. I made my choice long ago."

Kilkenny slipped from the house and returned to his horse. The black stood patiently, and, when Lance touched his bridle, he jerked up his head and was ready to go. Yet, when he reached the turn, Lance swung the black horse down the street of Cedar Bluff.

Walking the horse, he rode slowly up to the ring. It had been set up in an open space near the corrals. Seats had been placed around, with several rows close to the ringside. That would be where King Bill would sit with his friends. The emperor would watch the gladiators. Kilkenny smiled wryly.

A light footstep sounded at the side of the ring, and Kilkenny's gun leaped from its holster. "Don't move," he whispered sharply.

"It's all right, Kilkenny." The man stepped closer, his hands held wide. "It's Dan Cooper."

"So you know I'm Kilkenny?"

Cooper chuckled. "Yeah, I recognized your face that first day, but couldn't tie it to a name. It came to me just now. Hale will be wild when he hears."

"You're a good man, Cooper," Kilkenny said suddenly. "Why stay on the wrong side?"

"Is the winnin' side the wrong side? Not for me it ain't. I ain't sayin' as to who's right in this squabble, but for a gun hand the winnin' side is the right one."

"No conscience, Cooper?" Kilkenny questioned, trying to see the other man's eyes through the darkness. "Dick Moffitt was a good man. So were Jody Miller, Tot Wilson, an' Lije Hatfield."

"Then Lije died?" Cooper's voice quickened. "That's not good, for you or us. The Hales, they don't think much of the Hatfields. I do. I know 'em. The

Hales will have to kill every last Hatfield now, or die themselves. I know them."

"You could have tried a shot at me, Cooper," Kilkenny suggested.

"Me?" Cooper laughed lightly. "I'm not the kind, Kilkenny. Not in the dark, without a warnin'. I ain't so anxious to get you, anyway. I'd be the *hombre* that killed Kilkenny, an' that's like settin' yourself up in a shootin' gallery. Anyway, I want to see the fight."

"The fight?"

"Between you and Tombull. That should be good." Cooper leaned against the platform of the ring. "Between the two of us, I ain't envyin' you none. That *hombre*'s poison. He ain't human. Eats food enough for three men. Still"—Cooper shoved his hat back on his head—"you sure took King Bill, an' he was some shakes of a scrapper." Cooper straightened up. "Y'know, Kilkenny, just two men in town are bettin' on you."

"Two?"

"Uhn-huh. One's that Yaqui gunman, Brigo. The other's Cain Brockman."

"Cain Brockman?" Kilkenny was startled.

"Yeah. He says he's goin' to kill you, but he says you can whip Turner first. He told Turner to his face that you was the best man. Turner was sure mad." Dan Cooper hitched up his belt. "Almost time for my relief. If I was you, I'd take out. The next *hombre* might not be so anxious to see a good fight that he'd pass up five thousand dollars."

"You mean there's money on my head?" Kilkenny asked.

"Yeah. Five thousand. Dead or alive." Cooper shrugged. "Cub didn't like the idea of the reward. He figures you're staked out for him."

"OK, Dan. Enjoyed the confab."

"Thanks. Listen, make that fight worth the money, will you? An' by the way . . . watch Cub Hale. He's poison mean and faster than a strikin' rattler."

Kilkenny rode out of town and took to the hills. The route he took homeward was not the same as that by which he had approached the town. Long ago he had learned it was very foolhardy to retrace one's steps. Once at the Hatfields', he bedded down about daylight and slept until early afternoon.

So Cain Brockman was betting on him. For a long time, Kilkenny sat in speculation. He lived over again that bitter, bloody afternoon in the Trail House when he had whipped the huge Cain. It had seemed that great bulk was impervious to anything in the shape of a human fist. Yet he had brought him down, had beaten him into helplessness.

Parson and Quince strolled over and sat down. Their faces were grave. It was like these men to hide their grief, yet he knew that under the emotionless faces of the men there was a feeling of family and unity stronger than any he had ever known. These men loved each other and lived for each other.

"Kilkenny, you set on fightin' this Turner?" Parson inquired.

"Yes, I am," Kilkenny said quietly. "It's our big chance. It is more than a chance to talk to Halloran, too. It's a chance to hit Hale another wallop."

"To hurt him, you got to beat Turner," Quince said, staring at Kilkenny. "You got to win."

"That's right," Kilkenny agreed. "So I'm goin' in to win. I've changed my mind about some things. I was figurin' just on stayin' in there long enough to talk to the officials from Santa Fé, but now I am goin' in there to win. If I win, I make friends. People will like to see Hale beat again. Halloran is an Irishman, an' an Irishman loves a good fighter. Well, I got to win."

They were silent for a few minutes and Parson chewed on a straw. Then he looked up from under his bushy gray eyebrows. "It ain't the fight what worries me. If the good Lord wants you to win, you'll win. What bothers me is after . . . win or lose, what happens then? Think Hale will let you go?"

Kilkenny smiled grimly. "He will, or there'll be blood on the streets of Cedar Bluff. Hale blood!"

XV

The crowds had started coming to Cedar Bluff by daylight. The miners had come, drifting over for the rodeo and the fight. The gold camps had been abandoned for the day, as there was rarely any celebration for them, rarely any relief from the loneliness and the endless masculinity of the gold camps. The cowhands from the Hale Ranch were around in force. The bars were doing a rushing business even before noon, and the streets were jammed with people.

Kilkenny rode into town on the buckskin when the sun was high. For over an hour he had been lying on a hillside above the town, watching the movement. It was almost certain that King Bill would avoid trouble today. There were too many visitors, too many people who were beyond his control. He would be on his good behavior today, making an impression as the upright citizen and free-handed giver of celebrations.

A rider under a flag of truce had appeared in the cup the evening before with an invitation to Kilkenny and the actual challenge for the fight. Word of Kilkenny's willingness for the fight had seeped into town by the grapevine several days before, so no tricks were needed. Kilkenny was to report to a man named John Bartlett, at the Crystal Palace.

Kilkenny, accompanied by Parson Hatfield and Steve Runyon, rode down to the Palace and dismounted. Quince Hatfield and O'Hara had already arrived in town, and they moved up outside the Palace and loafed where they could watch the horses. Only a few of the Hale riders actually knew them by sight.

Pushing open the batwing doors, Kilkenny stepped inside, Parson at his elbow. The place was crowded, and all the games were going full blast. Kilkenny's quick eyes swept the place. Jaime Brigo was in his usual chair across the room, and their eyes met. Then Kilkenny located Price Dixon. He was dealing cards at a nearby table.

There was a warning in Dixon's eyes, and then Price made an almost imperceptible gesture of his head. Turning his eyes, Kilkenny felt a little chill go over him. Cain Brockman was standing at the bar, and Cain was watching him. Slowly, as though subtly aware of the tension in the room, eyes began to lift. As if by instinct they went from the tall, broad-shouldered man with the bronzed face, clad completely in black, to the towering bruiser in the checked shirt and the worn Levi's.

Then, his hands hanging carelessly at his sides, his flat-brimmed hat tipped just a little, Kilkenny started across the room toward Cain Brockman. A deadly hush fell over the room. Cain had turned, his wide unshaven face still marked by the scars of his former battle with Kilkenny, marked with scars he would carry to his grave. Through narrow eyes the big man looked at Kilkenny, watching his slow steps across the floor, the studied ease, the grace of the man in black, the two big guns at his hips. Unseen, Nita Riordan had come to the door of her room, and, eyes wide, she watched Kilkenny walk slowly among the tables and pause before Cain Brockman.

For a minute the two men looked at each other. Then Kilkenny spoke. "I hear you've come to town to kill me, Cain," he said quietly. Yet in the deathly hush of the room his voice carried to each corner. "Well, I've another fight on my hands, with Tombull Turner. If we shoot it out, I'm going to kill you, but you're a good man with a gun, and I reckon I'll catch some lead.

Fighting Tombull is going to be enough without carrying a crawful of lead when I do it. So how about a truce until afterward?"

For an instant, Cain hesitated. In the small gray eyes, chill and cold, there came a little light of reluctant admiration. He straightened. "I reckon I can wait," Cain drawled harshly. "Let it never be said that Cain Brockman broke up a good fight."

"Thanks." Abruptly Kilkenny turned away, turning his back fully on Cain Brockman, and with the same slow walk crossed the room to Price Dixon. A big red-headed man stood at the table near Price.

As he walked up to the table, the batwing doors pushed open and four men walked in. Kilkenny noticed them and felt the flash of recognition of danger go over him. It was King Bill Hale, Cub Hale, and the gold-dust twins, Dunn and Ravitz.

Ignoring them, Kilkenny walked up to the red-headed man. "You're John Bartlett?" he asked. "I'm Kilkenny."

"Glad to meet you." Bartlett thrust out a huge hand. "How'd you know me?"

"Saw you in Abilene. Again in New Orleans."

"Then you've seen Turner fight?" Bartlett demanded keenly. He glanced up and down Kilkenny with a quick, practiced eye.

"Yes. I've seen him fight."

"An' you're not afraid? He's a bruiser. He nearly killed Tom Hanlon."

Kilkenny smiled. "An' who was Tom Hanlon? A big

chunk of beef so slow he couldn't get out of his own way. I see nothing in Turner to fear."

"You'll actually fight him, then?" Bartlett was incredulous.

"Fight him?" Kilkenny asked. "Fight him? I'm going to whip him."

"That's the way to talk!" a big, black-bearded miner burst out. "I'm sick of this big bull of a Turner struttin' around. My money goes on Kilkenny."

"Mine, too," another miner said. "I'd rather he was a miner, but I'll even bet on a cowhand if he can fight."

Kilkenny turned and looked at the miner, and then he grinned. "Friend," he said, "I've swung a single-jack for many a day and tried a pan on half the creeks in Arizona."

Bartlett leaned forward. "This fight is for a prize of one thousand dollars in gold, put up by King Hale. However, if you want to make a side bet . . . ?"

"I do," Kilkenny said. He unbuttoned his shirt and took out a packet of bills. "Five thousand dollars of it."

"Five thousand?" Bartlett swallowed and saw Hale frown. "I don't think we can cover it."

"What?" Kilkenny looked up, and his eyes met those of King Bill. "I understood that Hale was offering three to one, and no takers. That's the money I want. Some of that three to one that Bill Hale is offering."

"Three to one?" Hale demanded. "Why, I never. . . ."

The astonishment in his voice was plain enough, but Kilkenny knew he had him, and every move was calculated to win the crowd, not for himself, but for the men he represented. To back down would mean loss of prestige to Hale; to declare he knew of no three-to-one offer would make many believe he had welshed on his bet. And if Kilkenny won, Hale would never dare order him killed because all would think it was revenge for losing the bet. And if Kilkenny lost, it would still put Hale in a bad light if he were suddenly murdered.

"What's the matter, Hale?" Kilkenny demanded sharply, and his voice rang loudly in the crowded room. "Are you backing down? Have you decided the man who whipped you on your own ground can whip Turner, too? Didn't you bring Tombull Turner here to whip me or to force me to back down? I'm calling you, Hale. Put up or shut up! I'm betting five thousand against your fifteen thousand that I win. I'm betting all I own, aside from that little claim you're trying to take away from me, against a mere fifteen thousand. Are you backing down?"

"No, by the Lord Harry, I'm not!" Hale's face was purple with anger. "I'm not going to let any fence-crawling nester throw money in my face. I'm covering you."

Kilkenny smiled slowly. "Looks like an interesting afternoon," he said cheerfully. Then he turned and walked slowly from the room, conscious that at every step he took the white cold eyes of Cub Hale followed him, their hatred almost a tangible thing.

When they got outside, Parson stared at him. "You sure made King Bill look bad in there. You made some friends."

"You mean *we* made friends," Kilkenny said quietly. "That's the point. We've got to make friends, we've got to get the sympathy of these miners and the outside people Hale can't touch. If we can get enough of them, we've got a fighting chance. Hale can't get too raw. There's law in this country now, an' he can win only so long as he can make what he's doin' seem right. If it stopped right here, an' he got me killed or took my land, a lot of people would be asking questions. They'll remember what I said. You see, Parson, we're little people buckin' a powerful an' wealthy man. That makes us the underdogs. I'm the smaller man in this fight, too. I'm a cowhand and a miner fightin' a trained prize fighter with my fists. A good part of that crowd is goin' to be with me for that reason, even some of Hale's cowhands."

It was mid-afternoon when Kilkenny walked down to the ring. The corral fence was covered with cowhands and miners, and the intervening space was filled with them. They were crowded along roofs and in every bit of space. Scanning the crowd, Kilkenny's eyes glinted. The miners were out in strength, and with them had come a number of gamblers, cowhands from outside the valley, and a few odds and ends of trappers.

The cluster of seats near the ring was empty, and two men guarded them. Kilkenny walked down to the ringside and stripped to the waist. He slipped off his boots and pulled on a pair of Indian moccasins that fitted snugly.

There was a roar from the crowd, and he saw Tombull Turner leaving the back door of Leathers's store and striding toward the ring, wrapped in a blanket. As he climbed through the ropes and walked to his corner, King Bill Hale, Cub Hale, and two men in store clothes left the Mecca and started toward the ring. Behind them walked Dunn and Ravitz.

Then, escorted by Jaime Brigo, Nita Riordan left the Palace and walked slowly through the crowd toward the ring. She was beautifully dressed, in the very latest of fashion, and carried her chin high. Men drew aside to let her pass, and those along the way she walked removed their hats. Nita Riordan had proved to Cedar Bluff that a woman could run a gambling joint and still remain a lady. Not one word had ever been said against her character. Even the most skeptical had been convinced, both by her own lady-like manner and by the ever-watchful presence of Brigo.

Price Dixon walked down to Kilkenny's corner. He hesitated, and then stepped forward. "I've had some experience as a handler," he said simply, "if you'll trust a gambling man."

Kilkenny looked at him, and then smiled. "Why, I reckon we're all gambling men after a fashion, sir. I'd be proud to have you."

He glanced around quickly. John Bartlett was to referee, and the big red-headed man was already in the ring. Parson Hatfield, wearing a huge Walker Colt, lounged behind Kilkenny's corner. Runyon was a short distance away, and near him was Quince Hatfield. O'Hara was to work in Kilkenny's corner, also.

XVI

Kilkenny climbed quickly into the ring and slipped off the coat he had hung around his shoulders. He heard a low murmur from the crowd. He knew they were sizing him up.

Tombull Turner was the larger by thirty pounds. He was taller, broader, and thicker, a huge man with a round, bullet head set on a powerful neck and mighty shoulders. His biceps and forearms were heavy with muscle, and the deltoid development on the ends of his shoulders was large. His stomach was flat and solid, his legs columns of strength.

Kilkenny was lean. His shoulders were broad and had the strength of years of living in the open, working, fighting, and struggling. His stomach was flat and corded with muscle and his shoulders splendidly muscled, yet beside the bigger man he appeared much smaller. Actually he weighed 200 pounds. Yet scarcely a man present, if asked to guess his weight, would have made it more than 180.

Bartlett walked to the center of the ring and raised a huge hand. "The rules is no punches below the belt.

Hit as long as they have one hand free. No gouging or biting allowed. Holding and hitting is fair. When a man falls, is thrown, or is knocked to the floor, the round ends. The fight is to a finish." He strode back, glancing with piercing eyes from Turner to Kilkenny.

The call of time was made, and the two men came forward to the scratch. Instantly Tombull rushed, swinging with both hands. Kilkenny weaved inside and smashed hard with a right and left to the body. Then Turner grabbed him and attempted to hurl him to the canvas, but Kilkenny twisted himself loose and struck with a lightning-like left to the bigger man's mouth.

Turner set himself and swung a left that caught Kilkenny in the chest and knocked him back against the ropes. The crowd let out a roar, but, unhurt, Kilkenny slipped away from Turner's charge and landed twice to the ribs. The big man closed in, feinted a left, and caught Kilkenny with a wicked overhand right that hit him on the temple.

Groggy, Kilkenny staggered into the ropes, and Turner charged like a bull and struck twice, left and right, to Kilkenny's head. Lance clinched and hung on tightly. Then, slipping a heel behind Turner's ankle, he tripped him up and threw him hard to the canvas!

He walked to his corner, seeing through a mist. They doused him with water, and at the call of time he came out slowly until almost up to the scratch. Then he lunged forward and landed with a hard left to the side of the neck. Tombull took it flat-footed and walked in, apparently unhurt. Kilkenny evaded a right and then lashed back with both hands, staggering the big man again.

Turner lunged forward, hitting Kilkenny with a short right, and then, slipping Kilkenny's left, he grabbed him and threw him to the canvas. The third round opened with both men coming out fast, and, walking right together, they began to slug. Then Kilkenny blocked Turner's left and hit him in the body with a right. They broke free, and, circling, Kilkenny got a look at the two men sitting with Hale.

One was Halloran. The other was a leaner, taller man. Lance evaded a rush, and then clipped Turner with a right. He had been doing well, but he was no fool. Turner was a fighter, and the big man had not been trying yet, was just getting warmed up now. He was quite sure Tombull was under orders to beat him, to pound him badly, but to keep him in the ring as long as possible. Hale was to have his revenge, his blood-letting.

Tombull Turner moved in, landing a powerful left to the head and then a right to the body. Kilkenny circled away from Turner's heavy-hitting right. Turner bored in, striving to get his hands on the lighter man and to get his fists where he could hit better. He liked to use short punches when standing close. Kilkenny slid away, stabbed a long left to Turner's mouth, feinted, and, when Tombull swung his right, stepped in and smashed both hands to the body.

For all the effect the punches had he might have

been hitting a huge drum. Turner rushed, crowding Kilkenny against the ropes, where he launched a storm of crashing, battering blows. One fist caught Kilkenny over the eye, and another crashed into the pit of his stomach. Then a clubbing right hit Kilkenny on the kidney. He staggered away, and Turner, his big fists poised, crowded closer.

He swung for the head, and Kilkenny ducked the right but caught a chopping blow from the left that started blood flowing from a cut over one eye. Kilkenny backed away, and Turner rushed and floored Kilkenny with a smashing right.

Dixon worked over the eye rapidly and skillfully. Kilkenny found time to be surprised at his skill. "Watch that right," O'Hara said. "It's bad."

Kilkenny moved up to scratch and then side-stepped just in time to miss Turner's bull rush. He stepped in and stabbed a left to the head, and then Tombull got in close and hurled him to the canvas again.

Taking the rest on the stool, Kilkenny relaxed. Then at the call, he came to the scratch again, and, suddenly leaping in, he smashed two rocking punches to Turner's jaw. The bigger man staggered, and, before he could recover, Kilkenny stepped in, stabbed a hard left to the mouth, and then hooked a powerful right to the body. Turner tried to get his feet under him, but Kilkenny was relentless. He smashed a left to the mouth and a right to the body, and then landed both hands to the body as Turner hit the ropes.

Tombull braced himself and, summoning his

tremendous strength, bulled in close, literally hurling Kilkenny across the ring, and then followed with a rush. The crowd was on its feet now. Kilkenny feinted, and then smashed a powerful right to the ribs. Turner tried a left, and, pushing it aside, Kilkenny stepped in with a wicked left uppercut to the wind. Turner staggered.

The crowd, still on its feet, was yelling for Kilkenny. He shook Turner with a right, but Tombull set himself and threw a mighty right that caught Kilkenny coming in and flattened him on the canvas.

When he got to his corner, he could see the crowd was excited. He was badly shaken, but not dazed by the blow. Suddenly he was on his feet, and before anyone could realize what was happening, he had stepped across to the ringside where Hale sat with the two officials.

"Gentlemen," he said swiftly, "I've little time. I am fighting here today because it is the only way I could get to speak to you. I am one of a dozen nesters who have filed on claims among the peaks, claims from which Hale is unlawfully trying to drive us. One man has been cruelly murdered. . . ."

The call of time interrupted. He wheeled to see Tombull charging, and he slid away along the ropes. Then Turner hit him and he staggered, but Turner lunged close, unwilling to let him fall. Shoving him back against the ropes, Turner shoved a left to his chin and then clubbed a powerful right.

Blasting pain seared across Kilkenny's brain. He

saw that right go up again and knew he could never survive another such punch. With all his strength, he jerked away. Turner intended to kill him now.

In a daze, he could see Hale was on his feet, as were the officials. Cub Hale had a hand on his gun, and Parson Hatfield was facing him across the ring. Then Kilkenny jerked loose.

But Turner was on him like a madman, clubbing, striking with all his mighty strength, trying to batter Kilkenny into helplessness before the round ended. The crowd was in a mighty uproar, and in a haze of pain and waning consciousness Kilkenny saw Steve Runyon had slipped behind Cub Hale and had a gun on him.

Somebody was shouting outside the ring, and then Turner hit him again and he broke away from Tombull and crashed to the canvas.

O'Hara carried him bodily to his corner, where Dixon worked over him like mad. The call of time came, and Kilkenny staggered to his feet and had taken but one step toward the mark when Tombull hit him like a hurricane, sweeping him back into the ropes with a whirlwind of staggering, pounding, battering blows. Weaving, swaying, slipping, and ducking punches, Kilkenny tried to weather the storm.

Somehow he slipped under a right to the head and got in close. Spreading his legs wide, he began to slug both hands into the big man's body. The crowd had gone mad now, but he was berserk. The huge man was fighting like a madman, eager for the kill, and

Kilkenny was suddenly lost to everything but the battering fury of the fight and the lust to put the big man down and to keep him down.

Slipping a left, he smashed a wicked right to the ribs and then another and another. Driving in, he refused to let Turner get set and smashed him with punch after punch. Turner threw him off, but he leaped in again, got Tombull's head in chancery with a crude headlock, and proceeded to batter blow after blow into the big man's face before Turner did a back somersault to break free and end the round.

Panting, gasping for every breath when each stabbed like a knife, Kilkenny swung to the ropes. "We've been refused food in Cedar Bluff!" Kilkenny shouted hoarsely at the officials. "We sent a wagon to Blazer, and three men were waylaid and killed. On a second attempt, we succeeded in getting a little, but only after a pitched battle."

The call of time came and he wheeled. Turner was on him with a rush, his face bloody and wild. Kilkenny set himself and struck hard with a left that smashed Turner's nose, and then with a wicked right that rocked Turner to his heels. Faster than the big man, he carried less weight and was tiring less rapidly. Also, the pounding of his body blows had weakened the bigger man.

Close in, they began to slug, but here, too, despite Turner's massive strength, Kilkenny was the better man. He was faster, and he was beating the big man to the punch. Smashing a wicked left to the chin,

Kilkenny stepped in and hooked both hands hard to the body. Then he brought up an uppercut that ripped a gash across Turner's face. Before Tombull could get set, Kilkenny drove after him with a smashing volley of hooks and swings that had the big man reeling.

Everyone was yelling now, yelling like madmen, but Turner was gone. Kilkenny was on him like a panther. He drove him into the ropes and, holding him there, struck the big man three times in the face. Then Tombull broke loose and swung a right that Kilkenny took in his stride. He smashed Turner back on his heels with a right of his own.

The big man started to fall, and Kilkenny whipped both hands to his face with cracking force! Turner went down, rolled over, and lay still.

In an instant, Kilkenny was across the ring. Grabbing his guns, he strapped them on. His fists were battered and swollen, but he could still hold a gun. He caught a quick glimpse of Nita and saw Brigo was hurrying her from the crowd. Parson and Quincy Hatfield closed in beside him, guns drawn.

"I'll have to go with you," Dixon said. "If I stay now, they'll kill me."

"Come on," Kilkenny said grimly. "We can use you."

Backing after them, Runyon kept Cub Hale at the end of his gun. The younger Hale's face was white. Then, as the Hale cowhands began to gather, a mob of miners surged between them.

"Go ahead!" a big miner shouted. "We'll stand by you!"

Kilkenny smiled suddenly, and, swinging away from his men, he walked directly toward the crowding cowhands. Muttering sullenly, they broke ahead of him, and he strode up to King Bill Hale. The big rancher was pale, and his eyes were cold as ice and bitter. Halloran stood behind him, and the tall, cool-eyed man stood nearby.

"I will take my fifteen thousand dollars now," Kilkenny said quietly.

His face sullen and stiff, Hale counted out the money and thrust it at him.

Kilkenny turned then, bowed slightly to Halloran and the other man, and said quietly: "What I have told you here, gentlemen, is true. I wish you would investigate the claims of Hale to our land, and our own filings upon that land."

Turning, he walked back to the miners, mounted, and rode off with the Hatfields, O'Hara, and Runyon close about him.

"We'll have to move fast!" Kilkenny said. "What happens will happen quick now!"

"What can he do?" Runyon asked. "We got our story across."

"Supposin', when they come back to investigate, there aren't any of us left?" Kilkenny demanded. "What could anybody do about that? There'd be no witnesses, an', even if they asked a lot of questions, it wouldn't do us any good. The big fight will come now."

They rode hard and fast, sticking to little-known

trails through the brush. They threaded the bottom of a twisted, broken cañon and curled along a path that led along the sloping shoulder of a rocky hill among the cedars.

Kilkenny rode with his rifle across the saddle in front of him and with one hand always ready to swing it up. He was under no misapprehension about King Bill. The man had been defeated again, and he would be frantic now. His ego was being sadly battered, and to prove to himself that he was still the power in the Cedar Valley country he must wipe this trouble from the earth. He would have lost much. Knowing the man, and knowing the white lightning that lay beneath the surface of Cub Hale, he knew the older man must more than once have cautioned the slower, surer method. Now Cub would be ranting for a shoot-out. Kilkenny knew he had gauged that young man correctly. He was spoiled. The son of a man of power, he had ridden, wild and free, and had grown more arrogant by the year, taking what he wanted and killing those who thwarted him. Dunn and Ravitz would be with him, he knew. That trio was poison itself. He was no fool. He believed he could beat Hale. Yet he had no illusions about beating all three. There was, of course, the chance of catching them off side as he had caught the Brockmans that day in Cottonwood. The Brockmans! Like a flash he remembered Cain. The big man was free to come gunning for him now!

XVII

Winding around a saddle trail leading into a deep gorge, they came out on the sandy bottom, and he speeded their movement to a rapid trot. Despite himself, he was worried. At the cup, there were only Jesse and Saul Hatfield, Bartram, and Jackie Moffitt. Suppose Hale had taken that moment to sweep down upon them and shoot it out? With luck, the defenders might hold the cup, but if the breaks went against them . . . ?

He turned his horse up a steep slope toward the pines. Ahead of him, suddenly, there was a rifle shot, just one. It sounded loudly and clearly in the cañon, yet he heard no bullet. As if by command, the little cavalcade spread out and rode up through the trees. It was Kilkenny who swept around a clump of scrub pine and saw several men scrambling for their horses. He reined in and dropped to the ground.

A rifle shot chunked into the trunk of the pine beside him, but he fired. One of the riders dropped his rifle and grabbed for the saddle horn, and then they swept into the trees. He got off three carefully spaced shots, heard Runyon, off to his left, opening up, and then, farther along, Parson himself.

He wheeled the buckskin and rode the yellow horse toward the cañon, yelling his name as he swept into the cup. What he saw sent his face white with fear! Jesse Hatfield lay sprawled full length on the hard-packed ground of the cup, a slow curl of blood trickling from under his arm, a bloody gash on his head.

As he reined in alongside Jesse, the door of the house burst open and Jackie Moffitt came running out. "They hit us about two hour ago!" Jackie said excitedly. "They nicked Bart, too!"

Kilkenny dropped to his knees beside Hatfield and turned him gently. One bullet had grazed his scalp; another had gone through his chest, high up. He looked at the wound and the bubbling froth on the man's lips, and his jaws tightened.

Price Dixon swung down beside him. Kneeling over Hatfield, he examined the wound. Kilkenny's eyes narrowed as he saw the gambler's fingers working over him with almost professional skill. He quickly cut away the cloth and examined the wound.

"We'll have to get him inside," he said gravely. "I've got to operate."

"Operate?" Parson Hatfield stared at him. "You a doc?"

Dixon smiled wryly. "I was once," he said. "Maybe I still am."

Ma Hatfield came to the door, bearing a rifle. Then, putting it down, she turned and walked back inside, and, when they brought the wounded man in, a bed was ready for him. Her long, thin-cheeked face was grave, and only her eyes showed pain and shock. She worked swiftly and without hysteria. Sally Crane was working over a wound in Bartram's arm, her own face white.

Kilkenny motioned to Parson and stepped outside.

"I've got to go back tonight an' get Nita," he said quietly. "I'll go alone."

"You better take help. There's enough of us now to hold this place. You'll have you a fight down to Cedar Bluff. An' don't forget Cain Brockman."

"I won't. By night I can make it, I think. This is all comin' to a head, Parson. They can't wait now. We've called their hand an' raised 'em. They never figured on me talkin'. They never figured on me winnin' that fight."

"All right," Parson said, "we'll stand by." He looked down at the ground a moment. "I reckon," he said slowly, "we've done a good day's work. I got me a man back on the trail, too. Jackie says Jesse got one up on the rim. A couple more nicked. That's goin' to spoil their appetite for fightin', an' spoil it a heap."

"Yeah," Kilkenny agreed. "I'm ridin' at sundown, Parson."

Yet it was after sundown before he got started. Jesse Hatfield was in a bad way. Price Dixon had taken a compact packet of tools from his saddlebags, and his operation had been quick and skilled. His gambler's work had kept his hands well, and he showed it now. Kilkenny glanced at him, curiosity in his eyes. At one time this man had been a fine surgeon.

He was never surprised. In the West you found strange men—noblemen from Europe, wanderers from fine old families, veterans of several wars, schoolboys, and boys who had grown up along the cattle trails. Doctors, lawyers, men of brilliance, and men with none, all had thronged West, looking for what the romantic called adventure and the experienced knew was trouble, or looking for a new home, for a change, or escaping from something. Price Dixon was one of these. The man was observant, shrewd, and cultured. He and Kilkenny had known each other from the first, not as men who came from the same life, but men who came from the same stratum of society. They were men of the lost legion, the kind who always must move.

Despite his lack of practice, Dixon's moves were sure and his hands skilled. He removed the bullet from dangerously near the spine. When he finished, he washed his hands and looked up at Parson.

"He'll live, with rest and treatment. Beef broth, that's what he needs now, to build strength in him."

Parson grinned behind his gray mustache. "He'll get it," he said dryly. "He'll get it as long as King Bill Hale has a steer on the range."

Sally Crane caught Kilkenny as he was saddling the little gray horse he was riding that night. She hurried up to him and then stopped suddenly and stood there, shifting her feet from side to side. Kilkenny turned and looked at her curiously from under his flat-brimmed hat.

"What's the trouble, Sally?"

"I wanted to ask. . . ." She hesitated, and he could sense her shyness. "Do you think I'm old enough to marry?"

"To marry?" He stopped, startled. "Why, I don't know, Sally. How old are you?"

"I'm sixteen, 'most nigh seventeen."

"That's young," he conceded, "but I've heard Ma Hatfield say she was just sixteen when she married, an' down in Kentucky and Virginia many a girl marries at that age. Why?"

"I reckon I want to marry," Sally said shyly. "Ma Hatfield said I should ask you. Said you was Daddy Moffitt's friend, an' you was sort of my guardian."

"Me?" He was thunderstruck. "Well, I reckon I never thought of it that way. Who wants to marry you, Sally?"

"It's Bart."

"You love him?" he asked. He suddenly felt strangely old, and yet, looking at the young girl standing there so shyly, he felt more than ever before the vast loneliness there was in him, and also a strange tenderness such as he had never known before.

"Yes." Her voice was shy, but he could sense the excitement in her, and the happiness.

"Well, Sally," he said slowly, "I reckon I'm as much a guardian as you've got now. I think, if you love Bartram an' he loves you, that's all that's needed. I know him. He's a fine, brave, serious young fellow who's goin' to do right well as soon as this trouble clears up. Yes, I reckon you can marry him."

She was gone, running.

For a few minutes he stood there, one foot in the stirrup. Then he swung his leg over the gray horse and shook his head in astonishment. *That's one thing, Lance*, he told himself, *you never expected to happen to you!*

But as he turned the horse into the pines, he remembered the Hatfields digging the grave for their brother. Men died, men were married, and the fighting and living and working went on. So it would always go. Lije Hatfield was gone, Miller and Wilson were gone, and Jesse Hatfield lay near to death in the cabin in the cup. Yet Sally was to marry Tom Bartram, and they were to build a home. Yes, this was the country, and these were its people. They had the strength to live, the strength to endure. In such a country men would be born, men who loved liberty and would ever fight to preserve it.

The little gray was as sure-footed as a mountain goat. Even the long-legged yellow horse could walk no more silently, no more skillfully than this little mountain horse. He talked to it in a low whisper and watched the ears flick backward with intelligence. This was a good horse.

Yet, when he reached the edge of Cedar Bluff, he reined in sharply. Something was wrong. There was a vague smell of smoke in the air, and an atmosphere of uneasiness seemed to hang over the town. He looked down, studying the place. Something was wrong. Something had changed. It was not only the emptiness left after a crowd is gone, it was something else, something that made him uneasy.

He moved the gray horse forward slowly, keeping to

sandy places where the horse would make no sound. The black bulk of a building loomed before him, and he rode up beside it and swung down. The smell of wood smoke was stronger. Then he peered around the corner of the building. Where the Mecca had stood was only a heap of charred ruins.

Hale's place—burned! He scowled, trying to imagine what could have happened. An accident? It could be, yet something warned him it was not that, and more, that the town wasn't asleep.

Keeping to the side of the buildings, he walked forward a little. There was a faint light in Bert Leathers's store. The Crystal Palace was dark. He went back to the gray horse and, carefully skirting the troubled area, came in from behind the building, and then swung down.

A man loomed ahead of him, a huge bulk of man. His heart seemed to stop, and he froze against the building. It was Cain Brockman!

Watching, Kilkenny saw him moving with incredible stealth, slip to the side of the Crystal Palace, work for an instant at the door, and then disappear inside. Like a ghost, Kilkenny crossed the alley and went in the door fast. There he flattened against the wall. He could hear the big man ahead of him, but only his breathing. Stealthily he crept after.

What could Brockman be doing here? Was he after Nita? Or hoping to find him? He crept along, closed a door after him, and lost Brockman in the stillness. Then suddenly a candle gleamed, and another. The first person he saw was Nita. She was standing there, in riding costume, staring at him.

"You've come, Lance?" she said softly. "Then it was you I heard?"

"No," he spoke softly, "it wasn't me. Cain Brockman's here."

A shadow moved against the curtain at the far side of the big room, and Cain Brockman stepped into the open. "Yeah," he said softly, "I'm here."

He continued to move, coming around the card tables until he stood near, scarcely a dozen feet away. The curtains were drawn on all the windows, thick drapes that kept all light within. If he lived to be a thousand, Lance Kilkenny would never forget that room. It was large and rectangular. Along one side ran the bar; the rest, except for the small dance floor where they stood now, was littered with tables and chairs. Here and there were fallen chips, cards, cigarette butts, and glasses. A balcony surrounded the room on three sides, a balcony with curtained booths. Only the candles flickered in the great room, candles that burned brightly but with a wavering, uncertain light. The girl held the candles—Nita Reardon, with her dark hair gathered against the nape of her neck, her eyes unusually large in the dimness.

Opposite Kilkenny stood the bulk of Cain Brockman. His big black hat was shoved back on his huge head. His thick neck descended into powerful shoulders, and the checkered shirt was open to expose a hairy chest. Crossed gun belts and big pistols completed the picture, guns that hung just beneath the open hands. Cain stood there, his flat face oily and unshaven in the vague light, his stance wide, his feet in their riding boots seeming unusually small.

"Yeah," Cain repeated. "I'm here."

Kilkenny drew a deep breath. Suddenly a wave of hopelessness spread over him. He could kill this man. He knew it. Yet why kill him? Cain Brockman had come looking for him, had come because it was the code of the life he had lived and because the one anchor he had, his brother Abel, had pulled loose. Suddenly Kilkenny saw Cain Brockman as he had never seen him before, as a big man, simple and earnest, a man who had drifted along the darker trails because of some accident of fate, and whose one tie, his brother, had been cut loose. He saw him now as big, helpless, and rather lost. To kill Kilkenny was his only purpose in life

Abruptly Kilkenny dropped his hands away from his guns. "Cain," he said, "I'm not going to shoot it out with you. I'm not going to kill you. I'm not even goin' to try. Cain, there's no sense in you an' me shootin' it out. Not a mite."

"What d'you mean?" The big man's brow was furrowed, his eyes narrowed with thought as he tried to decide what deception was in this.

"I don't want to kill you, Cain. You an' your brother teamed up with the wrong crowd in Texas. Because of that, I had to kill him. You looked for me, an' I had to fight you an' whip you. I didn't want to then, an' I don't now. Cain, I owe somethin' to those people up there, the Hatfields an' the rest. They want homes out here. I've got a reason to fight for them. If I kill, it'll be for that. If I die, it'll be to keep their land for them. There's nothin' to gain for you or me by shootin' it out. Suppose you kill me? What will you do then?"

Cain hesitated, staring, puzzled. "Why, ride out of here. And go back to Texas."

"An' then?"

"Go to ridin', I guess."

"Maybe, for a while. Then some *hombre*'ll come along, an' you'll rustle a few cows. Then you'll rob a stage, an' one time they'll get you like they got Sam Bass. You'll get shot down or you'll hang. I'm not goin' to shoot you, Cain. An' you're too good a man to draw iron on a man who won't shoot. You're a good man, Cain. Just a good man on the wrong trail. You've got too much good stuff in you to die the way you'll die."

Cain Brockman stared at him, and, in the flickering candlelight, Kilkenny waited. He was afraid for the first time, afraid his words would fail, and the big man would go for his gun. He didn't want to kill him, and he knew that his own gunman's instinct would make him draw if Cain went for a gun.

Cain Brockman stood stockstill in the center of the room, and then he lifted a hand to his face and pawed at his grizzled chin.

"Well, I'll be damned," he muttered. "I'll be eternally damned."

He shook his head, turned unsteadily, and lurched into the darkness toward the door.

XVIII

Kilkenny stepped back and wiped the sweat from his brow. Nita crossed the room to him, her face radiant with relief.

"Oh, Lance!" she exclaimed. "That was wonderful! Wonderful!"

Kilkenny grinned dazedly. "It was awful . . . just plain awful." He glanced around. "What's happened here? Where's Brigo?"

"He's in my room, Lance," Nita said quickly. "I was going to tell you, but Brockman came. He's hurt, very badly."

"Brigo? Hurt?" It seemed impossible. "What happened?"

"It was those two gunmen of Hale's. Cub sent them here after me. Brigo met them right here, and they shot it out. He killed both Dunn and Ravitz, but he was hit three times, once through the body."

"What happened to the Mecca? What happened in town?"

"That was before Dunn and Ravitz came. Some miners were in the Mecca, and they were all drinking. A miner had some words with a Hale gunman about the fight and about the nesters. The miner spoke very loudly, and I guess he said what he thought about Hale. The gunman reached for a gun, and the miner hit him with a bottle, and it was awful. It was a regular battle, miners against the Hale hands, and it was bloody and terrible. Some of the Hale riders liked your fight and your attitude, and they had quit. The miners drove the others out of the Mecca and burned it to the ground. Then the miners and the Hale riders fought all up and down the streets. But no one was killed. Nobody used a gun then. I guess all of them were afraid what might happen."

"And the miners?" Kilkenny asked quickly.

"They mounted up and got into wagons and rode out of town on the way back to their claims. It was like a ghost town then. Nobody stirred on the streets. They are littered with bottles, broken windows, and clubs. Then everything was quiet until Dunn and Ravitz came."

"What about Hale? King Bill, I mean?"

"We've only heard rumors. Some of the cowhands who quit stopped by here to get drinks. They said that Hale acts like a man who'd lost his mind. He had been here after the fight, before he went home. He asked me to marry him, and I refused. He said he would take me, and I told him Brigo would kill him if he tried. Then he went away. It was afterward that Cub sent the gunmen for me. He wanted me for himself. Something has happened to Hale. He doesn't even look like the same man. You won fifteen thousand dollars from him, and he paid you. He lost money to the miners, too, and to Cain Brockman. It hit him hard. He's a man who has always won, always had things his own way. He isn't used to being thwarted, isn't used to adversity, and he can't take it. Then before he left, Halloran told him he would have to let the law decide about the nesters, and Hale declared that he was the law. Halloran told him he would find out he was not and that, if he had ordered the killing of Dick Moffitt, he would hang."

"And then?"

"He seemed broken. He just seemed to go to pieces. I think he had ruled here these past ten years and that he actually believed he was king, that he had the power and that nothing could win against him. Everything had gone just as he wanted until you came along."

"You mean," Kilkenny said dryly, "until he tried to turn some good Americans out of their homes."

"Well, anyway, you'd managed to get food from here right under his nose. Then, when the attempt along the Blazer trail was tried, and he practically wiped your men out, he was supremely confident. But his attack on the cup failed. What really did it all was your defeat of Turner, and at the moment, when he had finished paying off, he was told for the first time of the death of Sodermann at Blazer. Then some of the cowhands who quit took the opportunity to drive off almost a thousand head of cattle. These defeats and what Halloran told him have completely demoralized the man."

"What about Cub?"

"He's wild. He hated you, and he was furious that

some of the men quit. He doesn't care about Halloran, for he's completely lawless. He's taken a dozen of the toughest men and gone after the stolen cattle."

"Good! That means we have time." Kilkenny took her by the arms. "Nita, you can't stay here. He might just come back. You must go to the cup and send Price Dixon down here. He can do something for Brigo. Tell him to get here as fast as he can. And you'll be safe there."

"But you?" Nita protested.

He smiled gently and put his hand on her head. "Don't worry about me, Nita. I've lived this way for years. I'll do what I can for Jaime. But hurry."

She hesitated only an instant. Then, suddenly on tiptoe, she kissed him lightly on the lips and turned toward the door.

"Just take my horse," he said. "It'll be quicker. The little gray. Give him his head and he'll go right back to the cup. I got him from Parson Hatfield."

Nita was gone.

Kilkenny turned swiftly and took a quick look around the darkened room. Then he walked through the door and over to the bed where Brigo lay.

The big Yaqui was asleep. He was breathing deeply, and his face was pale. When Kilkenny laid a hand on his brow, it was hot to the touch. Yet he was resting and was better left alone.

Kilkenny walked back into the main room and checked his guns by the candles. Then he got Brigo's guns, reloaded them, and hunted around. He found two more rifles, a double-barreled shotgun and many shells, and two more pistols. He loaded them all and placed the pistols in a neat row on the bar. One he thrust into his waistband, leaving his own guns in their holsters.

Then he doused the candles and sat down in Brigo's chair by the door. It would be a long time until morning.

Twice during the long hours he got up and paced restlessly about the great room, staring out into the vague dimness of the night at the ghostly street. It was deathly still. Once, something sounded outside, and he was out of his chair, gun in hand. But when he tiptoed to the window, he saw it was merely a lonely burro wandering aimlessly in the dead street.

Toward morning he slept a little, only restlessly and in snatches, every nerve alert for trouble or some sound that would warn of danger. When it was growing gray in the street, he went in to look at the wounded man. Brigo had opened his eyes and was lying there. He looked feverish. Kilkenny changed the dressing on the wound after bathing it, and then checked the two flesh wounds.

"¿Señor? Is it bad?" Brigo asked, turning his big black eyes toward Kilkenny.

"Not very. You lie still. Dixon is coming down."

"Dixon?" Brigo was puzzled.

"Yeah, he used to be a doctor. Good, too."

"A strange man." Sudden alarm came into Brigo's eyes. "And the *señorita?*"

"I sent her to the cup, to the Hatfields. She'll be safe there."

"*Bueno*. Cub, he has not come?"

"No. You'd better rest and lay off the talk. Don't worry if they come. I've got plenty of guns."

He put the water bucket close by the bed, and a tin cup on the table. Then he went out into the saloon.

In the gray light of dawn it looked garish and tawdry. Empty glasses lay about, and scattered poker chips. Idly he began to straighten things up a little. Then, after making a round of the windows, he went to the kitchen and started a fire. Then he put on water for coffee.

Cub Hale would come. It might take him a few hours or a few days to find the herd. He might grow impatient and return here first. He would believe Nita was still here, and his gunmen had not returned. Or he might send some men. Nita would not go over the trail as fast as he or the Hatfields. If all was well at the cup, the earliest Price could get here would be midday.

No one moved in the street. The gray dawn made it look strange and lonely in its emptiness. Somewhere, behind one of the houses, he heard the squeaking of a pump handle, and then the clatter of a tin pail. His eyelids drooped and he felt very tired. He shook himself awake and walked to the kitchen. The water was ready, so he made coffee, strong and black.

Brigo was awake when he came in and the big man took the coffee gratefully. "*Bueno*," he said.

Kilkenny noticed the man had somehow managed to reach his gun belt and had his guns on the table.

"Any pain?" he asked.

Brigo shrugged, and, after a look at him, Kilkenny walked out. Out in the main room of the saloon, he looked thoughtfully around. Then he searched until he found a hammer and nails. Getting some loose lumber from the back room, he nailed boards over the windows, leaving only a narrow space as a loophole from which each side of the building might be observed. Then he prepared breakfast.

The work on breakfast showed him how dangerously short of food they were. He thrust his head in the door and saw Brigo's eyes open.

"We're short of grub an' might have to stand a siege. I'm goin' down to Leathers's store."

The street was empty when he peered out of the door. He took a step out onto the porch. One would have thought the town was deserted. There was no sound now. Even the squeaky pump was still. He stepped down into the street and walked along slowly, little puffs of dust rising at every step. Then he went up on the boardwalk. There was still no sign of life.

The door to Leathers's store was closed. He rattled the knob, and there was no response. Without further hesitation, he put his shoulder to the door, picked up on the knob, and shoved. It held, but then he set himself and lunged. The lock burst and the door swung inward. Almost instantly, Leathers appeared from the back of the store.

"Here!" he exclaimed angrily. "You can't do this!"

"When I rattled the door, you should have opened it," Kilkenny said quietly. "I need some supplies."

"I told you once I couldn't sell to you," Leathers protested.

Kilkenny looked at him with disgust. "You're a yellow-belly, Leathers," he said quietly. "Why did you ever come West? You're built for a neat little civilized community where you can knuckle under to authority and crawl every time somebody looks at you. We don't like that in the West."

He picked up a slab of bacon and thrust it into a sack, and then he began piling more groceries into the burlap sack, until it was full. He took out some money and dropped it on the counter. He turned then to go. Leathers stood watching him angrily.

"Hale will get you for this," he snapped out.

Kilkenny turned patiently. "Leathers, you're a fool. Can't you realize that Hale is finished? That whole set-up is finished and you sided with him, so you're finished. You're the kind that always has to bow to authority. You think money is everything and power is everything. You've spent your life living in the shadows and cringing before bigger men. A good part of it's due to that sanctimonious wife of yours. If King Bill smiled at her, she'd walk in a daze for hours. It's because she's a snob and you're a weakling. Take a tip from me. Take what cash you've got, load up some supplies, and get out of here . . . but fast."

"An' leave my store?" Leathers wailed. "What do you mean?"

"What I say." Kilkenny's voice was harsh. "There's going to be some doin's in this town before another day. Hale's riders are comin' back, an' Cub Hale will be leadin' 'em. You know how much respect he has for property or anythin'. If he doesn't clear you out, the Hatfields will. There's no place for you in Cedar Bluff any more. We want to build from the ground up here, an' we want men who'll fight for what they believe. You won't, an' you were against us, so get out!"

He walked back down the silent street, went into the saloon, and stored his grub. Despite himself, he was worried. The morning was early yet, and he was expecting some of the Hale riders, and soon. The longer he waited, the more worried he became.

Brigo needed medical attention, and Doc Pollard, the Hale henchman, had gone to the Hale Ranch. He was little better than useless, anyway.

Seated at a table, he riffled the cards, and the sound was loud in the room. No one moved in the deserted street, and he played silently, smoking endless cigarettes and waiting. Again and again his thoughts returned to Nita. After all, should he wait? Supposing he was killed eventually? Why not have a little happiness first? He knew without asking that she was the girl for him, and he knew she would marry him in an instant and be completely happy to live in a house built among the high peaks. She was lovely, tender, thoughtful. A man could ask no more of any woman than she had for the giving. Yet he remembered the faces of other gunmen's wives when word came that their men had died. He remembered their faces when their men went down into the streets, when they waited through every lonely hour, never sure whether he would come back or not. Bartram had Sally Crane. He remembered her sweet, youthful face, flushed with happiness. It made him feel old and lonely.

He slipped his guns out and checked them once more. Then he took up the cards and shuffled them again. Suddenly an idea came to him. He got up and went to the back door, took a quick look around, and slipped out to the stable. There were still horses there. He had a hunch he might need them, and saddled two.

Then he went back inside and closed the door. The place was deathly still and the air close and hot. It felt like a storm was impending. He brushed the sweat from his brow and crossed to have a look at Brigo. The big man was sleeping, but his face was flushed and feverish. He looked poorly.

He glanced out the door at the empty street. Clouds were building up around the peaks. If it rained, it was going to make it tough to move Jaime Brigo. Thunder rumbled like a whimper of far-off trumpets, and then deeper like a rolling of gigantic casks along the floor of a cavern. He walked back inside, and sat down.

XIX

They came down the dusty street at high noon, a tight little cavalcade of men expecting no trouble. They rode as tired men ride, for there was dust on their horses and dust on their clothing and dust on their wide-brimmed hats. It was only their guns that had no dust. There was no humor in them, for they were men for whom killing was the order of business. The softer members of the Hale outfit were gone. These were the pick of the tough, gun-handy crew.

Lee Wright was in the lead, riding a blood bay. At his right and a bit behind was Jeff Nebel, and a bit behind him were gun-slick Tandy Wade and Kurt Wilde. There were ten in all, ten tough, gun-belted men riding into Cedar Bluff when the sun was high.

Dunn and Ravitz had not returned. What that meant, they could not know, nor did they care. They had come to get a woman, and, if Dunn and Ravitz had decided to keep her, these men would take her away. If those two had failed in their mission, they were to take her from the protection of Brigo. They had their orders and they knew what to do.

Near Leathers's store the group broke, and three men rode on down to the Crystal Palace. Lee Wright, big, hard-faced, and cruel, was in the lead. With him were Kurt Wilde and Tandy Wade.

His eyes slanting up the street at the scattering men,

Kilkenny let the three come on. When they reined in and were about to swing down, Kilkenny stopped them.

"Hold it!" he said sharply. "What do you want, Wright?"

Wright froze, and then settled back in the saddle. "Who is that?" he demanded, peering to see under the darkness of the sheet-metal awning and into the vagueness of the doorway.

"It's Kilkenny," he said. "What do you want?"

"We've come for that woman. Cub wants her," Wright said harshly. "What are you doin' here?"

"Me?" Kilkenny chuckled quietly. His eyes were cold and watchful. He knew these men were uncertain. They hadn't expected him. Now they did not know what the situation was. How many men were inside? Was Brigo there? The Hatfields? Kilkenny knew their lack of knowledge was half his strength. "Why, I've been waitin' for you boys to show up. Wanted to tell you that I'd slope, if I were you. The Hales are through."

"Are they?" Wright's eyes swept the building. Those boarded windows bothered him. "We came after the woman. We'll get her."

Kilkenny began building a smoke. "With only ten men? It ain't enough, Wright." He touched his tongue to the paper. "You're a fightin' man, Wright. Ever try to take a place like this with no more men than you got?"

"You're bluffin'!" Wright said. "You're alone."

Kilkenny chuckled. "You reckon I'd come down here alone? Or that the Hatfields would let me? They are right careful of me, Wright."

"Where are they?" Wright declared. "You. . . ." The words died on his lips as there was a tinkle of glass from down the building. Wright looked, and Kilkenny saw his face darken. It could mean but one thing. Brigo had gotten out of bed and thrust a rifle through the window at the right moment. But how long could he stand there? The man was weak. . . .

Kilkenny laughed. "Well, you can start comin' any time you want, Wright, but a lot of you boys are goin' to die for nothin'. If you think Hale can pay off now, you're wrong."

Kurt Wilde had been sitting quietly. Now he exploded suddenly: "To hell with this! Let's go in there!" He jumped his horse to one side and grabbed for his gun.

Kilkenny's hand swept down, and his gun was barking before it reached belt high. The first shot cut the rearing horse's bridle at the bit and whined off into the street. The second took Wilde in the shoulder and knocked him, sprawling, into the dust.

At the same instant, Brigo fired, and Tandy Wade's horse backed up suddenly and went down. Wade leaped clear and sprinted with Lee Wright for the shelter of the nearest building. From up the street, there was a volley of shots, but Kilkenny was safely inside.

With one quick look, he dodged away from the door

and ran to Brigo in the other room. The big man's face was deathly pale, and his movements had started his wounds bleeding.

"Lie down, damn it!" Kilkenny commanded. "You did your part. You fooled 'em. Now lie down!"

"No, *señor*, not when you fight."

"I can hold 'em now. Lie down an' rest till I need you. When they rush, I'll need help."

Brigo hesitated, and then sank back on the bed. From where he lay, he could see through a crack in the boards without moving. Lance grabbed a box of shells and dropped them on the bed beside him and handed him another rifle. Then he went back and made a round of the loopholes. He fired from one, skipped one, and fired from the next. He made the rounds, hunting for targets, but trying to keep the shots mixed so they would be in doubt.

Wilde was getting up. Kilkenny watched him, letting him go. Suddenly the man wheeled and blasted at the door, and Brigo, lying on his bed, drilled him through the chest!

One down, Kilkenny told himself, *an' nine to go!*

He was under no illusions. They could trade shots for a while, and he could fool Wright and the Hale riders for a few hours, perhaps. But they were much too shrewd to be fooled for long. Sooner or later they would guess, and then under cover of an attack from one direction, they would drive from the other, and the whole thing would end in a wicked red-laced blasting inside the Palace.

Kilkenny found a good place near a window where he could watch up the street toward Leathers's store. The dusty street was empty. He waited, and suddenly he saw a man slip around the corner of the store and dart for the door. He fired quickly, twice.

The first shot hit the man about waist high, but on the outside and probably near his holster. He staggered, and Kilkenny fired again and saw the fellow go to one knee. He crawled through the door. The first shot had not been a disabling one, he was sure, but the second, when he aimed at the thigh, had brought the man down.

He got up restlessly and started for the back of the saloon. There was no movement, but when he moved to the door, a bullet clipped the doorjamb right over his head, and, had he not been crouched, it would probably have been dead center. No chance to get to the horses then, not by day, anyway.

The afternoon wore on, and there were only occasional shots. They came with a rush finally. It had been quiet. Then suddenly a volley blasted at the back of the store. Taking a chance, Kilkenny rushed to the front just in time to see a half dozen men charging across the street. He dropped his rifle, whipped out both guns, and leaped into the doorway.

His first shot was dead center, a bullet fired from the hip that hit the Hale man and knocked him rolling. His guns roaring and blasting, he smelled the acrid odor of gunpowder, felt a red-hot whip laid across his cheek, and knew he'd been grazed. Then he blasted again, felt a gun go empty, and, still triggering the first gun, jerked out his belt gun and opened up again.

They fell back, and he saw two men were down. He knew neither of them. His cheek bone was burning like fire and he lifted a hand. It came away bloody. He sopped the wound with his handkerchief, and then dropped it and began reloading his guns. This time he brought the shotgun up to the door and stuffed his pockets with shotgun shells. The waiting was what got a man. He didn't want to wait. He wanted to go out there.

There was no firing now. The attacking party was down to seven, and one of those was wounded. They would hesitate a little now. And he still had the shotgun. That was his pay-off weapon. He knew what it would do to a man and hated to use it. At close range a shotgun wouldn't just make a wound. It would blast a man in two.

He showed himself at a window and got no action. He could hear loud voices in Leathers's store. There was some kind of an argument. After all, what had they to gain? Suddenly Kilkenny had an idea. He wheeled and went into the bedroom. Brigo was lying on the bed, breathing hoarsely. He looked terrible.

"Lie still an' watch," Kilkenny said. "I'm goin' out."

"Out?" Brigo's eyes fired. "You after them?"

"*Sí*. With this." He touched the shotgun. "They are all in Leathers's store. I'm goin' to settle this once an' for all."

He went to the door. For a long time he studied the terrain. He was worried. Price Dixon should be here by now. The Hale men probably knew he had joined Kilkenny and the Hatfields, so, if he came back, they would shoot him. And if Jaime Brigo was to live, he would need Dixon's attention.

Kilkenny waited. The sun was making a shadow under the awning, even if not much of a one. He eased outside, listening to the loud voices, and then he left the porch with a rush.

There was no shot. He got to the side of Leathers's store. From here it was four good steps to the door, and there was no window to pass. He stepped up on the porch, knowing that, if they had a man across the street, he was a gone gosling.

He took another step, and waited. Inside, the voices continued, and he could hear Lee Wright's voice above all the others. "Cub'll pay off, all right. If he don't, we can always take some cows ourselves!"

"Blazes!" somebody said disgustedly. "I don't want any cows! I want money! An'," he added, "I want out of this with a whole skin!"

"Personally," a voice drawled, "I don't see no percentage in gettin' a hide full of lead because some other *hombre* wants a woman. I'll admit that Riordan gal is somethin' to look at, but I think, if she wanted to have a Hale, she'd take one. I think the gal's crazy for this Kilkenny, an' for my money she's got the best of the lot."

"What's it to you, Tandy?" Wright demanded.

"Hale's got the money. He pays us. Besides, that Kilkenny figgers he's too durned good."

Tandy laughed. "Why, Lee, I reckon, if you'd go out there an' tell him you wanted a shoot-out, he'd give it to you."

"Say!" Wright jumped to his feet. "That's it! That's the way we'll get him. I'll go out and challenge him. Then when he comes out, pour it into him."

There was a moment of silence, but Kilkenny was just outside the screened door now. "Lee, that sure is a polecat's idea. You know durned well I wouldn't have no part of that. I'm a fightin' man, not a murderer."

"Tandy Wade, someday you'll . . . !" Wright began, angrily.

"Suppose," Kilkenny said, "that I take over from here?" Wright froze, his mouth open, his face slowly turning white. Only Tandy turned, and he turned very slowly, keeping his hands wide. He looked at the double-barreled shotgun for just an instant.

"Well, Kilkenny," he said softly, "I reckon that shotgun calls my hand."

"Shotgun?" Wright gasped. Kilkenny let him turn. He knew how ugly a double-barreled shotgun can seem when seen at close quarters.

"Buckshot in it, too," Kilkenny said lazily. "I might not be able to get more'n four or five of you *hombres*. Might be even one or two, but I'm sure goin' to get them good. Who wants a hot taste of buckshot?"

Wright backed up, licking his lips. He didn't want

259

any trouble now. You could see it in his eyes that he knew that shotgun was meant for him, and he didn't want any part of it.

"Leathers!" Kilkenny's voice cracked like a whiplash. "Come around here and get their guns. Slap their shirts, too. I don't want any sneak guns."

The storekeeper, his face dead white, came around and began lifting the guns, and no one said a word. When the guns were collected and all laid at Kilkenny's feet, he stood there for a moment, looking at the men.

"Wright, you wanted to trick me an' kill me. Didn't you?"

Lee Wright's eyes were wide and dark in the sickly moon of his face. "I talked too much," he said, tight-lipped, "I wouldn't've had nerve enough for that."

"Well. . . ."

There was a sudden rattle of horses' hoofs in the street, and Kilkenny saw Lee Wright's eyes brighten, but, as he looked at Kilkenny, his face went sick.

"Careful, Lee!" Kilkenny said quietly. "Don't get uneasy. If I go, you go with me."

"I ain't movin," Wright said hoarsely. "For heaven's sake, don't shoot!"

XX

Now the horses were walking. They stopped before the Crystal Palace. Kilkenny dared not turn. He dared not look. Putting a toe behind the stack of guns, he pushed them back. Then, still keeping his eyes on the men, he dragged them back farther. Then he waited.

Sweat came out on his forehead, and he felt his mouth go dry. They could slip up and come in. They could just walk up. And he dared not turn, or one of these men would leap and have a gun. His only way out was to go out fighting. Looking at the men before him, he could see what was in their minds. Their faces were gray and sick. A shotgun wasn't an easy way to die, and, once that gun started blasting, there was no telling who would get it. And Kilkenny, with an empty shotgun, was still closer to the guns on the floor than they were.

The flesh seemed to crawl on the back of Kilkenny's neck, and he saw Wright's tongue feeling his dry lips. Only Tandy Wade seemed relaxed. The tension was only in his eyes. Any moment now might turn this room into a bloody bit of hell. The shotgun was going to. . . . A door slammed at the Crystal Palace.

Had Brigo passed out? There was no sound, but Kilkenny knew someone was crossing the dusty space between the buildings. He was drawing closer now. The sound of a foot on the boardwalk made them all jump. Suddenly Leathers slipped to the floor in a dead faint. Tandy looked down amusedly, and then lifted his eyes as a board creaked.

Any moment now. When that door opened, if a friendly voice didn't speak. . . .

The door creaked just a little. That was only when it opened wide. Kilkenny remembered that door. He had eased through a crack himself. He lifted the shotgun slightly, his own face gray.

Suddenly he knew that, if this was Cub Hale, he would turn this store into a shambles. Kilkenny was going to go out taking a bloody dozen with him. He had these guns, and, if the first shot didn't get him, he wasn't going alone. He clicked back the hammers.

"No!" He didn't know who spoke. "No, Kilkenny! My God, no!"

These men who could stand a shoot-out with perfect composure were frightened and pale at the gaping muzzles of the shotgun.

"Kilkenny?" The voice was behind him, and it was Parson Hatfield.

"Yeah, Parson. I got me a few restless *hombres* here."

Hatfield came in, and behind him were Bartram and Steve Runyon. "Where's Cub?" Parson demanded sharply.

"He cut off for the ranch. He figured Dunn would have the girl there."

"We didn't find him," Parson said. "He must've stopped off on the way. Hale shot hisself."

"He did?" Kilkenny turned. "What happened at the place?"

"She was plumb deserted," Runyon offered. "Not a soul around. Looks as if they all deserted like rats from a sinkin' ship. He was all alone, an', when he seen us comin', he shot hisself."

"What happened then?" Kilkenny asked.

"We set fire to the place. Too big for any honest rancher. It's burnin' now."

"What happens to us?" Tandy demanded.

Kilkenny looked at them for a minute, but, before he could speak, Parson spoke up. "We want Jeff Nebel an' Lee Wright. They done murdered Miller, Wilson, an' Lije. They got Smithers, too. Jeff Nebel killed him. An' they was in on the killin' of Dick Moffitt. We got a rope for 'em!"

"Take them, then," Kilkenny said. He looked at Tandy Wade. "You're too good a man to run with this owlhoot crowd, Wade. You better change your ways before they get a rope on you. Get goin'!"

Wade looked at him. "Thanks, man," he said. "It's more'n I deserve."

"You," Kilkenny said to the others, "ride! If you ever come into this country again, we'll hang you."

They scrambled for the door. The Hatfields were already gone with Wright and Nebel. Kilkenny turned away and looked at Leathers, who had recovered from his faint. "You got twenty-four hours," he said quietly. "Take what you can an' get out of here. Don't come back."

He walked out of the store into the dusty street. A man was coming down the street on a rangy sorrel horse. He looked, and then looked again. It was Dan Cooper. A short distance behind him, another man rounded the corner. It was Cain Brockman. They rode straight on until they came up to Kilkenny.

Cooper reined in and began to roll a smoke. "Looks like I backed the wrong horse," he said slowly. "What's the deal? Got a rope for me? Or do I draw a ticket out of here?"

"What do you want?" Kilkenny demanded sharply. He had his thumbs in his belt, watching the two men.

"Well," Dan said, looking up at Kilkenny, "we talked it over. We both won money on your fight, an' we sort of had an idea we'd like to join you-all an' take up some claims ourselves."

"Right pretty places up in them meadows," Cain suggested. He sat his horse, looking at Kilkenny.

For a long minute Kilkenny glanced from one to the other. "Sure," he said finally. "You might find a good place up near mine, Cain. And the Moffitt place is empty now."

He turned and walked back to the Palace. He had forgotten Brigo. Yet, when he entered the place, his worry left him. Price Dixon had come, and Nita had returned with him. She met Kilkenny at the door.

"He's asleep," she whispered. "Dixon got the bullet out, and he's going to be all right."

"Good." Kilkenny looked at the girl, and then he

took her in his arms. He drew her close and her lips melted into his, and for a long time they stood there, holding each other.

"Oh, Lance," she whispered, "don't let me go. Keep me now. It's been so long, and I've been so lonely."

"Sure," he said quietly, "I'll keep you now. I don't want to let you go . . . ever!"

Slowly, in the days that followed, the town came back to itself. Widows of two of the nesters moved into the Leathers' house and took over the store. Kilkenny and Bartram helped them get things arranged and get started. The ruins of the Mecca were cleared away. Van Hawkins, a former actor from San Francisco, came in and bought the Crystal Palace from Nita. Kilkenny started to build a bigger, more comfortable house on the site of the old one that the Hales had burned for him.

Yet, over it all, there was restlessness and uneasiness. Kilkenny talked much with Nita in the evenings and saw the dark circles under her eyes. She was sleeping little, he knew.

The Hatfields carried their guns all the time, and Steve Runyon came and went with a pistol strapped on. It was because of Cub Hale. No one ever mentioned his name, yet his shadow lay over them all. He had vanished mysteriously, leaving no trace, nothing to tell them of where he had gone, what he planned to do, or when he would return.

Then one day Saul Hatfield rode up to Kilkenny's

claim. He leaned on the saddle horn and looked down at Lance.

"How's things?" he asked. "Seems you're doin' right well with the house."

"Yeah," Kilkenny admitted. "It's goin' up." He looked up at Saul. "How's your dad?"

"Right pert."

"Jesse goin' to dig those potatoes of Smithers's?"

"I reckon."

"He'd like it. He was a savin' man." Kilkenny straightened and their eyes met. "What's on your mind, Saul?"

"I was ridin' this mornin', down on the branch," Saul said thoughtfully. "Seen some tracks where a horse crossed the stream. I was right curious. I followed him a ways. Found some white hairs on the brush."

Cub Hale always rode a white horse. An albino, it was.

"I see." Kilkenny rubbed his jaw. "Which way was he headin'?"

"Sort of circlin'. Sizin' up the town, like."

Kilkenny nodded. "I reckon I better go down to Cedar Bluff," he said thoughtfully. "I want to stick around town a while."

"Sure." Saul looked at him. "A body could follow them tracks," he suggested. "It was a plain trail."

"Dangerous. He's a bad one. Maybe later. We'll see."

Kilkenny mounted the long-legged yellow horse and

headed for town. Cub Hale was mean. He wasn't going to leave. It wasn't in him to leave. He was a man who had to kill, even if he died in the process. Kilkenny had known that. He knew that some of the men believed Cub had lit out and left the country. He had never believed that. Cub was prowling, licking his wounds, waiting. And the hate in him was building up.

Kilkenny rode the yellow buckskin to the little cottage where Nita Riordan and Sally Crane were living together while Sally prepared for her wedding with Bartram. Nita came to the door, her sewing in her hand.

"Lance," she said quickly, "is it . . . ?"

"He's close by." He swung down from the horse. "I reckon you've got a guest for dinner."

Sitting by the window with a book, he glanced occasionally down the street. He saw two Hatfields ride in—Quince and Saul. They dismounted at the store, and then Steve Runyon rode in and, after him, Cain Brockman.

Brockman rode right on to the Palace, dismounted, and went in for a drink. Then he came out and loafed on a bench by the door. He was wearing two guns.

The room was bright and cheery with china plates and curtains at the windows. Nita came in, drying her hands on an apron, and called him to lunch. He took a last look down the street, and then got up and walked in to the table. Sally's face was flushed and she looked very pretty, yet he had eyes only for Nita.

He had never seen her so lovely as now. Her face

looked softer and prettier than he had ever seen it. She was happy, too, radiantly happy. Even the news of the nearness of Cub Hale had not been able to wipe it from her face.

Bartram came in and joined them. He grinned at Kilkenny. "Not often a man gets a chance to try his wife's cooking as much as I have before he marries her!" He chuckled. "I'll say this for her, she can sure make biscuits!"

"I didn't make them!" Sally protested. "Nita did!"

"Nita?" Kilkenny looked up, smiling. "I didn't know you could cook."

There was a low call from the door. "Kilkenny?" It was Cain Brockman. "He's comin'. Shall I take him?"

"No." Kilkenny touched his mouth with a napkin and drew back from the table. "It's my job." His eyes met Nita's across the table. "Don't pour my coffee," he said quietly. "I like it hot."

He turned and walked to the door. Far down the street he could see Cub Hale. He was on foot, and his hat was gone, his yellow hair blowing in the wind. He was walking straight up the center of the street, looking straight ahead.

Kilkenny stepped down off the porch. The roses were blooming, and their scent was strong in his nostrils. He could smell the rich odor of fresh earth in the sunlight, and somewhere a magpie shrieked. He opened the gate and, stepping out, closed it carefully behind him. Then he began to walk.

He took his time. There was no hurry. There was

never any hurry at a time like this. Everything always seemed to move by slow motion, until suddenly it was over and you wondered how it all could have happened. Saul Hatfield was standing on the steps, his rifle in the hollow of his arm. He and Quince were just there in case he failed.

Failed? Kilkenny smiled. He had never failed. Yet, they all failed soon or late. There was always a time when they were too slow, when their guns hung or missed fire. The dust smelled hot, and in the distance thunder rumbled. Then a few scattered drops fell. Odd, he hadn't even been aware it was clouding up.

Little puffs of dust lifted from his boots when he walked. He could see Cub more clearly now. He was unshaven, and his face was scratched by brush. His fancy buckskin jacket was gone. Only the guns were the same, and the white eyes, eyes that seemed to burn.

Suddenly Hale stopped, and, when he stopped, Kilkenny stopped, too. He stood there perfectly relaxed, waiting. Cub's face was white, dead. Only his eyes seemed alive, and that burning white light was in them. "I'm goin' to kill you!" he said, his voice sharp and strained.

It was all wrong. Kilkenny felt no tension, no alertness. He was just standing there, and in him suddenly there welled up a tremendous feeling of pity. Why couldn't they ever learn? There was nothing in a gun but death.

Something flickered in those white, blazing eyes,

and Kilkenny, standing perfectly erect, slapped the butt of his gun with his palm. The gun leaped up, settled into a rock-like grip, and then bucked in his hand, once, twice. The gun before him flowered with flame, and something stabbed, white hot, low down on his right side. The gun flowered again, but the stabbing flame wasted itself in the dust and Cub's knees buckled and there was a spot of blood on his chest, right over the heart. He fell face down and then straightened his legs, and there was silence in the long dusty street of Cedar Bluff.

Kilkenny thumbed shells into his gun, holstered it, and then turned. Steadily, quietly, looking straight ahead, he walked back up the hill toward the cottage. It was just a little hill, but it suddenly seemed steep. He walked on, and then he could see Nita opening the gate and running toward him.

He stopped then, and waited. There was a burning in his side, and he felt something wet against his leg. He looked down, puzzled, and, when he looked, he fell flat on his face in the dust.

Then Nita was turning him over, and her face was white. He tried to sit up, but they pushed him down. Cain Brockman came over, and with Saul Hatfield they carried him up the hill. It was only a few steps, and it had seemed so far.

He was still conscious when Price Dixon came in. Dixon made a brief examination, and then shrugged.

"He's all right. The bullet went into his side, slid off a rib, and narrowly missed his spine. But it's nothing that we can't fix up. Shock, mostly . . . and bleeding."

Later, Nita came in. She looked at him and smiled. "Shall I put the coffee on now?" she asked lightly. Her eyes were large and dark.

"Let Sally put it on," he said gently. "You stay here."

Center Point Publishing
600 Brooks Road • PO Box 1
Thorndike ME 04986-0001 USA

(207) 568-3717

US & Canada:
1 800 929-9108
www.centerpointlargeprint.com